Deemed 'the father of the scientific detective story', **Richard Austin Freeman** had a long and distinguished career, not least as a writer of detective fiction. He was born in London, the son of a tailor who went on to train as a pharmacist. After graduating as a surgeon at the Middlesex Hospital Medical College, Freeman taught for a while and joined the colonial service, offering his skills as an assistant surgeon along the Gold Coast of Africa. He became embroiled in a diplomatic mission when a British expeditionary party was sent to investigate the activities of the French. Through his tact and formidable intelligence, a massacre was narrowly avoided. His future was assured in the colonial service. However, after becoming ill with blackwater fever, Freeman was sent back to England to recover and, finding his finances precarious, embarked on a career as acting physician in Holloway Prison. In desperation, he turned to writing and went on to dominate the world of British detective fiction, taking pride in testing different criminal techniques. So keen were his powers as a writer that part of one of his best novels was written in a bomb shelter.

CW00953139

BY THE SAME AUTHOR
ALL PUBLISHED BY HOUSE OF STRATUS

Mr Polton Explains

R Austin Freeman

This edition published in 2001 by House of Stratus, an imprint of
Stratus Books Ltd., 21 Beeching Park, Kelly Bray,
Cornwall, PL17 8QS, UK.

www.houseofstratus.com

Typeset, printed and bound by House of Stratus.

A catalogue record for this book is available from the British Library
and the Library of Congress.

ISBN 0-7551-0367-X

TO

LIEUT-COM RUPERT T GOULD
RN (Retd)

THE DISTINGUISHED HOROLOGIST,
THIS STORY OF A SIMPLE CLOCKMAKER
IS DEDICATED BY HIS OLD
FRIEND, THE AUTHOR

CONTENTS

Part One
The Antecedents

Part Two
The Case of Moxdale Deceased
(*Narrated by Christopher Jervis, MD*)

PART ONE
The Antecedents

Introductory Observations
by Mr Polton

Friends of Dr Thorndyke who happen to have heard of me as his servant and technical assistant may be rather surprised to see me making my appearance in the character of an author. I am rather surprised, myself; and I don't mind admitting that of all the tools that I have ever used, the one that is in my hand at the present moment is the least familiar and the most unmanageable. But mere lack of skill shall not discourage me. The infallible method, as I have found by experience, of learning how to do anything is to do it, and keep on doing it until it becomes easy. Use is second nature, as a copy-book once informed me.

But I feel that some explanation is necessary. The writing of this record is not my own idea. I am acting on instructions; and the way in which the matter arose was this. My master, the Doctor, was commissioned to investigate the case of Cecil Moxdale deceased, and a very queer case it was. So queer that, as the Doctor assures me, he would never have been able to come to a definite conclusion but for one little fact that I was able to supply. I think he exaggerates my importance and that he would have found it out for himself. Still, that one little fact did certainly throw a new light on the case, so, when the time came for the record of it to be written, both the Doctor himself, and Dr Jervis decided that I was the proper person to set forth the circumstances that made the final discovery possible.

That was all very well, but the question was, what were the circumstances and when did they begin? And I could find no answer; for as soon as I thought that I had found the beginning of the train of circumstances, I saw that it would never have happened if something had not happened before it. And so it went on. Every event in my life was the result of some other event, and, tracing them back one after the other, I came to the conclusion that the beginning of the train of circumstances was also the beginning of me. For, obviously, if I had never been born, the experiences that I have to record could never have happened. I pointed this out to the Doctor, and he agreed that my being born was undoubtedly a contributory circumstance, and suggested that perhaps I had better begin with that. But, on reflection, I saw that this was impossible; for, although being born is undeniably a personal experience, it is, oddly enough, one which we have to take on hearsay and which it would therefore be improper to include in one's personal recollections.

Besides, although this history seems to be all about me, it is really an introduction to the case of Cecil Moxdale deceased; and my little contribution to the solving of that mystery was principally a matter of technical knowledge. There were some other matters; but my connection with the case arose out of my being a clock-maker. Accordingly, in these recollections, I shall sort out the incidents of my life, and keep, as far as possible, to those which present me in that character.

There is a surprising amount of wisdom to be gathered from copy-books. From one I learned that the boy is father to the man, and from another, to much the same effect, that the poet is born, not made. As there were twenty lines to the page, I had to repeat this twenty times, which was more than it merited. For the thing is obvious enough, and, after all, there is nothing in it. Poets are not peculiar in this respect. The truth applies to all other kinds of persons, including fools and even clock-makers; that is, if they are real clock-makers and not just common men with no natural aptitude who have drifted into the trade by chance.

Now, I was born a clock-maker. It may sound odd, but such, I am convinced, is the fact. As far back as I can remember, clocks have always had an attraction for me quite different from that of any other kinds of things. In later years my interests have widened, but I have still remained faithful to my old love. A clock (by which I mean a mechanical time-keeper of any kind) still seems to me the most wonderful and admirable of the works of man. Indeed, it seems something more: as if it were a living creature with a personality and a soul of its own, rather than a mere machine.

Thus I may say that by these beautiful creations my life has been shaped from the very beginning. Looking down the vista of years, I seem to see at the end of it the old Dutch clock that used to hang on the wall of our kitchen. That clock, and certain dealings with it on a particular and well-remembered day, which I shall mention presently, seem to mark the real starting-point of my journey through life. This may be a mere sentimental delusion, but it doesn't appear so to me. In memory, I can still see the pleasant painted face, changing in expression from hour to hour, and hear the measured tick that never changed at all; and to me, they are the face and the voice of an old and beloved friend.

Of my first meeting with that clock I have no recollection, for it was there when my Aunt Gollidge brought me to her home, a little orphan of three. But in that curious hazy beginning of memory when the events of our childhood come back to us in detached scenes like the pictures of a magic lantern, the old clock is the one distinct object; and as memories become more connected, I can see myself sitting in the little chair that Uncle Gollidge had made for me, looking up at the clock with an interest and pleasure that were never exhausted. I suppose that to a child any inanimate thing which moves of its own accord is an object of wonder, especially if its movements appear to have a definite purpose.

But of explanations I have given enough and of apologies I shall give none; for if the story of my doings should appear to the reader as little worth as it does to me, he has but to pass over it and turn to the case to which it forms the introduction.

CHAPTER ONE

The Young Horologist

"Drat that clock!" exclaimed my Aunt Judy. "Saturday night, too. Of course, it would choose Saturday night to stop."

She looked up malevolently, at the stolid face and the motionless pendulum that hung straight down like a plumb-bob, and then, as she hopped up on a chair to lift the clock off its nail, she continued:

"Get me the bellows, Nat."

I extricated myself with some difficulty from the little armchair. For dear Uncle Gollidge had overlooked the fact that boys grow and chairs do not, so that it was now a rather tight fit with a tendency to become, like a snail's shell, a permanent attachment. The separation accomplished, I took the bellows from the hook beside the fire-place and went to my aunt's assistance; she having, in her quick, brisk way, unhooked the pendulum and opened the little side doors of the case. Then I held the clock steady on the table while she plied the bellows with the energy of a village blacksmith, blowing out a most encouraging cloud of dust through the farther door-opening.

"We will see what that will do," said she, slapping the little doors to, fastening the catches and hooking on the pendulum. Once more she sprang up on the chair, replaced the clock on its nail, gave the pendulum a persuasive pat, and descended.

"What is the time by your watch, Dad?" she asked.

Old Mr Gollidge paused in the story that he was telling and looked at her with mild reproach. A great story-teller was old Mr Gollidge (he had been a ship's carpenter), but Aunt Judy had a way of treating his interminable yarns as mere negligible sounds like the ticking of a clock or the dripping of a leaky tap, and she now repeated her question; whereupon the old gentleman, having contributed to a large spittoon at his side, stuck his pipe in his mouth and hauled a bloated silver watch from the depths of his pocket as if he were hoisting out cargo from the lower hold.

"Watch seems to say," he announced, after looking at it with slight surprise, "as it's a quarter past six."

"Six!" shrieked Aunt Judy. "Why, I heard the church clock strike seven a full half-hour ago."

"Then," said the old gentleman, " 'twould seem to be about three bells, say half-past seven. Watch must have stopped."

He confirmed the diagnosis by applying it to his ear, and then, having fished up from another pocket an old-fashioned bronze, crank-shaped key, opened the front glass of the watch, which had the winding-hole in the dial like a clock, inserted the key and proceeded to wind as if he were playing a little barrel-organ.

"Half-past seven, you say," said he, transferring the key to the centre square preparatory to setting the hands.

Aunt Judy looked up at the clock, which was still sluggishly wagging its pendulum but uttering no tick, and shook her head impatiently.

"It's no use guessing," said she. "We shall want to know the time in the morning. If you put on your slipper, Nat, you can run round and have a look at Mr Abraham's clock. It isn't far to go."

The necessity for putting on my slipper arose from a blister on my heel which had kept me a bootless prisoner in the house. I began cautiously to insinuate my foot into the slipper and had nearly completed the operation when Aunt Judy suddenly interposed.

"Listen," said she; and as we all froze into immobility, the silence was broken by the church clock striking eight. Then old Mr

Gollidge deliberately set the hands of his watch, put it to his ear to make sure that it was going, and lowered it into his pocket; and Aunt Judy, mounting the chair, set the clock to time, gave the pendulum a final pat, and hopped down.

"We'll give it another chance," she remarked, optimistically; but I knew that her optimism was unfounded when I listened for the tick and listened in vain; and, sure enough, the oscillations of the pendulum slowly died away until it hung down as motionless as the weight.

In the ensuing silence, old Mr Gollidge took up the thread of his narrative.

"And then the boy comes up from the cuddy and says he seemed to hear a lot of water washin' about down below. So the mate he tells me for to sound the well, which I did; and, of course, I found there was a foot or two of water in it. There always was. Reg'ler old basket, that ship was. Always a-drainin' in, a-drainin' in, and the pumps a-goin' something crool."

"Ought to have had a windmill," said Uncle Gollidge, taking a very black clay pipe from his mouth and expectorating skilfully between the bars of the grate, "same as what the Dutchmen do in the Baltic timber trade."

The old gentleman shook his head. "Windmills is all right," said he, "if you've got a cargo of soft timber what'll float anyway. But they won't keep a leaky ship dry. Besides – "

"Now, Nat," said Aunt Judy, hooking a Dutch oven on the bar of the grate, "bring your chair over and keep an eye on the black pudding; and you, Sam, just mind where you're spitting."

Uncle Sam, who rather plumed himself on his marksmanship, replied with a scornful grunt; I rose to my feet (the chair rising with me) and took up my station opposite the Dutch oven, the back flap of which I lifted to make an interested inspection of the slices of black pudding (longitudinal sections, as the Doctor would say) which were already beginning to perspire greasily, in the heat. Meanwhile, Aunt Judy whisked about the kitchen (also the general sitting-room) busily making ready for the morrow, and old Mr Gollidge droned on tirelessly like the brook that goes on for ever.

Of the morrow's doings I must say a few words, since they formed a milestone marking the first stage of my earthly pilgrimage. It had been arranged that the four of us should spend the Sunday with Aunt Judy's younger sister, a Mrs Budgen, who lived with her husband in the country out Finchley way. But my unfortunate blistered heel put me out of the party, much to my regret, for these excursions were the bright spots in my rather drab existence. Aunt Budgen was a kindly soul who gave us the warmest of welcomes, as did her husband, a rather taciturn dairy-farmer. Then there was the glorious drive out of London on the front seat of the Finchley omnibus with its smart, white-hatted driver and the third horse stepping out gaily in front with jingling harness and swaying swingle-bar.

But the greatest delight of these visits was the meeting with my sister, Maggie, who had been adopted by Aunt Budgen at the time when Aunt Judy had taken me. These were the only occasions on which we met, and it was a joy to us both to ramble in the meadows, to call on the cows in the shippon, or to sit together on the brink of the big pond and watch the incredible creatures that moved about in its depths.

However, there were to be compensations. Aunt Judy expounded them to me as I superintended the black pudding, turning the Dutch oven when necessary to brown the opposite sides.

"I'm leaving you three pork sausages; they're rather small ones, but you are rather a small boy; and there are some cold potatoes which you can cut into slices and fry with the sausages, and mind you don't set the chimney on fire. Then there is a baked raisin pudding – you can hot that up in the oven – and a whole jar of raspberry jam. You can take as much of that as you like, so long as you don't make yourself ill; and I've left the key in the book-cupboard, but you must wash your hands before you take any of the books out. I am sorry you can't come with us, and Maggie will be disappointed, too; but I think you'll be able to make yourself happy. I know you don't mind being alone a bit."

Aunt Judy was right. I was a rather solitary boy; a little given to day-dreaming and, consequently, partial to my own society. But she prophesied better than she knew. Not only was I able to make myself happy in my solitude; but that Sunday stands out as one of the red-letter days of my life.

To be sure, the day opened rather cheerlessly. As I stood on the doorstep with my single boot and bandaged foot, watching the departure, I was sensible of a pang of keen disappointment and of something approaching loneliness. I followed the receding figures wistfully with my eyes as they walked away down the street in their holiday attire, Aunt Judy gorgeous in her silk dress and gaily-flowered bonnet and the two men in stiff black broadcloth and tall hats, to which old Mr Gollidge's fine, silver-topped malacca gave an added glory. At the corner Aunt Judy paused to wave her hand to me; then she followed the other two and was lost to view.

I turned back sadly into the house, which, when I had shut the door, seemed dark and gloomy, and made my way to the kitchen. In view of the early start to catch the omnibus, I had volunteered to wash up the breakfast things, and I now proceeded to get this job off my hands; but as I dabbled at the big bowl in the scullery sink, my thoughts still followed the holidaymakers. I saw them mounting the omnibus (it started from St Martin's Church), and visualized its pea-green body with the blessed word "Finchley" in big gold letters. I saw the driver gather up the reins and the conductor spring up to the monkey-board; and then away the omnibus rattled, and my thoughts went on ahead to the sweet countryside and to Maggie, waiting for me at the stile, and waiting in vain. That was the most grievous part of the affair, and it wrung my heart to think of it; indeed, if it had not been beneath the dignity of a young man of nine to shed tears, I think I should have wept.

When I had finished with the crockery, put the plates in the rack and hung the cups on their hooks, I tidied up the sink and then drifted through into the kitchen, where I looked about me vaguely, still feeling rather miserable and unsettled. From the kitchen I wandered into the parlour, or "best room", where I unlocked the book cupboard and ran my eye along the shelves. But their contents had no attractions for me. I didn't want books; I wanted to run in the fields with Maggie and look on all the things that were so novel and strange to a London boy. So I shut the cupboard and went back to the kitchen, where, once more, I looked about me, wondering what I should do to pass the time. It was too early to think of frying the sausages, and, besides, I was not hungry, having eaten a substantial breakfast.

It was at this moment that my wandering glance lighted on the clock. There it hung, stolid-faced, silent, and motionless. What, I wondered, could be the matter with it? Often enough before had it stopped, but Aunt Judy's treatment with the bellows had always set it ticking again. Now the bellows seemed to have lost their magic and the clock would have to have something different done to it.

But what? Could it be just a matter of old age? Clocks, I realized, grow old like men; and, thinking of old Mr Gollidge, I realized also that old age is not a condition that can be cured. But I was loth to accept this view and to believe that it had "stopped short, never to go again", like Grandfather's Clock in the song.

I drew up a high chair, and, mounting it, looked up earnestly at the familiar face. It was a pleasant old clock, comely and even beautiful in its homely way, reflecting the simple, honest outlook of the Black Forest peasants who had made it; the wooden dial painted white with a circle of fine bold hour-figures ("chapters" they call them in the trade), a bunch of roses painted on the arch above the dial, and each of the four corner-spaces, or spandrels, decorated with a sprig of flowers, all done quite skilfully and with the unerring good taste of the primitive artist.

From inspection I proceeded to experiment. A gentle pat at the pendulum set it swinging, but brought no sound of life from within; but when I turned the minute-hand, as I had seen Aunt

Judy do, while the pendulum still swung, a faint tick was audible; halting and intermittent, but still a tick. So the clock was not dead. Then I tried a gentle pull at the chain which bore the weight, whereupon the tick became quite loud and regular, and went on for some seconds after I ceased to pull, when it once more died away. But now I had a clue to the mystery. The weight was not heavy enough to keep the clock going; but since the weight had not changed, the trouble must be something inside the clock, obstructing its movements. It couldn't be dust because Aunt Judy had blown it out thoroughly. Then what could it be?

As I pondered this problem I was assailed by a great temptation. Often had I yearned to look into the clock and see what its mysterious "works" were really like, but beyond a furtive peep when the bellows were being plied, I had never had an opportunity. Now, here was a perfect opportunity. Aunt Judy, no doubt, would have disapproved, but she need never know; and, in any case, the clock wouldn't go, so there could be no harm. Thus reasoning, I unhooked the weight from the chain and set it down on the chair, and then, not without difficulty, reached up, lifted the clock off its nail, and, descending cautiously with my prize, laid it tenderly on the table.

I began by opening the little side doors and then lifting them bodily off the brass hooks that served as hinges. Now I could see how to take off the pendulum, and, when I had done this, I carried the clock to the small table by the window, drew up a chair, and, seating myself, proceeded to study the interior at my ease. Not that there was much to study in its simple, artless mechanism. Unlike most of these "Dutch" clocks, it had no alarum (or perhaps this had been removed), and the actual "train" consisted of no more than three wheels and two pinions. Nothing more perfect for the instruction of the beginner could be imagined. There were, it is true, some mysterious wheels just behind the dial in a compartment by themselves and evidently connected with the hands, but these I disregarded for the moment, concentrating my attention on what I recognized as the clock, proper.

It was here that my natural mechanical aptitude showed itself, for by the time that I had studied the train in all its parts, considering each wheel in connection with the pinion to which it was geared, I had begun to grasp the principle on which the whole thing worked. The next proceeding was to elucidate the matter by experiment. If you want to know what effects a wheel produces when it turns, the obvious thing is to turn the wheel and see what happens. This I proceeded to do, beginning with the top wheel, as the most accessible, and turning it very gently with my finger. The result was extremely interesting. Of course, the next wheel turned slowly in the opposite direction, but, at the same time, the wire pendulum-crutch wagged rapidly to and fro.

This was quite a discovery. Now I understood what kept the pendulum swinging and what was the cause of the tick; but, more than this, I now had a clear idea as to the function of the pendulum as the regulator of the whole movement. As to the rest of the mechanism, there was little to discover. I had already noticed the ratchet and pawl connected with the pulley, and now, when I drew the chain through, the reason why it moved freely in the one direction and was held immovable in the other was perfectly obvious; and this made clear the action of the weight in driving the clock.

There remained the group of wheels in the narrow space behind the dial. From their position they were less easy to examine, but when I turned the minute-hand and set them in motion, their action was quite easy to follow. There were three wheels and one small pinion, and when I moved the hand round they all turned. But not in the same direction. One wheel and the pinion turned in the opposite direction to the hand, while the other two wheels, a large one and a much smaller one, turned with the hand; and as the large one moved very slowly, being driven by the little pinion, whereas the small one turned at the same speed as the hand, I concluded that the small wheel belonged to the minute-hand, while the large wheel turned the hour-hand. And at this I had to leave it, since the actual connections could not be ascertained without taking the clock to pieces.

But now that I had arrived at a general understanding of the clock, the original problem reappeared. Why wouldn't it go? I had ascertained that it was structurally complete and undamaged. But yet when it was started it refused to tick and the pendulum did nothing but wag passively and presently cease to do even that. When it had stopped on previous occasions, the bellows had set it going again. Evidently, then, the cause of the stoppage had been dust. Could it be that dust had at last accumulated beyond the powers of the bellows? The appearance of the inside of the clock (and my own fingers) lent support to this view. Wheels and case alike presented a dry griminess that seemed unfavourable to easy running. Perhaps the clock simply wanted cleaning.

Reflecting on this, and on the difficulty of getting at the wheels in the narrow space, it suddenly occurred to me that my tooth-brush would be the very thing for the purpose. Instantly, I hopped off to my little bedroom and was back in a few moments with this invaluable instrument in my hand. Pausing only to make up the fire, which was nearly out, I fell to work on the clock, scrubbing wheels and pinions and whatever the brush would reach, with visible benefit to everything, excepting the brush. When the worst of the grime had been removed, I blew out the dislodged dust with the bellows and began to consider how I should test the results of my efforts. There was no need to hang the clock on its nail (and, indeed, I was not disposed to part with it so soon), but it must be fixed up somehow so that the weight and the pendulum could hang free. Eventually, I solved the problem by drawing the small table towards the large one, leaving a space of about nine inches between them, and bridging the space with a couple of narrow strips of wood from a broken-up packing-case. On this bridge I seated the clock, with its chain and the rehung pendulum hanging down between the strips. Then I hooked on the weight and set the pendulum swinging.

The result was disappointing, but yet my labour had not been all in vain. Start of itself the clock would not, but a slight pull at the chain elicited the longed-for tick, and thereafter for a full minute it continued and I could see the scape wheel turning. But there was no enthusiasm. The pendulum swung in a dead-alive fashion, its excursions growing visibly shorter, until, at length, the ticking stopped and the wheel ceased to turn.

It was very discouraging. As I watched the pendulum and saw its movements slowly die away, I was sensible of a pang of keen disappointment. But still I felt that I had begun to understand the trouble and perhaps I might, by taking thought, hit upon some further remedy. I got up from my chair and wandered restlessly round the room, earnestly cogitating the problem. Something in the clock was resisting the pull of the weight. Now, what could it be? Why had the wheels become more difficult to turn?

So delightfully absorbed was I in seeking the solution of this mystery that all else had faded out of my mind. Gone was all my depression and loneliness. The Finchley omnibus was forgotten; Aunt Budgen was as if she had never been; the green meadows and the pond, and even dear Maggie, had passed clean out of my consciousness. The clock filled the field of my mental vision and the only thing in the world that mattered was the question, what was hindering the movement of its wheels?

Suddenly, in my peregrinations I received an illuminating hint. Stowed away in the corner was Aunt Judy's sewing-machine. Now sewing-machines and clocks are not very much alike, but they both have wheels; and it was known to me that Aunt Judy had a little oil-can with which she used to anoint the machine. Why did she do that? Obviously, to make the wheels run more easily. But if the wheels of a sewing-machine needed oil, why should not those of a clock? The analogy seemed a reasonable one, and, in any case, there could be no harm in trying. Cautiously, and not without some qualms of conscience, I lifted the cover of the machine, and, having found the little, long-snouted oil-can, seized it and bore it away with felonious glee.

My proceedings with that oil-can will hardly bear telling; they would have brought tears to the eyes of a clock-maker. I treated my patient as if it had been an express locomotive with an unlimited thirst for oil. Impartially, I flooded every moving part, within and without: pallets, wheel-teeth, pivots, arbors, the chain-pulley, the "motion wheels" behind the dial, and the centres of the hands. I even oiled the pendulum rod as well as the crutch that held it. When I had finished, the whole interior of the clock seemed to have broken out into a greasy perspiration, and even the woodwork was dark and shiny. But my thoroughness had one advantage: if I oiled all the wrong places, I oiled the right ones as well.

At length, when there was not a dry spot left anywhere, I put down the oil-can, and "in trembling hope" proceeded to make a fresh trial; and even now, after all these years, I can hardly record the incident without emotion. A gentle push at the pendulum brought forth at once a clear and resonant tick, and, looking in eagerly, I could see the scape wheel turning with an air of purpose and the centre wheel below it moving steadily in the opposite direction. And it was no flash in the pan this time. The swing of the pendulum, instead of dying away as before, grew in amplitude and liveliness to an extent almost beyond belief. It seemed that, under the magical influence of the oil-can, the old clock had renewed its youth.

To all of us, I suppose, there have come in the course of our lives certain moments of joy which stand out as unique experiences. They never come a second time; for though the circumstances may seem to recur, the original ecstasy cannot be recaptured. Such a moment was this. As I sat and gazed in rapture at the old clock, called back to vigorous life by my efforts, I enjoyed the rare experience of perfect happiness. Many a time since have I known a similar joy, the joy of complete achievement (and there is no pleasure like it); but this was the first of its kind, and, in its perfection, could never be repeated.

Presently, there broke in upon my ecstasy the sound of the church clock, striking two. I could hardly believe it, so swiftly had the hours sped. And yet certain sensations of which I suddenly became conscious confirmed it. In short, I realized that I was ravenously hungry and that my dinner had yet to be cooked. I set the hands of the clock to the incredible time and rose to seek the frying-pan. But, hungry as I was, I could not tear myself away from my darling, and in the end I compromised by substituting the Dutch oven, which required less attention. Thus I alternated between cookery and horology, clapping the pudding in the large oven and then sitting down once more to watch the I clock until an incendiary sausage, bursting into flame with mighty sputterings, recalled me suddenly to the culinary department.

My cookery was not equal to my horology, at least in its results; yet never have I so thoroughly enjoyed a meal. Black and brittle the sausages may have been and the potatoes sodden and greasy. It was no matter. Hunger and happiness imparted a savour beyond the powers of the most accomplished chef. With my eyes fixed adoringly on the clock (I had "laid my place" where I could conveniently watch the movement as I fed), I devoured the unprepossessing viands with a relish that a gourmet might have envied.

Of the way in which the rest of the day was spent my recollection is rather obscure. In the course of the afternoon I washed up the plates and cleaned the Dutch oven so that Aunt Judy should be free when she came home; but even as I worked at the scullery sink, I listened delightedly to the tick of the clock, wafted to my ear through the open doorway. Later, I made my tea and consumed it, to an *obbligato* accompaniment of raspberry jam, seated beside the clock; and, when I was satisfied unto repletion, I washed the tea-things (including the tea-pot) and set them out tidily in their places on the dresser. That occupied me until six o'clock, and left me with a full three hours to wait before Aunt Judy should return.

Incredibly long hours they were, in strange contrast to the swift-footed hours of the morning. With anxious eyes I watched the minute-hand creeping sluggishly from mark to mark. I even counted the ticks (and found them ninety-six to the minute), and listened eagerly for the sound of the church clock, at once relieved and disappointed to find that it told the same tale. For now my mood had changed somewhat. The joy of achievement became mingled with impatience for its revelation. I was all agog to see Aunt Judy's astonishment when she found the clock going and to hear what she would say. And now, in my mind's eye, the progress of the Finchley omnibus began to present itself. I followed it from stage to stage, crawling ever nearer and nearer to St Martin's Church. With conscious futility I went out, again and again, to look up the street along which the revellers would approach, only to turn back for another glance at the inexorable minute-hand.

At length, the sound of the church clock striking eight admonished me that it was time to return the clock to its place on the wall. It was an anxious business, for, even when I had unhooked the weight, it was difficult for me, standing insecurely on the chair, to reach up to the nail and find the hole in the backplate through which it passed. But at last, after much fumbling, with up-stretched arm and my heart in my mouth, I felt the clock supported, and, having started the pendulum, stepped down with a sigh of relief and hooked on the weight. Now, all that remained to do was to put away the oil-can, wash my tooth-brush at the scullery sink and take it back to my bedroom; and when I had done this and lit the gas, I resumed my restless flittings between the kitchen and the street door.

Nine o'clock had struck when, at long last, from my post on the doorstep, I saw the home-comers turn the corner and advance up the lamp-lighted street. Instantly, I darted back into the house to make sure that the clock was still going, and then, returning, met them almost on the threshold. Aunt Judy greeted me with a kindly smile and evidently misinterpreted my eagerness for their return, for, as she stooped to kiss me, she exclaimed:

"Poor old Nat! I'm afraid it has been a long, dull day for you, and we were all sorry that you couldn't come. However, there is something to make up for it. Uncle Alfred has sent you a shilling and Aunt Anne has sent you some pears; and Maggie has sent you a beautiful pocket-knife. She was dreadfully disappointed that she couldn't give it to you herself, because she has been saving up her pocket-money for weeks to buy it, and you will have to write her a nice letter to thank her."

Now this was all very gratifying, and when the big basket was placed on the kitchen table and the treasures unloaded from it, I received the gifts with proper acknowledgements. But they aroused no enthusiasm, not even the pocket-knife, for I was bursting with impatience for someone to notice the clock.

"You don't seem so particularly grateful and pleased," said Aunt Judy, looking at me critically; and then, as I fidgeted about restlessly, she exclaimed,

"What's the matter with the boy? He's on wires!"

She gazed at me with surprise, and Uncle Sam and the old gentleman turned to look at me curiously. And then, in the momentary silence, Aunt Judy's quick ear caught the tick of the clock. She looked up at it and then exclaimed:

"Why, the clock's going; going quite well, too. Did you start it, Nat? But, of course, you must have done. How did you get it to go?"

With my guilty consciousness of the tooth-brush and the borrowed oil-can, I was disposed to be evasive.

"Well, you see, Aunt Judy," I explained, "it was rather dirty inside, so I just gave it a bit of a clean and put a little oil on the wheels. That's all."

Aunt Judy smiled grimly, but asked no further questions.

"I suppose," said she, "I ought to scold you for meddling with the clock without permission, but as you've made it go we'll say no more about it."

"No," agreed old Mr Gollidge, "I don't see as how you could scold the boy for doing a useful bit of work. The job does him credit and shows that he's got some sense; and sense is what gets a man on in life."

With this satisfactory conclusion to the adventure, I was free to enter into the enjoyment of my newly acquired wealth; and, having sampled the edible portion of it and tested the knife on a stick of fire-wood, spent the short remainder of the evening in rapturous contemplation of my new treasures and the rejuvenated clock. I had never possessed a shilling before, and now, as I examined Uncle Alfred's gift and polished it with my handkerchief, visions of its immense potentialities floated vaguely through my mind; and continued to haunt me, in company with the clock, even when I had blown out my candle and snuggled down into my narrow bed.

CHAPTER TWO

The Pickpocket's Leavings

It was shortly after my eleventh birthday that I conceived a really brilliant idea. It was generated by a card in the shop window of our medical attendant, Dr Pope (in those days, doctors practising in humble neighbourhoods used to keep what were euphemistically described as "Open Surgeries", but which were, in effect, druggists' shops), bearing the laconic announcement, "Boy wanted". I looked at the card and debated earnestly the exact connotation of the word "wanted". It was known to me that some of my schoolfellows contrived to pick up certain pecuniary trifles by delivering newspapers before school hours or doing small jobs in the evenings. Was it possible that the boy wanted by Dr Pope might thus combine remunerative with scholastic industry? There would be no harm in enquiring.

I entered, and, finding the Doctor secretly compounding medicine in a sort of hiding-place at the end of the counter, proceeded to state my case without preamble.

The Doctor put his head round the corner and surveyed me somewhat disparagingly.

"You're a very small boy," he remarked.

"Yes, Sir," I admitted, "but I am very strong for my size."

He didn't appear much impressed by this, but proceeded to enquire:

"Did Mrs Gollidge tell you to apply?"

"No, Sir," I replied, "it's my own idea. You see, Sir, I've been rather an expense to Aunt Judy — Mrs Gollidge, I mean — and I thought that if I could earn a little money, it would be useful."

"A very proper idea, too," said the Doctor, apparently more impressed by my explanation than by my strength.

"Very well. Come round this evening when you leave school. Come straight here, and you can have some tea, and then you can take a basket of medicine and see how you get on with it. I expect you will find it a bit heavy."

"It will get lighter as I go on, Sir," said I; on which the Doctor smiled quite pleasantly, and, having admonished me to be punctual, retired to his hiding-place, and I departed in triumph.

But the Doctor's prediction turned out to be only too correct; for when I lifted the deep basket, stacked with bottles of medicine, I was rather shocked by its weight and had to remind myself of my own prediction that the weight would be a diminishing quantity. That was an encouraging reflection. Moreover, there had been agreeable preliminaries in the form of a Gargantuan tea, including a boiled egg and marmalade, provided by Mrs Stubbs, the Doctor's fat and jovial housekeeper. So I hooked the basket boldly on my arm — and presently shifted it to the other one — and set forth on my round, consulting the written list provided for me and judiciously selecting the nearest addresses to visit first and thereby lighten the basket for the more distant ones.

Still, there was no denying that it was heavy work for a small boy, and when I had made a second round with a fresh consignment, I felt that I had had enough for one day; and when I returned the empty basket, I was relieved to learn that there was nothing more to deliver.

"Well," said the Doctor as I handed in the basket, "how did you get on?"

"All right, thank you, Sir," I replied, "but I think it would be easier if I put rather less in the basket and made more journeys."

The Doctor smiled approvingly. "Yes," he agreed, "that's quite a sensible idea. Give your legs a bit more to do and save your arms. Very well; you think you can do the job?"

"I am sure I can, Sir, and I should like to."

"Good," said he. "The pay will be three and sixpence a week. That suit you?"

It seemed to me an enormous sum, and I agreed gleefully; which closed the transaction and sent me homewards rejoicing and almost oblivious of my fatigue.

A further reward awaited me when I arrived home. Aunt Judy, it is true, had professed disapproval of the arrangement as interfering with my "schooling"; but the substantial hot supper seemed more truly to express her sentiments. It recognized my new status as a working man and my effort to pull my weight in the family boat.

The next day's work proved much less arduous, for I put my plan into operation by sorting out the bottles into groups belonging to particular localities, and thus contrived never to have the basket more than half full. This brought the work well within my powers, so that the end of the day found me no more than pleasantly tired; and the occupation was not without its interest, to say nothing of the dignity of my position as a wage-earner. But the full reward of my industry came when, returning home on Saturday night, I was able to set down my three shillings and sixpence on the kitchen table before Aunt Judy, who was laying the supper. The little heap of silver coins, a florin, a shilling, and a sixpence, made a quite impressive display of wealth. I looked at it with proud satisfaction – and also with a certain wistful curiosity as to whether any of that wealth might be coming my way. I had faint hopes of the odd sixpence, and watched a little anxiously as Aunt Judy spread out the heap with a considering air. Eventually, she picked up the florin and the sixpence, and, pushing the shilling towards me, suddenly put her arm round my neck and kissed me.

"You're a good boy, Nat," said she; and as she released me and dropped the money in her pocket, I picked up my shilling and turned away to hide the tears that had started to my eyes. Aunt

Judy was not a demonstrative woman; but, like many undemonstrative persons, could put a great deal of meaning into a very few words. Half a dozen words and a kiss sweetened my labours for many a day thereafter.

My peregrinations with the basket had, among other effects, that of widening the range of my knowledge of the geography of London. In my early days that knowledge was limited to the few streets that I traversed on my way to and from school, to certain quiet backwaters in which one could spin tops at one's convenience or play games without undue interruption, and certain other quiet streets in which one was likely to find the street entertainer: the acrobat, the juggler, the fire-eater, or, best of all, the Punch and Judy show.

But now the range of my travels coincided with that of Dr Pope's practice and led me far beyond the limits of the familiar neighbourhood; and quite pleasant these explorations were, for they brought me into new streets with new shops in them which provided new entertainment. I think shops were more interesting then than they are in these days of mass-production and uniformity, particularly in an old-fashioned neighbourhood where the crafts were still flourishing. A special favourite was Wardour Street, with its picture-frame makers, its antique shops filled with wonderful furniture and pictures and statuettes and gorgeous clocks.

But the shop that always brought me to a halt was that of M Chanot, the violin-maker, which had, hanging on the door-jamb by way of a trade sign, a gigantic bow (or fiddlestick, as I should have described it). It was stupendous. As I gazed at it with the fascination that the juvenile mind discovers in things gigantic or diminutive, my imagination strove to picture the kind of fiddle that could be played with it and the kind of Titan who could have held the fiddle. And then, as a foil to its enormity, there hung in the window an infant violin, a "kit" such as dancing-masters were wont to carry in the skirt pockets of their ample frock-coats.

A few doors from M Chanot's was the shop of a second-hand bookseller which was also one of the attractions of the street; for it was from the penny and twopenny boxes that my modest library was chiefly recruited. On the present occasion, having paid my respects to the Lilliputian fiddle and the Brobdingnagian bow, I passed on to see what treasures the boxes had to offer. Naturally, I tried the penny box first as being more adapted to my financial resources. But there was nothing in it which specially attracted me; whereupon I turned my attention to the twopenny box.

Now, if I were disposed to moralize, I might take this opportunity to reflect on the momentous consequences which may emerge from the most insignificant antecedents. For my casual rooting about in the twopenny box started a train of events which profoundly influenced my life in two respects, and in one so vitally that, but for the twopenny box, this story could never have been written.

I had turned over nearly all the contents of the box when from the lowest stratum I dredged up a shabby little volume the spine of which bore in faded gold lettering the title, "Clocks and Locks; Denison." The words instantly riveted my attention. Shifting the basket to free both my hands, I opened the book at random and was confronted by a beautiful drawing of the interior of a common house-clock, clearly displaying the whole mechanism. It was a wonderful drawing. With fascinated eyes I pored over it, comparing it rapidly with the well-remembered Dutch clock at home and noting new and unfamiliar features. Then I turned over the leaves and discovered other drawings of movements and escapements on which I gazed in rapture. I had never supposed that there was such a book in the world.

Suddenly I was assailed by a horrible doubt. Had I got twopence? Here was the chance of a lifetime; should I have to let it slip? Putting the basket down on the ground, I searched feverishly through my pockets; but search as I might even in the most unlikely pockets, the product amounted to no more than a single penny. It was an awful predicament. I had set my heart on that book, and the loss of it was a misfortune that I shuddered to contemplate. Yet there was the grievous fact; the price of the book was twopence and I had only a penny.

Revolving this appalling situation, I thought of a possible way out of the difficulty. Leaving my basket on the pavement (a most reprehensible thing to do; but no one wants to steal medicine, and there were only three bottles left), I stepped into the shop with the book in my hand and deferentially approached the book-seller, a stuffy-looking elderly man.

"I want to buy this book, Sir," I explained, timorously, "but it is twopence, and I have only got a penny. Will you keep it for me if I leave the penny as a deposit? I hope you will, Sir. I very much want to have the book."

He looked at me curiously, and, taking the little volume from me, glanced at the title and then turned over the leaves.

"Clocks, hey," said he. "Know anything about clocks?"

"Not much, Sir," I replied, "but I should like to learn some more."

"Well," said he, "you'll know all about them when you have read that book; but it is stiffish reading for a boy."

He handed it back to me, and I laid my penny on it and put it down on the counter.

"I will try to call for it this evening, Sir," said I, "and pay the other penny; and you'll take great care of it, Sir, won't you?"

My earnestness seemed to amuse him, but his smile was a kindly and approving smile.

"You can take it away with you," said he, "and then you will make sure of it."

Tears of joy and gratitude rose to my eyes, so that I had nearly taken up the penny as well as the book. I thanked him shyly but warmly and, picking up the precious volume, went out with it in my hand. But even now I paused to take another look at my treasure before resuming charge of the neglected basket. At length I bestowed the book in my pocket, and, returning to my proper business, took up the basket and was about to sort out the remaining three bottles when I made a most surprising discovery. At the bottom of the basket, beside the bottles, lay a leather wallet. I gazed at it in astonishment. Of course, it was not mine, and I had not put it there, nor, I was certain, had it been there when I went into the shop. Someone must have put it in during my short absence. But why should anyone present me with a wallet? It could hardly have been dropped into the basket by accident; but yet –

I picked it out and examined it curiously, noting that it had an elastic band to keep it closed but that nevertheless it was open. Then I ventured to inspect the inside, but, beyond a few stamps and a quantity of papers, it seemed to contain nothing of interest to me. Besides, it was not mine. I was still puzzling over it when I became aware of a policeman approaching down the street in company with a short, wrathful-looking elderly gentleman who appeared to be talking excitedly while the constable listened with an air of resignation. Just as they reached me, the gentleman caught sight of the wallet and immediately rushed at me and snatched it out of my hand.

"Here you are, Constable," he exclaimed, "here is the stolen property and here is the thief, taken red-handed."

"Red-handed be blowed," said the constable. "You said just now that you saw the man run away, and you've led me a dance a-chasing him. You had better see if there is anything missing."

But the wrathful gentleman had already seen that there was.

"Yes!" he roared, "there were three five-pound notes, and they're gone! Stolen! Fifteen pounds! But I'll have satisfaction. I give this young villain in charge. Perhaps he has the notes on him still. We'll have him searched at the station."

"Now, now," said the constable, soothingly, "don't get excited, Sir. Softly, softly, you catch the monkey. You said that you saw the man run off."

"So I did; but, of course, this young rascal is a confederate, and I give him in charge."

"Wait a minute, Sir. Let's hear what he's got to say. Now, young shaver, tell us how you came by that pocket-book."

I described the circumstances, including my absence in the shop, and the constable, having listened patiently, went in and verified my statement by questioning the bookseller.

"There, Sir, you see," said he when he came out, "it's quite simple. The pickpocket fished the notes out of your wallet and then, as he was making off, he looked for some place where he could drop the empty case out of sight, and there was this boy's basket with no one looking after it, just the very place he wanted. So he dropped it in as he passed. Wouldn't have done to drop it in the street where someone might have seen it and run after him to give it back."

The angry gentleman shook his head. "I can't accept that," said he. "It's only a guess, and an unlikely one at that."

"But," the constable protested, "it's what they always do: drop the empty purses or pocket-books in a doorway or a dark corner or post them in pillar-boxes – anywhere to get the incriminating stuff out of sight. It's common sense."

But the gentleman was obdurate. "No, no," he persisted, "that won't do. The common sense of it is that I found this boy with the stolen property in his possession, and I insist on giving him in charge."

The constable was in a dilemma, but he was a sensible man and he made the best of it.

"Well, Sir," he said, "if you insist, I suppose we must walk round to the station and report the affair. But I can tell you that the inspector won't take the charge."

"He'll have to," retorted the other, "when I have made my statement."

The constable looked at him sourly and then turned to me almost apologetically.

"Well, sonny," said he, "you'll have to come along to the station and see what the inspector has to say."

"Can't I deliver my medicines first?" I pleaded. The people may be wanting them, and there are only three bottles."

The policeman grinned but evidently appreciated my point of view, for he replied, still half-apologetically: "You're quite right, my lad, but I don't suppose they'll be any the worse for a few minutes more without their physic, and the station is quite handy. Come, now; step out."

But even now the irate gentleman was not satisfied.

"Aren't you going to hold him so that he doesn't escape?" he demanded.

Then, for the first time, the patient constable showed signs of temper. "No, Sir," he replied, brusquely, "I am not going to drag a respectable lad through the streets as if he had committed a crime when I know he hasn't."

That settled the matter, and we walked on with the manner of a family party. But it was an uncomfortable experience. To a boy of my age, a police station is a rather alarming sort of place; and the fact that I was going to be charged with a robbery was a little disturbing. However, the constable's attitude was reassuring, and, as we traversed Great Marlborough Street and at last entered the grim doorway, I was only moderately nervous.

The proceedings were, as my constabulary friend had foreseen, quite brief. The policeman made his concise report to the inspector, I answered the few questions that the officer asked, and the gentleman made his statement, incriminating me.

"Where did the robbery take place?" the inspector asked.

"In Berwick Street," was the reply. "I was leaning over a stall when I felt myself touched, and then a man moved away quickly through the crowd; and then I missed my wallet and gave chase."

"You were leaning over a stall," the inspector repeated. "Now, how on earth did he get at your wallet?"

"It was in my coat-tail pocket," the gentleman explained.

"In your coat-tail pocket!" the inspector repeated, incredulously; "with fifteen pounds in it, and you leaning over a stall in a crowded street! Why, Sir, it was a free gift to a pickpocket."

"I suppose I can carry my wallet where I please," the other snapped.

"Certainly you can – at your own risk. Well, I can't accept the charge against this boy. There is no evidence; in fact, there isn't even any suspicion. It would be only wasting the magistrate's time. But I will take the boy's name and address and make a few inquiries. And I will take yours too and let you know if anything transpires."

He took my name and address (and my accuser made a note of them), and that, so far as I was concerned, finished the business. I took up my basket and went forth a free boy in company with my friend the policeman. In Great Marlborough Street we parted, he to return to his beat, and I to the remainder of my round of deliveries.

So ended an incident that had, at one time, looked quite threatening. And yet it had not really ended. Perhaps no incident ever does truly end. For every antecedent begets consequences. Coming events cast their shadows before them; but those shadows usually remain invisible until the events which have cast them have, themselves, come into view. Indeed, it befalls thus almost from necessity; for how can a shadow be identified otherwise than by comparison with the substance?

But I shall not here anticipate the later passages of my story. The consequences will emerge in their proper place. I may, however, refer briefly to the more immediate reactions, though these also had their importance later. The little book which I had purchased (and paid for the same evening) was a treatise on clocks and locks by that incomparable master of horology and mechanism, Edmund Beckett Denison (later to be known as Lord Grimthorpe). It was an invaluable book, and it became my chiefest treasure. Carefully wrapped in a protective cover of brown paper, the precious volume was henceforth my constant companion. The abstruse mathematical sections I had regretfully to pass over, but the descriptive parts were read and reread until I could have recited them from memory. Even the drawings of the Great Westminster Clock, which had at first appeared so bewildering, became intelligible by repeated study, and the intricacies of gravity escapements and maintaining powers grew simple by familiarity.

Thus did the revered E B Denison add a new delight to my life. Not only was every clock-maker's window a thing of beauty and a provider of quiet pleasure, but an object so lowly as the lock of the scullery door – detached by Uncle Sam and by me carefully dismembered – was made to furnish an entertainment compared with which even the Punch and Judy show paled into insignificance.

CHAPTER THREE

Out of the Nest

A certain philosopher, whose name I cannot recall, has, I understand, discovered that there are several different kinds of time. He is not referring to those which are known to astronomers, such as sidereal mean or apparent time, which differ only in terms of measurement, but to time as it affects the young, the middle-aged and the old.

The discovery is not a new one. Shakespeare has told us that "Time travels in divers paces with divers persons", and, for me, the poet's statement is more to the point (and perhaps more true) than the philosopher's. For I am thinking of one "who Time ambles withal", or even "who he stands still withal"; to wit, myself in the capacity of Dr Pope's bottle-boy. That stage of my existence seemed, and still seems, looking back on it, to have lasted for half a life-time; whereas it occupied, in actual fact, but a matter of months.

It came to an end when I was about thirteen, principally by my own act. I had begun to feel that I was making unfair inroads on the family resources, for, though the school that I attended was an inexpensive one, it was not one of the cheapest. Aunt Judy had insisted that I should have a decent education and not mix with boys below our own class, and accordingly she had sent me to the school conducted by the clergyman of our parish, the Reverend Stephen Page, which was attended by the sons of the local shopkeepers and better-class working men. But modest as the school fees were, their payment entailed some sacrifice; for, though we were not poor, still Uncle Sam's earnings as a journeyman cabinet-maker were only thirty shillings a week. Old Mr Gollidge, who did light jobs in a carpenter's shop, made a small contribution, and there was half-a-crown a week from my wages; but, when all was said, it was a tight fit and must have taxed Aunt Judy's powers of management severely to maintain the standard of comfort in which we lived.

Moved by these considerations (and perhaps influenced by the monotonous alternation of school and bottle-basket), I ventured to put the case to Aunt Judy and was relieved to find that she took my suggestions seriously and was obviously pleased with me for making them.

"There is something in what you say, Nat," she admitted. "But remember that your schooling has got to last you for life. It's the foundation that you've got to build on, and it would be bad economy to skimp that."

"Quite right," Uncle Sam chimed in. "You can't make a mahogany table out of deal. Save on the material at the start and you spoil the job."

"Still," I urged, "a penny saved is a penny earned," at which Aunt Judy laughed and gave me a playful pat on the head.

"You are a queer, old-fashioned boy, Nat," said she, "but perhaps you are none the worse for that. Well, I'll see Mr Page and ask him what he thinks about it, and I shall do exactly what he advises. Will that satisfy you?"

I agreed readily enough, having the profoundest respect and admiration for my schoolmaster. For the Reverend Stephen Page, though he disdained not to teach the sons of working men, was a distinguished man in his way. He was a Master of Arts – though of what arts I never discovered – and a Senior Wrangler. That is what was stated on the School prospectus, so it must have been true; but I could never understand it, for a less quarrelsome or contentious man you could not imagine. At any rate, he was a most unmistakable gentleman, and, if he had taught us nothing else, his example of good manners, courtesy and kindliness would have been, a liberal education in itself.

I was present at the interview, and very satisfactory I found it. Aunt Judy stated the problem and Mr Page listened sympathetically. Then he pronounced judgement in terms that rather surprised me as coming from a schoolmaster.

"Education and schooling, Mrs Gollidge, are not quite the same thing. When a boy leaves school to learn a trade, he is not ending his education. Some might say that he is only beginning it. At any rate, the knowledge and skill by which he will earn his living and maintain his family when he has one, and be a useful member of society, is the really indispensable knowledge. Our young friend has a good groundwork of what simple folk call book-learning, and, if he wants to increase it, there are books from which he can learn. Meanwhile, I don't think that he is too young to begin the serious business of life."

That question, then, was settled, and the next one was how the beginning was to be made. As a temporary measure, "while we were looking about", Uncle Sam managed to plant me on his employer, Mr Beeby, as workshop boy at a salary of five shillings a week. So it came about that I made my final round with the bottles, handed in the basket for the last time, drew my wages and, on the following morning, set forth in company with Uncle Sam en route for Mr Beeby's workshop in Broad Street. There was only one occupant when we arrived: a round-shouldered, beetle-browed, elderly man with rolled-up shirt-sleeves, a linen apron and a square brown-paper cap such as workmen commonly wore in those days, who was operating with a very small saw on a piece of wood that was clamped in the bench-vice. He looked up as we entered and remarked:

"So this is the young shaver, is it? There ain't much of him. He'll have to stand on six pennorth of coppers if he is going to work at a bench. Never mind, youngster. You'll be a man before your mother," and with this he returned to his work with intense concentration (I discovered, presently, that he was cutting the pins of a set of dovetails), and Uncle Sam, having provided me with a broom, set me to work at sweeping up the shavings, picking up the little pieces of waste wood and putting them into the large open box in which they were thriftily stored for use in odd jobs. Then he took off his coat, rolled up his sleeves and put on his apron and paper cap; in which costume he seemed to me to be invested with a new dignity; and when he fell to work with a queer-looking, lean-bodied plane on the edge of a slab of mahogany, miraculously producing on it an elegant moulding, I felt that I had never properly appreciated him. Presently the third member of the staff arrived, a young journeyman named Will Foster. He had evidently heard of me, for he saluted me with a friendly grin and a few words of welcome while he was unrobing and getting into working trim. Then he, too, set to work with an air of business on his particular job, the carcase of a small chest of drawers; and I noticed that each of the three men was engaged on his own piece of work, independently of the others. And this I learned later was Mr Beeby's rule, so far as it was practicable. "If a man carries his own job right through," he once explained to me, "and does it well, he gets all the credit; and if he does it badly, he takes all the blame." It seemed a sensible rule. But that was an age of individualism.

I shall not follow in detail my experiences during the few months that I spent in Mr Beeby's workshop. My service there was but an interlude between school and my real start in life. But it was a useful interlude, and I have never regretted it. As I was not an apprentice, I received no formal instruction. But little was needed when I had the opportunity of watching three highly expert craftsmen and following their methods from the preliminary sketch to the finished, work; and I did, in fact, get a good many useful tips besides the necessary instruction in my actual duties.

As to these, they gradually extended as time went on from mere sweeping, cleaning and tidying to more technical activities, but, from the first, the glue-pots were definitely assigned to me. Once for all, the whole art and mystery of the preparation and care of glue was imparted to me. Every night I emptied and cleaned the glue-pots and put the fresh glue in to soak, for Mr Beeby would have nothing to do with stale glue; and every morning, as soon as I arrived, I set the pots of fresh glue on the workshop stove. Then, by degrees, I began to learn the use of tools; to saw along a pencil line, to handle a chisel and a jack-plane (with the aid of an improvised platform to bring my elbows to the bench level) and to use the marking gauge and the try-square, so that, presently, I became proficient enough to be given small, rough jobs of sawing and planing to save the time of the skilled workmen.

It was all very interesting (what creative work is not?), and I was happy enough in the workshop with its pleasant atmosphere of quiet, unhurried industry. I liked to watch these three skilful craftsmen doing difficult things with unconscious case and a misleading appearance of leisureliness, and I learned that this apparently effortless precision was really the result of habitual concentration. The fact was expounded to me by Mr Beeby on an appropriate occasion.

"You've given yourself the trouble, my lad, of doing that twice over. Now the way to work quickly is to work carefully. Attend to what you are doing and see that you make no mistakes."

It was a valuable precept, which I have never forgotten and have always tried to put into practice; indeed, I find myself, to this day, profiting from Mr Beeby's practical wisdom.

But though I was interested and happy in my work, my heart was not in cabinet-making. Clocks and watches still held my affections, and, on most evenings, the short interval between supper and bedtime was occupied in reading and re-reading the books on horology that I possessed. I now had a quite respectable little library; for my good friend, Mr Strutt, the Wardour Street bookseller, was wont to put aside for me any works on the subject that came into his hands, and I suspect that, in the matter of price, he frequently tempered the wind to the shorn lamb.

Thus, though I went about my work contentedly, there lurked always at the back of my mind the hope that some day a chance might present itself for me to get a start on the career of a clock-maker. Apprenticeship was not to be thought of, for the family resources were not equal to a premium. But there might be other ways. Meanwhile, I tended the glue-pots and cherished my dream in secret; and in due course, by very indirect means, the dream became a reality.

The chance came, all unperceived at first, on a certain morning in the sixth month of my servitude, when a burly, elderly man came into the workshop carrying a brown-paper parcel. I recognized him instantly as Mr Abraham, the clock-maker, whose shop in Foubert's Place had been familiar to me since my earliest childhood, and I cast an inquisitive eye on the parcel as he unfastened it on the bench, watched impassively by Mr Beeby. To my disappointment, the unwrapping disclosed only an empty clock-case, and a mighty shabby one at that. Still, even an empty case had a faint horological flavour.

"Well," said Mr Beeby, turning it over disparagingly, "it's a bit of a wreck. Shockingly knocked about, and some fool has varnished it with a brush. But it has been a fine case in its time, and it can be again. What do you want us to do with it? Make it as good as new, I suppose."

"Better," replied Mr Abraham with a persuasive smile.

"Now, you mustn't be unreasonable," said Beeby. "That case was made by a first-class tradesman and no one could make it any better. No hurry for it, I suppose? May as well let us take our time over it."

To this Mr Abraham agreed, being a workman himself; and, after some brief negotiations as to the cost of the repairs, he took his departure. When he had gone, Mr Beeby picked up the "wreck", and, exhibiting it to Uncle Sam, remarked:

"It wants a lot of doing to it, but it will pay for a bit of careful work. Care to take it on when you've finished that table?"

Uncle Sam took it on readily, having rather a liking for renovations of good old work; and when he had clamped up some glued joints on his table, fell to work forthwith on the case, dismembering it, as a preliminary measure, with a thoroughness that rather horrified me, until it seemed to be reduced to little more than a collection of fragments. But I realised the necessity for the dismemberment when I saw him making the repairs and restorations on the separated parts, unhampered by their connections with the others.

I followed his proceedings from day to day with deep interest as the work grew; first, when all the old varnish had been cleaned off, the cutting away of damaged parts, then the artful insetting of new pieces and their treatment with stain until from staring patches they became indistinguishable from the old. So it went on, the battered old parts growing newer and smarter every day with no visible trace of the repairs, and, at last, when the fresh polish was hard, the separated parts were put together and the transformation was complete. The shabby old wreck had been changed into a brand-new case.

"Well, Sam," said Mr Beeby, looking at it critically as its restorer stood it on the newly finished table, "you've made a job of that. It's good now for another hundred years. Ought to satisfy Abraham. Nat might as well run round presently and let him know that it's finished."

"Why shouldn't he take it with him?" Uncle Sam suggested.

Mr Beeby considered the suggestion and eventually, having admonished me to carry the case carefully, adopted it. Accordingly, the case was wrapped in one or two clean dusters and tied up with string, leaving the gilt top handle exposed for convenience of carrying, and I went forth all agog to see how Mr Abraham would be impressed by Uncle Sam's wizardry.

I found that gentleman seated at his counter writing on a card, and, as the inscription was in large Roman capitals, my eye caught at a glance the words, "Smart youth wanted". He rounded off the final D and then looked up at me and enquired:

"You are Mr Beeby's apprentice, aren't you? Is that the case?"

"This is the case, Sir," I replied, "but I am not an apprentice. I am the workshop boy."

"Oh!" said he, "I thought you were an apprentice, as you were working at the bench. Well, let's see what sort of a job they've made of the case. Bring it in here."

He preceded me into a small room at the back of the shop which was evidently the place where he worked, and here, having cleared a space on a side bench, he took the case from me and untied the string. When the removal of the dusters revealed the case in all its magnificence, he regarded it with a chuckle of satisfaction.

"It looks a bit different from what it did when you saw it last, Sir," I ventured to remark.

He seemed a little surprised, for he gave me a quick glance before replying.

"You're right, my boy; I wouldn't have believed it possible. But there, every man to his trade, and Mr Beeby is a master of his."

"It was my uncle, Mr Gollidge, that did the repairs, Sir," I informed him, bearing in mind Mr Beeby's rule that the doer of a good job should have the credit. Again Mr Abraham looked at me, curiously, as he rejoined:

"Then your uncle is a proper tradesman and I take my hat off to him."

I thanked him for the compliment, the latter part of which was evidently symbolical, as he was bareheaded, and then asked:

"Is that the clock that belongs to the case, Sir?" and I pointed to a bracket clock with a handsome brass, silver-circled dial which stood on a shelf, supported by a movement-holder.

"You're quite right," he replied. "That's the clock; all clean and bright and ready for fixing. Would you like to see it in its case? Because, if so, you may as well help me to put it in."

I agreed, joyfully, and as he released the movement from the holder, I unlocked and opened the back door of the case and "stood by" for further instructions, watching intently every stage of the procedure. There was not much for me to do beyond steadying the case and fetching the screws and the screwdriver; but I was learning how a bracket clock was fixed into its case, and when, at last, the job was finished and the fine old clock stood complete in all its beauty and dignity, I had the feeling of, at least, having been a collaborator in the achievement.

It had been a great experience. But all the time, a strong undercurrent of thought had been running at the back of my mind. "Smart youth wanted". Was I a smart youth? Honest self-inspection compelled me to admit that I was not. But perhaps the smartness was only a rhetorical flourish, and in any case, it doesn't do to be too modest. Eventually I plucked up courage to ask:

"Were you wanting a boy, Sir?"

"Yes," he replied. "Do you know of one who wants a job?"

"I was wondering, Sir, if I should be suitable."

"You!" he exclaimed. "But you've got a place. Aren't you satisfied with it?"

"Oh, yes, Sir, I'm quite satisfied. Mr Beeby is a very good master. But I've always wanted to get into the clock trade."

He looked down at me with a broad smile. "My good boy," said he, "cleaning a clock-maker's window and sweeping a clock-maker's floor won't get you very far in the clock trade."

It sounded discouraging, but I was not put off. Experience had taught me that there are boys and boys. As Dr Pope's bottle boy I had learned nothing and gained nothing but the weekly wage. As Mr Beeby's workshop boy I had learned the rudiments of cabinet-making and was learning more every day.

"It would be a start, Sir, and I think I could make myself useful," I protested.

"I daresay you could," said he (he had seen me working at the bench), "and I would be willing to have you. But what about Mr Beeby? If you suit him, it wouldn't be right for me to take you away from him."

"Of course, I should have to stay with him until he had got another boy."

41

"And there is your uncle. Do you think he would let you make the change?"

"I don't think he would stand in my way, Sir. But I'll ask him."

"Very well," said he. "You put it to him, and I'll have a few words with Mr Beeby when I call to settle up."

"And you won't put that card in the window, Sir," I urged.

He smiled at my eagerness but was not displeased; indeed, it was evident to me that he was well impressed and very willing to have me.

"No," he agreed, "I'll put that aside for the present."

Much relieved, I thanked him and took my leave; and as I wended homeward to dinner I prepared myself, a little nervously, for the coming conference.

But it went off more easily than I had expected. Uncle Sam, indeed, was strongly opposed to the change ("just as the boy had got his foot in and was beginning to learn the trade"), and he was disposed to enlarge on the subject of rolling stones. But Aunt Judy was more understanding.

"I don't know, Sam," said she, "but what the boy's right. His heart is set on clocks, and he'll be happier working among things that he likes than going on with the cabinet-making. But I'm afraid Mr Beeby won't be pleased."

That was what I was afraid of. But here again my fears proved to be unfounded. On the principle of grasping the nettle, I attacked him as soon as we returned to the workshop after dinner; and certainly, as he listened to my proposal with his great eyebrows lowered in a frown of surprise, he seemed rather alarming, and I began to "look out for squalls". But when I had finished my explanations, he addressed me so kindly and in such a fatherly manner that I was quite taken aback and almost regretful that I had thought of the change.

"Well, my son," said he, "I shall be sorry to lose you. If you had stayed with me I would have given you your indentures free, because you have got the makings of a good workman. But if the clock trade is your fancy and you have a chance to get into it, you are wise to take that chance. A tradesman's heart ought to be in his trade. You go to Mr Abraham and I'll give you a good character. And you needn't wait for me. Take the job at once and get a start, but look us up now and again and tell us how you are getting on."

I wanted to thank Mr Beeby, but was too overcome to say much. However, he understood. And now – such is human perversity – I suddenly discovered an unsuspected charm in the workshop and an unwillingness to tear myself away from it; and when "knocking-off time" came and I stowed my little collection of tools in the rush basket to carry away, my eyes filled and I said my last "good night" in an absurd, tremulous squeak.

Nevertheless, I took Mr Abraham's shop in my homeward route and found it still open; a fact which I noted with slight misgivings as suggestive of rather long hours. As I entered, my prospective employer rose from the little desk at the end of the counter and confronted me with a look of enquiry; whereupon I informed him briefly of the recent developments and explained that I was now a free boy.

"Very well," said he; "then I suppose you want the job. It's five shillings a week and your tea – unless," he added as an afterthought, "you'd rather run round and have it at home. Will that suit you? Because, if it will, you can come tomorrow morning at half-past eight and I will show you how to take down the shutters."

Thus, informally, were my feet set upon the road which I was to tread all the days of my life; a road which was to lead me, through many a stormy passage, to the promised land which is now my secure abiding-place.

CHAPTER FOUR

The Innocent Accessory

The ancient custom of hanging out a distinctive shop sign still struggles for existence in old-fashioned neighbourhoods. In ours there were several examples. A ham-and-beef merchant proclaimed the nature of his wares by a golden ham dangled above his shop front; a gold-beater more appropriately exhibited a golden arm wielding a formidable mallet; several barbers in different streets displayed the phlebotomist's pole with its spiral hint of blood and bandages; and Mr Abraham announced the horologer's calling by a large clock projecting on a bracket above his shop.

They all had their uses, but it seemed to me that Mr Abraham's was most to the point. For whereas the golden ham could do no more for you than make your mouth water, leaving you to seek satisfaction within, and the barber's offer to "let blood" was a pure fiction (at least, you hoped that it was), Mr Abraham's sign did actually make you a free gift of the time of day. Moreover, for advertising purposes the clock was more efficient. Ham and gold leaf supply only occasional needs; but time is a commodity in constant demand. Its sign was a feature of the little street observed by all wayfarers, and thus conferred distinction on the small, antiquated shop that it surmounted.

At the door of that shop the tenant was often to be seen, looking up and down the street with placid interest and something of a proprietary air; and so I found him, refreshing himself with a pinch of snuff, when I arrived at twenty-six minutes past eight on the morning after my engagement. He received me with unexpected geniality, and, putting away the tortoiseshell snuff-box and glancing up approvingly at the clock, proceeded forthwith to introduce me to the art and mystery of taking down the shutters, including the secret disposal of the padlock. The rest of the daily procedure – the cleaning of the small-paned window, the sweeping of the floor, and such dusting as was necessary – he indicated in general terms, and, having shown me where the brooms and other cleaning appliances were kept, retired to the little workshop which communicated with the retail part of the premises, seated himself at the bench, fixed his glass in his eye, and began some mysterious operations on a watch. I observed him furtively in the intervals of my work, and when I had finished, I entered the workshop for further instructions; but by that time the watch had dissolved into a little heap of wheels and plates which lay in a wooden bowl covered by a sort of glass dish-cover, and that was the last that I saw of it. For it appeared that, when not otherwise engaged, my duty was to sit on a stool behind the counter and "mind the shop".

In that occupation, varied by an occasional errand, I spent the first day; and mighty dull I found it after the life and activity of Mr Beeby's establishment, and profoundly was I relieved when, at half-past eight, Mr Abraham instructed me to put up the shutters under his supervision. As I took my way home, yawning as I went, I almost wished myself back at Beeby's.

But it was a false alarm. The intolerable dullness of that first day was never repeated. On the following morning I took the precaution to provide myself with a book, but it was not needed; for, while I was cleaning the window, Mr Abraham went forth, and presently returned with an excessively dirty "grandfather" clock – without its case – which he carried into the workshop and at once began to "take down" (i.e., to take to pieces). As I had finished my work, I made bold to follow him and hover around to watch the operation; and, as he did not seem to take my presence amiss, but chatted in quite a friendly way as he worked, I ventured to ask one or two questions, and meanwhile kept on the alert for a chance to "get my foot in".

When he had finished the "taking down" and had put away the dismembered remains of the movement in a drawer, leaving the two plates and the dial on the bench, he proceeded to mix up a paste of rotten-stone and oil, and then, taking up one of the plates, began to scrub it vigorously with a sort of overgrown toothbrush dipped in the mixture. I watched him attentively for a minute or two, and then decided that my opportunity had come.

"Wouldn't it save you time, Sir, if I were to clean the other plate?" I asked.

He stopped scrubbing and looked at me in surprise.

"That's not a bad idea, Nat," he chuckled. "Why shouldn't you? Yes, get a brush from the drawer. Watch me and do exactly as I do."

Gleefully, I fetched the brush and set to work, following his methods closely and observing him from time to time as the work progressed. He gave an eye to me now and again, but let me carry out the job completely, even to the final polishing and the "pegging out" of the pivot-holes with the little pointed sticks known as peg-wood. When I had finished, he examined my work critically, testing one or two of the pivot-holes with a clean peg, and finally, as he laid down the plate, informed me that I had made quite a good job of it.

That night I went home in a very different frame of mind. No longer did I yearn for Beeby's. I realised that I had had my chance and taken it. I had got my foot in and was now free of the workshop. Other jobs would come my way and they would not all be mere plate-cleaning. I should see to that. And I did. Cautiously and by slow degrees I extended my offers of help from plates to wheels and pinions, to the bushing of worn pivot-holes and the polishing of pivots on the turns. And each time Mr Abraham viewed me with fresh surprise, evidently puzzled by my apparent familiarity with the mechanism of clocks, and still more so by my ability to make keys and repair locks, an art of which he knew nothing at all.

Thus, the purpose that had been in my mind from the first was working out according to plan. My knowledge of the structure and mechanism of timekeepers was quite considerable. But it was only paper knowledge, book-learning. It had to be supplemented by that other kind of knowledge that can be acquired only by working at the bench, before I could hope to become a clock-maker. The ambition to acquire it had drawn me hither from Mr Beeby's, and now the opportunity seemed to be before me.

In fact, my way was made unexpectedly easy, for Mr Abraham's inclinations marched with mine. Excellent workman as he was, skilful, painstaking and scrupulously conscientious, he had no enthusiasm. As Mr Beeby would have said, his heart was not in his trade. He did not enjoy his work, though he spared no pains in doing it well. But by nature and temperament he was a dealer, a merchant, rather than a craftsman, and it was his ability as a buyer that accounted for the bulk of his income. Hence he was by no means unwilling for me to take over the more laborious and less remunerative side of the business, in so far as I was able, for thereby he was left with more free time to devote to its more profitable aspects.

Exactly how he disposed of this free time I could never quite make out. I got the impression that he had some other interests which he was now free to pursue, having a deputy to carry on the mere retail part of the business and attend to simple repairs. But however that may have been, he began occasionally to absent himself from the shop, leaving me in charge; and as time went on and he found that I managed quite well without him, his absences grew more frequent and prolonged until they occurred almost daily, excepting when there were important repairs on hand. It seemed an anomalous arrangement, but there was really nothing against it. He had instructed me in the simple routine of the business, had explained the artless "secret price marks" on the stock, and ascertained (I think from Beeby) that I was honest and trustworthy, and if he was able to employ his free time more profitably, there was nothing further to be said.

It was on the occasion of one of these absences that an incident occurred which, simple as it appeared to be at the time, was later to develop unexpected consequences. This was one of the days on which Mr Abraham went down into the land of Clerkenwell to make purchases of material and stock. Experience had taught me that a visit to Clerkenwell meant a day off; and, there being no repairs on hand, I made my arrangements to pass the long, solitary day as agreeably as possible. It happened that I had recently acquired an old lock of which the key was missing; and I decided to pass the time pleasantly in making a key to fit it. Accordingly, I selected from the stock of spare keys that I kept in my cupboard a lever key the pipe of which would fit the drill-pin of the lock, but of which the bit was too long to enter; and with this and a small vice and one or two tools, I went out into the shop and prepared to enjoy myself.

I had fixed the vice to the counter, taken off the front plate of the lock (it was a good but simple lock with three levers), clamped the key in the vice and was beginning to file off the excess length of the bit, preparatory to cutting the steps, when a man entered the shop, and, sauntering up to the counter, fixed an astonished eye on the key.

"Guvnor in?" he enquired.

I replied that he was not.

"Pity," he commented. "I've broke the glass of my watch. How long will he be?"

"I don't think he will be back until the evening. But I can fit you a new glass."

"Can you, though?" said he. "You seem to be a handy sort of bloke for your size. How old are you?"

"Getting on for fourteen," I replied, holding out my hand for the watch which he had produced from his pocket.

"Well, I'm blowed," said he; "fancy a blooming kid of fourteen running a business like this."

I rather resented his description of me, but made no remark. Besides, it was probably meant as a compliment, though unfortunately expressed. I glanced at his watch, and, opening the drawer in which watch-glasses were kept, selected one of the suitable size, tried it in the bezel after removing the broken pieces, and snapped it in.

"Well, I'm sure!" he exclaimed as I returned the watch to him. "Wonderful handy cove you are. How much?"

I suggested sixpence, whereupon he fished a handful of mixed coins out of his pocket and began to sort them out. Finally he laid a sixpence on the counter and once more fixed his eyes on the vice.

"What are you doing to that lock?" he asked.

"I am making a key to fit it," I replied.

"Are you, reely?" said he with an air of surprise. "Actooally making a key? Re-markable handy bloke you are. Perhaps you could do a little job for me. There is a box of mine what I can't get open. Something gone wrong with the lock. Key goes in all right but it won't turn. Do you think you could get it to open if I was to bring it along here?"

"I don't know until I have seen it," I replied. "But why not take it to a locksmith?"

"I don't want a big job made of it," said he. "It's only a matter of touching up the key, I expect. What time did you say the guvnor would be back?"

"I don't expect him home until closing time. But he wouldn't have anything to do with a locksmith's job, in any case."

"No matter," said he. "You'll do for me. I'll just cut round home and fetch that box"; and with this he bustled out of the shop and turned away towards Regent Street.

His home must have been farther off than he had seemed to suggest, for it was nearly two hours later when he reappeared, carrying a brown-paper parcel. I happened to see him turn into the street, for I had just received a shop dial from our neighbour, the grocer, and had accompanied him to the door, where he paused for a final message.

"Tell the governor that there isn't much the matter with it, only it stops now and again, which is a nuisance."

He nodded and turned away, and at that moment the other customer arrived with the unnecessary announcement that "here he was". He set the parcel on the counter, and, having untied the string, opened the paper covering just enough to expose the keyhole; by which I was able to see that the box was covered with morocco leather and that the keyhole guard seemed to be of silver. Producing a key from his pocket, he inserted it and made a show of trying to turn it.

"You see?" said he. "It goes in all right, but it won't turn. Funny, isn't it? Never served me that way before."

I tried the key and then took it out and looked at it, and, as a preliminary measure, probed the barrel with a piece of wire. Then, as the barrel was evidently clean, I tried the lock with the same piece of wire. It was a ward lock, and the key was a warded key, but the wards of the lock and those of the key were not the same. So the mystery was solved; it was the wrong key.

"Well, now," my friend exclaimed, "that's very singler. I could have swore it was the same key what I have always used, but I suppose you know. What's to be done? Do you think you can make that key fit?"

Now, here was a very interesting problem. I had learned from the incomparable Mr Denison that the wards of a lock are merely obstructions to prevent it from being opened with the wrong key, and that, since the fore edge of the bit is the only acting part of such a key, a wrong key can be turned into a right one by simply cutting away the warded part and leaving the fore edge intact. I had never tried the experiment; but here was an opportunity to put the matter to a test.

"I'll try, if you like," I replied – "that is, if you don't mind my cutting the key about a little."

"Oh, the key is no good to me if it won't open the lock. I don't care what you do to it."

With this, I set to work gleefully, first making a further exploration of the lock with my wire and then carrying the key into the workshop, where there was a fixed vice. There I attacked it with a hack-saw and a file, and soon had the whole of the bit cut away excepting the top and fore edge. All agog to see how it worked, I went back to the shop with a small file in my hand in case any further touches should be necessary, and, inserting the key, gave a gentle turn. It was at once evident that there was now no resistance from the wards, but it did not turn freely. So I withdrew it and filed away a fraction from the fore edge to reduce the friction. The result was a complete success, for when I re-inserted it and made another trial, it turned quite freely and I heard the lock click.

My customer was delighted (and so was I). He turned the key backwards and forwards several times and once opened the lid of the box; but only half an inch – just enough to make sure that it cleared the lock. Then he took out the key, put it in his pocket, and proceeded to replace the paper cover and tie the string.

"Well," said he, "you are a regler master craftsman, you are. How much have I got to pay?"

I suggested that the job was worth a shilling, to which he agreed.

"But who gets that shilling?" he enquired.

"Mr Abraham, of course," I replied. "It's his shop."

"So it is," said he, "but you have done the job, so here's a bob for yourself, and you've earned it."

He laid a couple of shillings on the counter, picked up his parcel and went out, whistling gleefully.

Now, all this time, although my attention had been concentrated on the matter in hand, I had been aware of something rather odd that was happening outside the shop. My customer had certainly had no companion when he arrived, for I had seen him enter the street alone. But yet he seemed to have some kind of follower; for hardly had he entered the shop when a man appeared, looking in at the window and seeming to keep a watch on what was going on within. At first he did not attract my attention – for a shop window is intended to be looked in at. But presently he moved off, and then returned for another look; and while I was working at the key in the workshop, I could see him on the opposite side of the street, pretending to look in the shop windows there, but evidently keeping our shop under observation.

I did not give him much attention while I was working at my job; but when my customer departed, I went out to the shop door and watched him as he retired down the street. He was still alone. But now, the follower, who had been fidgeting up and down the pavement opposite, and looking in at shop windows, turned and walked away down the street, slowly and idly at first, but gradually increasing his pace as he went, until he turned the corner quite quickly.

It was very queer; and, my curiosity being now fairly aroused, I darted out of the shop and ran down the street, where, when I came to the corner, I could see my customer striding quickly along King Street, while the follower was "legging it" after him as hard as he could go. What the end of it was I never saw, for the man with the parcel disappeared round the corner of Argyll Place before the follower could come up with him.

It was certainly a very odd affair. What could be the relations of these two men? The follower could not have been a secret watcher, for there he was, plainly in view of the other. I turned it over in my mind as I walked back to the shop, and as I entered the transaction in the day-book ("key repaired, 1/-") and dropped the two shillings into the till, having some doubt as to my title to the "bob for myself". (But its presence was detected by Mr Abraham when we compared the till with the day-book, and it was, after a brief discussion, restored to me.) Even when I was making a tentative exploration of the shop dial and restoring the vanished oil to its dry bearings and pallets, I still puzzled over this mystery until, at last, I had to dismiss it as insoluble.

But it was not insoluble, though the solution was not to appear for many weeks. Nor, when my customer disappeared round the corner, was he lost to me for ever. In fact, he re-visited our premises less than a fortnight after our first meeting, shambling into the shop just before dinner-time and greeting me as before with the enquiry:

"Guvnor in?"

"No," I replied, "he has just been called out on business, but he will be back in a few minutes." (He had, in fact, walked round, according to his custom about this time, to inspect the window of the cook's shop in Carnaby Street.) "Is there anything that I can do?"

"Don't think so," said he. "Something has gone wrong with my watch. Won't go. I expect it is a job for the guvnor."

He brought out from his pocket a large gold watch, which he passed across the counter to me. I noted that it was not the watch to which I had fitted the glass and that it had a small bruise on the edge. Then I stuck my eyeglass in my eye, and, having opened first the case and then the dome, took a glance at the part of the movement that was visible. That glance showed me that the balance-staff pivot was broken, which accounted sufficiently for the watch's failure to go. But it showed me something else — something that thrilled me to the marrow. This was no ordinary watch. It was fitted with that curious contrivance that English watch-makers call a "tourbillion" – a circular revolving carriage on which the escapement is mounted, the purpose being the avoidance of position errors. Now, I had never seen a tourbillion before, though I had read of them as curiosities of advanced watch construction, and I was delighted with this experience, and the more so when I read on the movement the signature of the inventor of this mechanism, Breguet à Paris. So absorbed was I with this mechanical wonder that I forgot the existence of the customer until he, somewhat brusquely, drew my attention to it. I apologized and briefly stated what was the matter with the watch.

"That don't mean nothing to me," he complained. "I want to know if there's much wrong with it, and what it will cost to put it right."

I was trying to frame a discreet answer when the arrival of Mr Abraham relieved me of the necessity. I handed him the watch and my eyeglass and stood by to hear his verdict.

"Fine watch," he commented. "French make. Seems to have been dropped. One pivot broken; probably some others. Can't tell until I have taken it down. I suppose you want it repaired."

"Not if it is going to be an expensive job," said the owner. "I don't want it for use. I got a silver one what does for me. I bought this one cheap, and I wish I hadn't now. Gave a cove a fiver for it."

"Then you got it very cheap," said Mr Abraham.

"S'pose I did, but I'd like to get my money back all the same. That's all I ask. Care to give me a fiver for it?"

Mr Abraham's eyes glistened. All the immemorial Semitic passion for a bargain shone in them. And well it might. Even I could tell that the price asked was but a fraction of the real value. It was a tremendous temptation for Mr Abraham.

But, rather to my surprise, he resisted it. Wistfully, he looked at the watch, and especially at the hall-mark, or its French equivalent, for nearly a minute; then, with a visible pang of regret, he closed the case and pushed the watch across the counter.

"I don't deal in second-hand watches," said he.

"Gor!" exclaimed our customer, "it ain't second-hand for you. Do the little repairs what are necessary, and it's a new watch. Don't be a mug, Mister. It's the chance of a lifetime."

But Mr Abraham shook his head and gave the watch a further push.

"Look here!" the other exclaimed, excitedly, "the thing's no good to me. I'll take four pund ten. That's giving it away, that is. Gor! You ain't going to refuse that! Well, say four pund. Four blooming jimmies! Why, the case alone is worth more than double that."

Mr Abraham broke out into a cold sweat. It was a frightful temptation, for what the man said was literally true. But even this Mr Abraham resisted; and eventually the owner of this priceless timepiece, realizing that "the deal was off", sulkily put it in his pocket and slouched out without another word.

"Why didn't you buy it, Sir?" I asked. "It was a beautiful watch."

"So it was," he agreed, "and a splendid case – twenty-two carat gold; but it was too cheap. I would have given him twice what he asked if I had known how he came by it."

"You don't think he stole it, Sir, do you?" I asked.

"I suspect someone did," he replied, "but whether this gent was the thief or only the receiver is not my affair."

It wasn't mine either; but as I recalled my former transaction with this "gent" I was inclined to form a more definite opinion; and thereupon I decided to keep my own counsel as to the details of that former transaction. But circumstances compelled me to revise that decision when the matter was reopened by someone who took a less impersonal view than that of Mr Abraham. That someone was a tall, military-looking man who strode into our shop one evening about six weeks after the watch incident. He made no secret of his business, for, as he stepped up to the counter, he produced a card from his pocket and introduced himself with the statement:

"You are Mr David Abraham, I think. I am Detective Sergeant Pitts."

Mr Abraham bowed graciously, and, disregarding the card, replied that he was pleased to make the officer's acquaintance; whereupon the sergeant grinned and remarked:

"You are more easily pleased than most of my clients."

Mr Abraham smiled and regarded the officer with a wary eye.

"What can I have the pleasure of doing for you?" he asked.

"That's what I want to find out," said the sergeant. "I have information that, on or about the thirteenth of May, you made a skeleton key for a man named Alfred Coomey, alias John Smith. Is that correct?"

"No," Abraham replied, in a startled voice, "certainly not. I never made a skeleton key in my life. Don't know how to, in fact."

The officer's manner became perceptibly more dry.

"My information," said he, "is that on the date mentioned, the said Coomey, or Smith, brought a jewel-case to this shop and that you made a skeleton key that opened it. You say that is not true."

"Wait a moment," said Abraham, turning to me with a look of relief; "perhaps the sergeant is referring to the man you told me about who brought a box here to have a key fitted when I was out. It would be about that date."

The sergeant turned a suddenly interested eye on me and remarked:

"So this young shaver is the operator, is he? You'd better tell me all about it; and first, what sort of box was it?"

"I couldn't see much of it, Sir, because it was wrapped in brown paper, and he only opened it enough for me to get at the keyhole. But it was about fifteen inches long by about nine broad, and it was covered with green leather and the keyhole plate seemed to be silver. That is all that I could see."

"And what about the key?"

"It was the wrong key, Sir. It went in all right, but it wouldn't turn. So I cut away part of the bit so that it would go past the wards and then it turned and opened the lock."

The sergeant regarded me with a grim smile.

"You seem to be a rather downy young bird," said he. "So you made him a skeleton key, did you? Now, how did you come to know how to make a skeleton key?"

I explained that I had read certain books on locks and had taken a good deal of interest in the subject, a statement that Mr Abraham was able to confirm.

"Well," said the sergeant, "it's a useful accomplishment, but a bit dangerous. Don't you be too handy with skeleton keys, or you may find yourself taking a different sort of interest in locks and keys."

But here Mr Abraham interposed with a protest.

"There's nothing to make a fuss about, Sergeant. The man brought his box here to have a key fitted, and my lad fitted a key. There was nothing incorrect or unlawful in that."

"No, no," the sergeant admitted, "I don't say that there was. It happens that the box was not his, but, of course, the boy didn't know that. I suppose you couldn't see what was in the box?"

"No, Sir. He only opened it about half an inch, just to see that it would open."

The sergeant nodded. "And as to this man, Coomey; do you think you would recognize him if you saw him again?"

"Yes, Sir, I am sure I should. But I don't know that I could recognise the other man."

"The other man!" exclaimed the sergeant. "What other man?"

"The man who was waiting outside"; and here I described the curious proceedings of Mr Coomey's satellite and so much of his appearance as I could remember.

"Ha!" said the sergeant, "that would be the footman who gave Coomey the jewel-case. Followed him here to make sure that he didn't nip off with it. Well, you'd know Coomey again, at any rate. What about you, Mr Abraham?"

"I couldn't recognize him, of course. I never saw him."

"You saw him later, you know, Sir, when he came in with the watch," I reminded him.

"But you never told me – " Abraham began, with a bewildered stare at me; but the sergeant broke in, brusquely:

"What's this about a watch, Mr Abraham? You didn't mention that. Better not hold anything back, you know."

"I am not holding anything back," Abraham protested. "I didn't know it was the same man"; and here he proceeded to describe the affair in detail and quite correctly, while the sergeant took down the particulars in a large, funereal note-book.

"So you didn't feel inclined to invest," said he with a sly smile. "Must have wrung your heart to let a bargain like that slip."

"It did," Abraham admitted, "but, you see, I didn't know where he had got it."

"We can take it," said the sergeant, "that he got it out of that jewel-case. What sort of watch was it? Could you recognize it?"

"I am not sure that I could. It was an old watch. French make, gold case, engine-turned with a plain centre. No crest or initials."

"That's all you remember, is it? And what about you, young shaver? Would you know it again?"

"I think I should, Sir. It was a peculiar watch; made by Breguet of Paris, and it had a tourbillion."

"Had a what!" exclaimed the sergeant. "Sounds like some sort of disease. What does he mean?" he added, gazing at Mr Abraham.

The latter gave a slightly confused description of the mechanism, explaining that he had not noticed it, as he had been chiefly interested in the case; whereupon the sergeant grinned and remarked that the melting-pot value was what had also interested Mr Coomey.

"Well," he concluded, shutting up his note-book, "that's all for the present. I expect we shall want you to identify Coomey, and the other man if you can; and when the case comes up for the adjourned hearing, you will both have to come and give evidence. But I will let you know about that later." With this and a nod to Mr Abraham and a farewell grin at me, he took his departure.

Neither to my employer nor myself was the prospect of visiting the prison and the court at all alluring, especially as our simultaneous absence would entail shutting up the shop; and it was a relief to us both when the sergeant paid us a second, hurried visit to let us know that, as the accused men had decided to plead guilty, our testimony would not be required. So that disposed of the business so far as we were concerned.

CHAPTER FIVE

Mr Parrish

It has been remarked, rather obviously, that it is an ill wind that blows nobody good, and also that one man's meat is another man's poison. The application of these samples of proverbial wisdom to this history is in the respective effects of a severe attack of bronchitis upon Mr Abraham and me. The bronchitis was his, with all its attendant disadvantages, an unmitigated evil, whereas to me it was the determining factor of a beneficial change.

While he was confined to his bed, under the care of the elderly Jewess who customarily "did for him", my daily procedure was, when I had shut up the shop, to carry the contents of the till with the day-book to his bedroom that he might compare them and check the day's takings; and it was on one of these occasions, when he was beginning to mend, that the change in my prospects came into view.

"I have been thinking about you, Nat," said he. "You're an industrious lad, and you've done your duty by me since I've been ill, and I think I ought to do something for you in return. Now, you're set on being a clock-maker, but you can't get into the trade without serving an apprenticeship in the regular way. Supposing I were willing to take you on as my apprentice, how would you like that?"

I jumped at the offer, but suggested that there might be difficulties about the premium.

"There wouldn't be any premium," said he. "I should give you your indentures free and pay the lawyer's charges. Think it over, Nat, and see what your uncle and aunt have to say about it."

It didn't require much thinking over on my part, nor, when I arrived home in triumph and announced my good fortune, was there any difference of opinion as to the practical issue, though the respective views were differently expressed. Uncle Sam thought it "rather handsome of the old chap" (Mr Abraham was about fifty-five), but Aunt Judy was inclined to sniff.

"He hasn't done badly all these months," said she, "with a competent journeyman for five shillings a week; and he'd be pretty well up a tree if Nat left him to get another job. Oh, he knows which side his bread's buttered."

There may have been some truth in Aunt Judy's comment, but I thought there was more wisdom in old Mr Gollidge's contribution to the debate.

"It may be a good bargain for Mr Abraham," said he, "but that don't make it a worse bargain for Nat. It's best that both parties should be suited."

In effect, it was agreed that the offer should be accepted; and when I conveyed this decision to Mr Abraham, the necessary arrangements were carried through forthwith. The indentures were drawn up, on Mr Abraham's instructions, by his solicitor, a Mr Cohen, who brought them to the shop by appointment; and when they had been submitted to and approved by Aunt Judy, they were duly signed by both parties on a small piece of board laid on the invalid's bed, and I was then and there formally bound apprentice for the term of seven years to "the said David Abraham hereinafter called the Master", who, for his part, undertook to instruct me in the art and mystery of clock-making. I need not recite the terms of the indenture in detail, but I think Aunt Judy found them unexpectedly liberal.

To my surprise, I was to be given board and lodging; I was to receive five shillings a week for the first year and my wages were to increase by half-a-crown annually, so that in my last year I should be receiving the full wage of a junior journeyman, or improver.

These were great advantages; for henceforth not only would Aunt Judy be relieved of the cost of maintaining me, but she would now have an additional room to dispose of profitably. But beyond these material benefits there were others that I appreciated even more. Now, as an apprentice, I was entitled to instruction in that part of the "art and mystery" which was concerned with the purchase of stock and material. It is true that, at the time, I did not fully realize the glorious possibilities contained in this provision. Only when, a week or so later, Mr Abraham (hereinafter called the Master) was sufficiently recovered to descend to the shop, did they begin to dawn on me.

"We seem to be getting short of material," said he after an exploratory browse round the workshop. "I am not well enough to go out yet, so you'll have to run down to Clerkenwell and get the stuff. We'd better draw up a list of what we want."

We made out the list together, and then "the Master" gave me the addresses of the various dealers with full directions as to the route, adding, as I prepared to set forth: "Don't be any longer than you can help, Nat. I'm still feeling a bit shaky."

The truth of the latter statement was so evident that I felt morally compelled to curtail my explorations to the utmost that was possible. But it was a severe trial. For as I hurried along Clerkenwell Road I found myself in a veritable Tom Tiddler's Ground. By sheer force of will, I had to drag myself past those amazing shop windows that displayed – better and more precious than gold and silver – all the wonders of the clock-maker's art. I hardly dared to look at them. But even the hasty glance that I stole as I hurried past gave me an indelible picture of those unbelievable treasures that I can recall to this day. I see them now, though the years have made familiar the subjects of that first, ecstatic, impression: the entrancing tools and gauges, bench-drills and wheel-cutters, the lovely little watch-maker's lathe, fairer to me than the Rose of Sharon or the Lily of the Valley, the polishing heads with their buffs and brushes, the assembled movements, and the noble regulator with its quicksilver pendulum, dealing with seconds as common clocks do with hours. I felt that I could have spent eternity in that blessed street.

However, my actual business, though it was but with dealers in "sundries", gave me the opportunity for more leisured observations. Besides Clerkenwell Road, it carried me to St John's Gate and Clerkenwell Green; from which, at last, I tore myself away and set forth at top speed towards Holborn to catch the omnibus for Regent Circus (now, by the way, called Oxford Circus). But all the way, as my carriage rumbled sleepily westward, the vision of those Aladdin caves floated before my eyes and haunted me until I entered the little shop and dismissed my master to his easy-chair in the sitting-room. Then I unpacked my parcels, distributed their contents in the proper receptacles, put away the precious price-lists that I had collected for future study, and set about the ordinary business of the day.

I do not propose to follow in detail the course of my life as Mr Abraham's apprentice. There would, indeed, be little enough to record; for the days and months slipped by unreckoned, spent with placid contentment in the work which was a pleasure to do and a satisfaction when done. But apart from the fact that there would be so little to tell, the mere circumstances of my life are not the actual subject of this history. Its purpose is, as I have explained, to trace the antecedents of certain events which occurred many years later when I was able to put my finger on the one crucial fact that was necessary to disclose the nature and authorship of a very singular crime. With the discovery of that crime, the foregoing chapters have had at least some connection; and in what follows I shall confine myself to incidents that were parts of the same train of causation.

Of these, the first was concerned with my uncle Sam. By birth he was a Kentish man, and he had served his time in a small workshop at Maidstone, conducted by a certain James Wright. When his apprenticeship had come to an end, he had migrated to

London; but he had always kept in touch with his old master and paid him occasional visits. Now, about the end of my third year, Mr Wright, who was getting too old to carry on alone, had offered to take him into partnership; and the offer being obviously advantageous, Uncle Sam had accepted and forthwith made preparations for the move.

It was a severe blow to me, and I think also to Aunt Judy. For though I had taken up my abode with Mr Abraham, hardly an evening had passed which did not see me seated in the familiar kitchen (but not in my original chair) facing the old Dutch clock and listening to old Mr Gollidge's interminable yarns. That kitchen had still been my home as it had been since my infancy. I had still been a member, not only of the family, but of the household, absent, like Uncle Sam, only during working hours. But henceforth I should have no home – for Mr Abraham's house was a mere lodging; no family circle, and, worst of all, no Aunt Judy.

It was a dismal prospect. With a sinking heart I watched the preparations for the departure and counted the days as they slid past, all too quickly; and when the last of the sands had run out and I stood on the platform with my eyes fixed on the receding train, from a window of which Aunt Judy's arm protruded, waving her damp handkerchief, I felt as might have felt some marooned mariner following with despairing gaze the hull of his ship sinking below the horizon. As the train disappeared round a curve, I turned away and could have blubbered aloud; but I was now a young man of sixteen, and a railway station is not a suitable place for the display of the emotions.

But in the days that followed, my condition was very desolate and lonely; and yet, as I can now see, viewing events with a restrospective eye, this shattering misfortune was for my ultimate good. Indeed, it yielded certain immediate benefits. For, casting about for some way of disposing of the solitary evenings, I discovered an institution known as the Working Men's College, then occupying a noble old house in Great Ormond Street; whereby it came about that the homely kitchen was replaced by austere but pleasant classrooms, and the voice of old Mr Gollidge recounting the mutiny on the *Mary Jane* by those of friendly young graduates explaining the principles of algebra and geometry, of applied mechanics and machine-drawing.

The next incident, trivial as it will appear in the telling, had an even more profound effect in the shaping of my destiny; indeed, but for that trifling occurrence, this history could never have been written. So I proceed without further apologies.

On a certain morning at the beginning of the fourth year of my apprenticeship, my master and I were in the shop together reviewing the stock when a rather irate-looking, elderly gentleman entered, and, fixing a truculent eye on Mr Abraham, demanded:

"Do you know anything about equatorial clocks?"

Now, I suspect that Mr Abraham had never heard of an equatorial clock, all his experience having been in the ordinary trade. But it would never do to say so. Accordingly he temporized.

"Well, Sir, they don't, naturally, come my way very often. Were you wanting to purchase one?"

"No, I wasn't, but I've got one that needs some slight repair or adjustment. I am a maker of philosophical instruments and I have had an equatorial sent to me for overhaul. But the clock won't budge; won't start at all. Now, clocks are not philosophical instruments and I don't pretend to know anything about 'em. Can you come round and see what's the matter with the thing?"

This was, for me, a rather disturbing question. For our visitor was none other than the gentleman who had accused me of having stolen his pocket-book. I had recognized him at the first glance as he entered, and had retired discreetly into the background lest he should recognize me. But now I foresaw that I should be dragged forth into the light of day. And so it befell.

"I am afraid," Mr Abraham said, apologetically, "that I can't leave my business just at the moment. But my assistant can come round with you and see what is wrong with your equa – with your clock."

Our customer looked at me, disparagingly, and my heart sank. But either I had changed more than I had supposed in the five years that had elapsed, or the gentleman's eyesight was not very acute (it turned out that he was distinctly near-sighted). At any rate, he showed no sign of recognition, but merely replied gruffly:

"I don't want any boys monkeying about with that clock. Can't you come yourself?"

"I am afraid I really can't. But my assistant is a perfectly competent workman, and I take full responsibility for what he does."

The customer grunted and scowled at me.

"Very well," he said, with a very bad grace. "I hope he's better than he looks. Can you come with me now?"

I replied that I could; and, having collected from the workshop the few tools that I was likely to want, I went forth with him, keeping slightly in the rear and as far as possible out of his field of view. But, to my relief, he took no notice of me, trudging on doggedly and looking straight before him.

We had not far to go, for, when we had passed halfway down a quiet street in the neighbourhood of Oxford Market, he halted at a door distinguished by a brass plate bearing the inscription,

"W Parrish, Philosophical Instrument Maker", and, inserting a latch-key, admitted himself and me. Still ignoring my existence, he walked down a long passage ending in what looked like a garden door but which, when he opened it, proved to be the entrance to a large workshop in which were a lathe and several fitted benches, but, at the moment, no human occupants other than ourselves.

"There," said he, addressing me for the first time, but still not looking at me, "that's the clock. Just have a look at it, and mind you don't do any damage. I've got a letter to write, but I'll be back in a few minutes."

With this he took himself off, much to my satisfaction, and I proceeded forthwith to make a preliminary inspection. The "patient" was a rather large telescope mounted on a cast-iron equatorial stand. I had never seen an equatorial before except in the form of a book-illustration, but from this I was able easily to recognize the parts and also the clock, which was perched on the iron base with its winding-handle within reach of the observer. This handle I tried, but found it fully wound (it was a spring-driven clock, fitted with governor balls and a fly, or fan), and I then proceeded to take off the loose wooden case so as to expose the movement. A leisurely inspection of this disclosed nothing structurally amiss, but it had an appearance suggesting long disuse and was desperately in need of cleaning.

Suspecting that the trouble was simply dirt and dry pivots, I produced from my bag a little bottle of clock-oil and an oiler and delicately applied a small drop of the lubricant to the empty and dry oil-sinks and to every point that was exposed to friction. Then I gave the ball-governor a cautious turn or two, whereupon my diagnosis was immediately confirmed; for the governor, after a few sluggish revolutions as the oil worked into the bearings, started off in earnest, spinning cheerfully and in an obviously normal fashion.

This was highly satisfactory. But now my curiosity was aroused as to the exact effect of the clock on the telescope. The former was geared by means of a long spindle to the right ascension circle, and on this was a little microscope mounted opposite the index. To the eyepiece of this microscope I applied my eye, and was thrilled to observe the scale of the circle creeping almost imperceptibly past the vernier. It was a great experience. I had read of these things in the optical textbooks, but here was this delightful mechanism made real and active before my very eyes. I was positively entranced as I watched that slow, majestic motion; in fact I was so preoccupied that I was unaware of Mr Parrish's re-entry until I heard his voice; when I sprang up with a guilty start.

"Well," he demanded, gruffly, "have you found out – Oh, but I see you have."

"Yes, Sir," I said, eagerly, "it's running quite well now, and the right ascension circle is turning freely, though, of course, I haven't timed it."

"Ho, you haven't, hey?" said he. "Hm. Seem to know all about it, young fellow. What was the matter with the clock?"

"It only wanted a little adjustment," I replied, evasively, for I didn't like to tell him that it was only a matter of oil. "But," I added, "it really ought to be taken to pieces and thoroughly cleaned."

"Ha!" said he, "I'll let the owner do that. If it goes, that is all that matters to me. You can tell your master to send me the bill."

He still spoke gruffly, but there was a subtle change in his manner. Evidently, my rapid performance had impressed him, and I thought it best to take the undeserved credit though I was secretly astonished that he, a practical craftsman, had not been able to do the job himself.

But I had impressed him more than I realized at the time. In fact he had formed a ridiculously excessive estimate of my abilities, as I discovered some weeks later when he brought a watch to our shop to be cleaned and regulated, and stipulated that I should do the work myself "and not let the old fellow meddle with it". I assured him that Mr Abraham (who was fortunately absent) was a really skilful watch-maker, but he only grunted incredulously.

"I want the job done properly," he insisted, "and I want you to do it yourself."

Evidently Mr Abraham's evasions in the matter of equatorial clocks had been noted and had made an unfavourable impression. It was unreasonable – but Mr Parrish was an unreasonable man – and, like most unreasonable beliefs, it was unshakable. Nor did he make any secret of his opinion when, on subsequent occasions during the next few months, he brought in various little repairs and renovations and sometimes interviewed my principal. For Mr Parrish had no false delicacy – nor very much of any other kind. But Mr Abraham took no offence. He knew (as Aunt Judy had observed) which side his bread was buttered; and as he was coming more and more to rely on me, he was willing enough that my merits should be recognized.

So, through those months, my relations with Mr Parrish continued to grow closer and my future to shape itself invisibly. Little did I guess at the kind of grist that the Mills of God were grinding.

CHAPTER SIX

Fickle Fortune

"The best-laid plans of mice and men gang aft agley." The oft-quoted words were only too apposite in their application to the plans laid by poor Mr Abraham for the future conduct of his own affairs and mine. Gradually, as the years had passed, it had become understood between us that, when the period of my apprenticeship should come to an end, I should become his partner and he should subside into the partial retirement suitable to his increasing age.

It was an excellent plan, advantageous to us both. To him it promised a secure and restful old age, to me an assured livelihood, and we both looked forward hopefully to the time, ever growing nearer, when it should come into effect.

But, alas! it was never to be. Towards the end of my fourth year, his old enemy, bronchitis, laid its hand on him and sent him, once more, to his bedroom. But this was not the customary sub-acute attack. From the first it was evident that it was something much more formidable. I could see that for myself; and the doctor's grave looks and evasive answers to my questions confirmed my fears. Nor was evasion possible for long. On the fifth day of the illness, the ominous word "pneumonia" was spoken, and Miriam Goldstein, Mr Abraham's housekeeper, was directed to summon the patient's relatives.

But, promptly as they responded to the call, they were too late for anything more than whispered and tearful farewells. When they arrived, with Mr Cohen, the solicitor, and I conducted them up to the sick room, my poor master was already blue-faced and comatose; and it was but a few hours later, when they passed out through the shop with their handkerchiefs to their eyes, that Mr Cohen halted to say to me in a husky undertone, "You can put up the shutters, Polton," and then hurried away with the others.

I shall not dwell on the miserable days that followed, when I sat alone in the darkened shop, vaguely meditating on this calamity, or creeping silently up the stairs to steal a glance at the shrouded figure on the bed. Of all the mourners, none was more sincere than I. Quiet and undemonstrative as our friendship had been, a genuine affection had grown up between my master and me. And not without reason. For Mr Abraham was not only a kindly man; he was a good man, just and fair in all his dealings, scrupulously honest, truthful and punctual, and strict in the discharge of his religious duties. I respected him deeply and he knew it; and he knew that in me he had a faithful friend and a dependable comrade. Our association had been of the happiest and we had looked forward to many years of pleasant and friendly collaboration. And now he was gone, and our plans had come to nought.

In those first days I gave little thought to my own concerns. It was my first experience of death, and my mind was principally occupied by the catastrophe itself, and by sorrow for the friend whom I had lost. But on the day after the funeral I was suddenly made aware of the full extent of the disaster as it affected me. The bearer – sympathetic enough – of the ill tidings was Mr Cohen, who had called to give me my instructions.

"This is a bad look-out for you, Polton," said he. "Mr Abraham ought to have made some provision on your behalf, and I think he meant to. But it was all so sudden. It doesn't do to put off making your will or drafting a new one."

"Then, how do I stand, Sir?" I asked.

"The position is that your apprenticeship is dissolved by your master's death, and I, as the executor, have to sell the business as a going concern, according to the provisions of the will, which was made before you were apprenticed. Of course, I shall keep you on, if you are willing, to run the business until it is sold; perhaps the purchaser may agree to take over your indentures or employ you as assistant. Meanwhile, I will pay you a pound a week. Will that suit you?"

I agreed, gladly enough, and only hoped that the purchaser might not make too prompt an appearance. But in this I was disappointed, for, at the end of the third week, Mr Cohen notified me that the business was sold, and on the following day brought the new tenant to the premises; a rather raffish middle-aged man who smelt strongly of beer and bore the name of Stokes.

"I have explained matters to Mr Stokes," said Mr Cohen, "and have asked him if he would care to take over your indentures; but I am sorry to say that he is not prepared to. However, I leave you to talk the matter over with him. Perhaps you can persuade him to change his mind. Meanwhile, here are your wages up to the end of the week, and I wish you good luck."

With this he departed, and I proceeded, forthwith, to try my powers of persuasion on Mr Stokes.

"It would pay you to take me on, Sir," I urged. "You'd get a very cheap assistant. For, though I am only an apprentice, I have a good knowledge of the trade. I could do all the repairs quite competently. I can take a watch down, and clean it; in fact, Mr Abraham used to give me all the watches to clean."

I thought that would impress him, but it didn't. It merely amused him.

"My good lad," he chuckled, "you are all behind the times. We don't take watches down, nowadays, to clean 'em. We just take off the dial, wind 'em up, wrap 'em in a rag soaked in benzine, and put 'em in a tin box and let 'em clean themselves."

I gazed at him in horror. "That doesn't seem a very good way, Sir," I protested. "Mr Abraham always took a watch down to clean it."

"Ha!" Mr Stokes replied with a broad grin, "of course he would. That's how they used to do 'em at Ur of the Chaldees when he was serving his time. Hey? Haw haw! No, my lad. My wife and I can run this business. You'll have to look elsewhere for a billet."

"And about my bedroom, Sir. Could you arrange to let me keep it for the present? I don't mean for nothing, of course."

"You can have it for half-a-crown a week until you have found another place. Will that do?"

I thanked him and accepted his offer; and that concluded our business, except that I spent an hour or two showing him where the various things were kept, and in stowing my tools and other possessions in my bedroom. Then I addressed myself to the problem of finding a new employer; and that very afternoon I betook myself to Clerkenwell and began a round of all the dealers and clock-makers to whom I was known.

It was the first of many a weary pilgrimage, and its experiences were to be repeated in them all. No one wanted a half-finished apprentice. My Clerkenwell friends were all master craftsmen and they employed only experienced journeymen, and the smaller tradesmen to whom the dealers referred me were mostly able to conduct their modest establishments without assistance. It was a miserable experience which, even now, I look back on with discomfort. Every morning I set out, with dwindling hope, to search unfamiliar streets for clock-makers' shops or to answer obviously inapplicable advertisements in the trade journals; and every evening I wended – not homewards, for I had no home – but to the hospitable common room of the Working Men's College, where, for a few pence, I could get a large cup of tea and a slab of buttered toast to supplement the scanty scraps of food that I had allowed myself during the day's wanderings. But presently even this was beyond my means, and I must needs, for economy, buy myself a half-quartern "household" loaf to devour in my cheerless bedroom to the accompaniment of a draught from the water-jug.

In truth, my condition was becoming desperate. My tiny savings – little more than a matter of shillings – were fast running out in spite of an economy in food which kept me barely above the starvation level. For I had to reserve the rent for my bedroom, that I might not be shelterless as well as famished, so long as any fraction of my little hoard remained. But as I counted the pitiful collection of shillings and sixpences at the bottom of my money-box – soon they needed no counting – I saw that even this was coming to an end and that I was faced by sheer destitution. Now and again the idea of applying for help to Aunt Judy or to Mr Beeby drifted through my mind; but either from pride or obstinacy or some more respectable motive, I always put it away from me. I suppose that, in the end, I should have had to pocket my pride, or whatever it was, and make the appeal; but it was ordained otherwise.

My capital had come down to four shillings and sixpence, which included the rent for my bedroom due in five days' time, when I took a last survey of my position. The end seemed to be fairly in sight. In five days I should be penniless and starving, without even a night's shelter. I had sought work in every likely and unlikely place and failed ever to come within sight of it. Was there anything more to be done? Any possibility of employment that I had overlooked? As I posed the question again and again, I could find no answer but a hopeless negative. And then, suddenly, I thought of Mr Parrish. He at least knew that I was a workman. Was it possible that he might find me something to do?

It was but a forlorn hope; for he was not a clock-maker, and of his trade I knew nothing. Nevertheless, no sooner had the idea occurred to me than I proceeded to give effect to it. Having smartened myself up as well as I could, I set forth for Oxford Market as briskly as if I had a regular appointment; and having the good luck to find him at home, put my case to him as persuasively as I was able in a few words.

He listened to me with his usual frown of impatience, and, when I had finished, replied in his customary gruff manner:

"But, my good lad, what do you expect of me? I am not a clock-maker and you are not an instrument-maker. You'd be no use to me."

My heart sank, but I made one last, despairing effort.

"Couldn't you give me some odd jobs, Sir, such as filing and polishing, to save the time of the skilled men? I shouldn't want much in the way of wages."

He began to repeat his refusal, more gruffly than before. And then, suddenly, he paused; and my heart thumped with almost agonized hope.

"I don't know," he said, slowly and with a considering air. "Perhaps I might be able to find you a job. I've just lost one of my two workmen and I'm rather short-handed at the moment. If you can use a file and know how to polish brass, I might give you some of the rough work to do. At any rate, I'll give you a trial and see what you can do. But I can't pay you a workman's wages. You'll have to be satisfied with fifteen shillings a week. Will that do for you?"

Would it do! It was beyond my wildest hopes. I could have fallen on his neck and kissed his boots (not simultaneously, though I was fairly supple in the joints in those days). Tremulously and gratefully, I accepted his terms, and would have said more, but he cut me short.

"Very well. You can begin work tomorrow morning at nine, and you'll get your wages when you knock off on Saturday. That's all. Off you go."

I wished him "good morning!" and off I went, in an ecstasy of joy and relief, reflecting incredulously on my amazing good fortune. Fifteen shillings a week! I could hardly believe that my ears had not deceived me. It was a competence. It was positive affluence.

But it was prospective affluence. My actual possessions amounted to four shillings and sixpence; but it was all my own, for the half-crown that had been earmarked for rent was now available for food. Still, this was Monday morning and wages were payable on Saturday night, so I should have to manage on ninepence a day until then. Well, that was not so bad. In those days, you could get a lot of food for ninepence if you weren't too particular and knew where to go. At the cook's shop in Carnaby Street where I used to buy Mr Abraham's mid-day meal and my own, we often fed sumptuously on sixpence apiece; and now the recollection of those simple banquets sent me hurrying thither, spurred on by ravenous hunger and watering at the mouth as imagination pictured that glorious, steamy window.

As I turned into Great Marlborough Street, I encountered Mr Cohen, just emerging from the Police Court, where he did some practice as advocate. He stopped to ask what I was doing; and, when I had announced my joyful tidings, he went on to cross-examine me on my experiences of the last few weeks, listening attentively to my account of them and looking at me very earnestly.

"Well, Polton," he said, "you haven't been putting on a great deal of flesh. How much money have you got?"

I told him, and he rapidly calculated the possibilities of expenditure.

"Ninepence a day. You won't fatten a lot on that. Where did you get the money?"

"I used to put by a little every week when I was at work, Sir," I explained; and I could see that my thrift commended itself to him. "Wise lad," said he, in his dry, legal way. "The men who grow rich are the men who spend less than they earn. Come and have a bit of dinner with me. I'll pay," he added, as I hesitated.

I thanked him most sincerely, for I was famished, as I think he had guessed, and together we crossed the road to a restaurant kept by a Frenchman named Paragot. I had never been in it, but had sometimes looked in with awe through the open doorway at the sybarites within, seated at tables enclosed in pews and consuming unimaginable delicacies. As we entered, Mr Cohen paused for a few confidential words with the proprietor's sprightly and handsome daughter, the purport of which I guessed when the smiling damsel deposited our meal on the table and I contrasted Mr Cohen's modest helping with the Gargantuan pile of roast beef, Yorkshire pudding and baked potatoes which fairly bulged over the edge of my plate.

"Have a drop of porter," said Mr Cohen. "Do you good once in a way"; and, though I would sooner have had water, I thought it proper to accept. But if the taste of the beer was disagreeable, the pleasant pewter tankard in which it was served was a refreshment to the eye. And I think it really did me good. At any rate, when we emerged into Great Marlborough Street, I felt like a giant refreshed; which is something to say for a young man of four feet eleven.

As we stood for a moment outside the restaurant, Mr Cohen put his hand in his pocket and produced a half sovereign.

"I'm going to lend you ten shillings, Polton," said he. "Better take it. You may want it. You can pay me back a shilling a week. Pay at my office. If I am not there, give it to my clerk and make him give you a receipt. There you are. That's all right. Wish you luck in your new job. So long."

With a flourish of the hand, he bustled off in the direction of the Police Court, leaving me grasping the little gold coin and choking with gratitude to this – I was going to say "Good Samaritan", but I suppose that would be a rather left-handed compliment to an orthodox Jew with the royal name of Cohen.

I spent a joyous afternoon rambling about the town and looking in shop windows, and, as the evening closed in, I repaired to a coffee-shop in Holborn and consumed a gigantic cup of tea and two thick slices of bread and butter ("pint of tea and two doorsteps", in the vernacular). Then I turned homeward, if I may use the expression in connection with a hired bedroom, resolving to get a long night's rest so as to be fresh for the beginning of my new labours in the morning.

CHAPTER SEVEN

Introduces a Key and a Calendar

When I entered the workshop which was to be the scene of my labours for the next few months, I found in it two other occupants: an elderly workman who was engaged at a lathe and a youth of about my own age who was filing up some brass object that was fixed in a vice. They both stopped work when I appeared, and looked at me with evident curiosity, and both greeted me in their respective ways; the workman with a dry "good morning", and the other with a most peculiar grin.

"You're the new hand, I suppose," the former suggested, adding, "I don't know what sort of a hand you are. Can you file flat?"

I replied that I could, whereupon he produced a rough plate of brass and handed it to me.

"There," said he, "that casting has got to be filed smooth and true and then it's got to be polished. Let's see what you can do with it."

Evidently, he had no extravagant expectations as to my skill, for he watched me critically as I put my toolbag on the bench and selected a suitable file from my collection (but I could see that he viewed the bag with approval); and every few minutes he left his work to see how I was getting on. Apparently, the results of his observations were reassuring, for his visits gradually became less frequent, and finally he left me to finish the job alone.

During that first day I saw Mr Parrish only once, for he did his own work in a small private workshop, which was always kept locked in his absence, as it contained a very precious dividing machine, with which he engraved the graduations on the scales of measuring instruments such as theodolites and sextants. This, with some delicate finishing and adjusting, was his province in the business, the larger, constructive work being done by his workmen. But on this occasion he came into the main workshop just before "knocking-off time" to hear the report on my abilities.

"Well, Kennet," he demanded in his gruff way, "how has your new hand got on? Any good?"

Mr Kennet regarded me, appraisingly, and after a brief consideration, replied:

"Yes, I think he'll do."

It was not extravagant praise; but Mr Kennet was a man of few words. That laconic verdict established me as a permanent member of the staff.

In the days that followed, a quiet friendliness grew up between us. Not that Mr Kennet was a specially prepossessing person. Outwardly a grey-haired, shrivelled, weasel-faced little man, dry and taciturn in manner and as emotionless as a potato, he had his kindly impulses, though they seldom came to the surface. But he was a first-class craftsman who knew his trade from A to Z, and measured the worth of other men in terms of their knowledge and skill. The liking that, from the first, he took to me, arose, I think, from his observation of my interest in my work and my capacity for taking pains. At any rate, in his undemonstrative way, he made me aware of his friendly sentiments, principally by letting me into the mysteries and secrets of the trade and giving me various useful tips from the storehouse of his experience.

My other companion in the workshop was the youth whom I have mentioned, who was usually addressed and referred to as Gus, which I took to represent Augustus. His surname was Haire, and I understood that he was some kind of relation of Mr Parrish's; apparently a nephew, as he always spoke of Mr Parrish as his uncle, though he addressed him as "Sir". His position in the workshop appeared to he that of a pupil, learning the business – as I gathered from him – with a view to partnership and succession. He lived on the premises, though he frequently went away for the weekends to his home, which was at Malden in Essex.

The mutual liking of Mr Kennet and myself found no counterpart in the case of Gus Haire. I took an instant distaste of him at our first meeting; which is rather remarkable, since I am not in the least addicted to taking sudden likes or dislikes. It may have been his teeth, but I hope not; for it would be unpardonable to allow a mere physical defect to influence one's judgement of a man's personal worth. But they were certainly rather unpleasant teeth and most peculiar. I have never seen anything like them, before or since. They were not decayed. Apparently, they were quite sound and strong, but they were covered with brown spots and mottlings which made them look like tortoiseshell. They were also rather large and prominent; which was unfortunate, as Gus was distinctly sensitive about them. Whence the remarkable grin which had so impressed me when we first met. It was habitual with him, and it startled me afresh every time. It began as a fine broad grin displaying the entire outfit of tortoiseshell. Then suddenly, he became conscious of his teeth, and in an instant the grin was gone. The effect was extraordinary, and not by any means agreeable.

Still, as I have said, I hope it was not the teeth that prejudiced me against him. There were other, and much better, reasons for my disliking him. But these developed later. My initial distaste of him may have been premonitory. In some unimaginable way, I seemed instinctively to have recognized an enemy.

As to his hardly-concealed dislike of me, I took it to be merely jealousy of Kennet's evident preference. For that thorough-going craftsman had no use for Gus. The lad was lazy, inattentive, and a superlatively bad workman; faults enough to damn him in Kennet's eyes. But there were other matters, which will transpire in their proper place.

In these early days I was haunted by constant anxiety as to the security of my position. There was really not enough for me to do. Mr Parrish was getting on in years and some of his methods were rather obsolete. Newer firms with more up-to-date plant were attracting orders that would formerly have come to him, so that his business was not what it had been. But even of the work that was being done I could, at first, take but a small share. Later, when I had learned more of the trade, Kennet was able to turn over to me a good deal of his own work, so that I became, in effect, something like a competent journeyman. But in the first few weeks I often found myself with nothing to do, and was terrified lest Mr Parrish should think that I was not earning my wage.

It was a dreadful thought. The idea of being set adrift once more to tramp the streets, hungry and despairing, became a sort of permanent nightmare. I worked with intense care and effort to learn my new trade and felt myself making daily progress. But still "Black Care rode behind the horseman". Something had to be done to fill up the hours of idleness and make me seem to be worth my pay. But what?

I began by taking down the workshop clock and cleaning it. Then I took off the lock of the workshop door, which had ceased to function, and made it as good as new; which seemed at the time to be a fortunate move, for, just as I was finishing it, Mr Parrish came into the workshop and stopped to watch my proceedings.

"Ha!" said he, "so you are a locksmith, too. That's lucky, because I have got a job for you. The key of my writing-table has broken in the lock and I can't get the drawer open. Come and see what you can do with it."

I picked up my tool-bag and followed him to his workshop (which also served as an office), where he showed me the closed drawer with the stem of the broken key projecting about a quarter of an inch.

"There must be something wrong with the lock," said he, "for the key wouldn't turn, and when I gave it an extra twist it broke off. Flaw in the key, I expect."

I began by filing a small flat on the projecting stump, and then, producing a little hand-vice from my bag, applied it to the stump and screwed it up tight. With this I was able to turn the key a little backwards and forwards, but there was evidently something amiss with the lock, as it would turn no further. With my oiler, I insinuated a touch of oil on to the bit of the key and as much of the levers as I could reach and continued to turn the key to and fro, watched intently by Mr Parrish and Gus (who had left his work to come and look on). At last, when I ventured to use a little more force, the resistance gave way and the key made a complete turn with an audible click of the lock.

As I withdrew the key, Mr Parrish pulled out the drawer, which, as I saw, contained, among other things, a wooden bowl half-filled with a most untidy collection of mixed money: shillings, half-crowns, coppers, and at least two half-sovereigns. I looked with surprise at the disorderly heap and thought how it would have shocked poor Mr Abraham.

"Well," said Mr Parrish, "what's to be done? Can you make a new key?"

"Yes, Sir," I replied, "or I could braze the old one together."

"No," he replied, "I've had enough of that key. And what about the lock?"

"I shall have to take that off in any case, because the ironmonger won't sell me a key-blank unless I show the lock. But it will have to be repaired."

"Very well," he agreed. "Take it off and get the job done as quickly as you can. I don't want to leave my cash-drawer unlocked."

I had the lock off in a few moments and took it away, with the broken key, to the workshop, where I spent a pleasant half-hour taking it to pieces, cleaning it, and doing the trifling repairs that it needed; and all the time, Gus Haire watched me intently, following me about like a dog and plying me with questions. I had never known him to be so interested in anything. He even accompanied me to the ironmonger's and looked on with concentrated attention while I selected the blank. Apparently, locksmithing was more to his taste than the making of philosophical instruments.

But the real tit-bit of the entertainment for him was the making of the new key. His eyes fairly bulged as he followed the details of the operation. I had in my bag a tin box containing a good-sized lump of stiff moulding-wax, which latter I took out, and, laying it on the bench, rolled it out flat with a file-handle. Then, on the flat surface, I made two impressions of the broken key, one of the profile of the bit and the other of the end, showing the hole in the "pipe"; and, having got my pattern, I fell to work on the blank. First, I drilled out the bore of the pipe, then I filed up the blank roughly to the dimensions with the aid of callipers, and, when I had brought it to the approximate size, I began carefully to shape the bit and cut out the "steps" for the levers, testing the result from time to time by fitting it into the impressions.

At length, when it appeared to fit both impressions perfectly, I tried it in the lock and found that it entered easily and turned freely to and fro, moving the bolt and levers without a trace of stiffness. Naturally, I was quite pleased at having got it right at the first trial. But my satisfaction was nothing compared with that of my watcher, who took the lock from me and turned the key to and fro with as much delight as if he had made it himself. Even Kennett, attracted by Gus' exclamations, left his work (he was making a reflecting level – just a simple mirror with a hole through it, mounted in a suspension frame) to come and see what it was all about.

But Gus' curiosity seemed now to be satisfied, for, when I took the lock and the new key to Mr Parrish's workroom, he did not accompany me. Apparently, he was not interested in the mere refixing of the lock; whereas Mr Parrish watched that operation with evident relief. When I had finished, he tried the key several times, first with the drawer open and then with it closed, finally locking the drawer and pocketing the key with a grunt of satisfaction.

"Where's the broken key?" he demanded as I prepared to depart. "I'd better have that."

I ran back to the workshop, where I found Gus back at his vice, industriously filing something, and Kennet still busy with his level. The latter looked round at me as I released the key from the hand-vice, and I explained that I had forgotten to give the broken key to Mr Parrish. He nodded and still watched me as I retired with it in my hand to return it to its owner; and when I came back to the workshop he put down his level and strolled across to my bench, apparently to inspect the slab of wax. I, also, inspected it, and saw at once that it was smaller than when I had left it; and I had no doubt that the ingenious Gus had "pinched" a portion of it for the purpose of making some private experiments. But I made no remark; and, having obliterated the key-impressions with my thumb, I peeled the wax off the bench, squeezed it up into a lump, and put it into my bag. Whereupon Kennet went back to his level without a word.

But my suspicions of Master Gus' depredations were confirmed a few days later when, Kennet and I happening to be alone in the workshop, he came close to me and asked, in a low tone:

"Did you miss any of that wax of yours the other day?"

"Yes, I did; and I'm afraid I suspected that Gus had helped himself to a bit."

"You were right," said Kennet. "He cut a piece off and pocketed it. But before he cut it off, he made two impressions of the key on it. I saw him. He thought I didn't, because my back was turned to him. But I was working on that level, and I was able to watch him in the mirror."

I didn't much like this, and said so.

"More don't I," said Kennet. "I haven't said anything about it, because it ain't my concern. But it may be yours. So you keep a look-out. And remember that I saw him do it."

With this and a significant nod he went back to the lathe and resumed his work.

The hardly-veiled hint that "it might be my concern" was not very comfortable to reflect on, but there was nothing to be done beyond keeping my tool-bag locked and the key in my pocket, which I was careful to do; and as the weeks passed, and nothing unusual happened, the affair gradually faded out of my mind.

Meanwhile, conditions were steadily improving. I had now learned to use the lathe and even to cut a quite respectable screw, and, as my proficiency increased, and with it my value as a workman, I began to feel my position more secure. And even when there was nothing for me to do in the workshop, Mr Parrish found me odd jobs about the house, repairing locks, cleaning his watch, and attending to the various clocks, so that I was still earning my modest wage. In this way I came by a piece of work which interested me immensely at the time and which had such curious consequences later that I venture to describe it in some detail.

It was connected with a long-case, or "grandfather" clock, which stood in Mr Parrish's workroom a few feet from his writing-table. I suspect that it had not been cleaned within the memory of man, and, naturally, there came a time when dirt and dry pivots brought it to a standstill. Even then, a touch of oil would probably have kept it going for a month or two, but I made no such suggestion. I agreed emphatically with Mr Parrish's pronouncement that the clock needed a thorough overhaul.

"And while you've got it to pieces," he continued, "perhaps you could manage to fit it with a calendar attachment. Do you think that would be possible?"

I pointed out that it had a date disc, but he dismissed that with contempt.

"Too small. Want a microscope to see it. No, no, I mean a proper calendar with the day of the week and the day of the month in good bold characters that I can read when I am sitting at the table. Can you do that?"

I suggested that the striking work would be rather in the way, but he interrupted:

"Never mind the striking work. I never use it. I hate a jangling noise in my room. Take it off if it's in the way. But I should like a calendar if you could manage it."

Of course, there was no difficulty. A modification of the ordinary watch-calendar movement would have answered. But when I described it, he raised objections.

"How long does it take to change?" he asked.

"About half an hour, I should think. It changes during the night."

"That's no use," said he. "The date changes in an instant, on the stroke of midnight. A minute to twelve is, say, Monday; a minute after twelve is Tuesday. That ought to be possible. You make a clock strike at the right moment; why couldn't you do the same with a calendar? It must be possible."

It probably was; but no calendar movement known to me would do it. I should have to invent one on an entirely different principle if my powers were equal to the task. It was certainly a problem; but the very difficulty of it was an attraction, and in the end I promised to turn it over in my mind, and meanwhile I proceeded to take the clock out of its case and bear it away to the workshop. There, under the respectful observation of Gus and Mr Kennet, I quickly took it down and fell to work on the cleaning operations; but the familiar routine hardly occupied my attention. As I worked, my thoughts were busy with the problem that I had to solve, and gradually my ideas began to take a definite shape. I saw, at once, that the mechanism required must be in the nature of an escapement; that is to say, that there must be a constant drive and a periodical release. I must not burden the reader with mechanical details, but it is necessary that I should give an outline of the arrangement at which I arrived after much thought and a few tentative pencil drawings.

Close to the top of the door of the case I cut two small windows, one to show the date numbers and the other the days of the week. Below these was a third window for the months, the names of which were painted in white on a band of black linen which travelled on a pair of small rollers. But these rollers were turned by hand and formed no part of the mechanism. There was no use in complicating the arrangements for the sake of a monthly change.

And now for the mechanism itself. The names of the days were painted in white on a black drum, or roller, three inches in diameter, and the date numbers were painted on an endless black ribbon which was carried by another drum of the same thickness but narrower. This drum had at each edge seven little pins, or pegs; and the ribbon had, along each edge, a series of small eyelet holes which fitted loosely on the pins, so that, as the drum turned, it carried the ribbon along for exactly the right distance. Both drums were fixed friction-tight on a long spindle, which also carried at its middle a star wheel with seven long, slender teeth, and at its end a ratchet pulley over which ran a cord carrying the small driving-weight. Thus the calendar movement had its own driving-power and made no demands on that of the clock.

So much for the calendar itself; and now for its connection with the clock. The mechanism "took off" from the hour-wheel which carries the hour-hand and makes a complete turn in twelve hours, and which, in this clock, had forty teeth. Below this, and gearing with it, I fixed another wheel, which had eighty teeth, and consequently turned once in twenty-four hours. I will call this "the day-wheel". On this wheel I fixed, friction-tight, so that it could be moved round to adjust it, what clock-makers call a "snail"; which is a flat disc cut to a spiral shape, so that it looks like the profile of a snail's shell. Connecting the snail with the calendar was a flat, thin steel bar (I actually made it from the blade of a hack saw) which I will call "the pallet-bar". It moved on a pivot near its middle and had at its top end a small pin which rested against the edge of the snail and was pressed against it by a very weak spring. At its lower end it had an oblong opening with two small ledges, or pallets, for the teeth of the star-wheel to rest on. I hope I have made this fairly clear. And now let us see how it worked.

We will take the top end first. As the clock "went", it turned the snail round slowly (half as fast as the hour-hand); and as the snail turned, it gradually pushed the pin of the pallet-bar, which was resting against it, farther and farther from its centre, until the end of the spiral was reached. A little further turn and the pin dropped off the end of the spiral ("the step") down towards the centre. Then the pushing-away movement began again. Thus it will be seen that the rotation of the snail (once in twenty-four hours) caused the top end of the pallet-bar to move slowly outwards and then drop back with a jerk.

Now let us turn to the lower end of the pallet-bar. Here, as I have said, was an oblong opening, interrupted by two little projecting ledges, or pallets. Through this opening the star-wheel projected, one of its seven teeth resting (usually) on the upper pallet, and held there by the power of the little driving weight. As the snail turned and pushed the top end of the pallet-bar outwards, the lower end moved in the opposite direction, and the pallet slid along under the tooth of the wheel. When the tooth reached the end the upper pallet, it dropped off on to the lower pallet and remained there for a few minutes. Then, when the pin dropped into the step of the snail, the lower pallet was suddenly withdrawn from under the tooth, which left the wheel free to turn until the next tooth was stopped by the upper pallet. Thus the wheel made the seventh of a revolution; but so, also, did the two drums which were on the same spindle, with the result that a new day and date number were brought to their respective windows; and the change occupied less than a second.

The above is only a rough sketch of the mechanism, omitting the minor mechanical details, and I hope it has not wearied the reader. To me, I need not say, the work was a labour of love which kept me supremely happy. But it also greatly added to my prestige in the workshop. Kennet was deeply impressed by it, and Gus followed the construction with the keenest interest and with a display of mechanical intelligence that rather surprised me. Even

Mr Parrish looked into the workshop from time to time and observed my progress with an approving grunt.

When the construction was finished, I brought the case into the workshop and there set the clock up – at first without the dial – to make the final adjustments. I set the snail to discharge at twelve noon, as midnight was not practicable, and the three of us used to gather round the clock as the appointed hour approached, for the gratification of seeing the day and date change in an instant at the little windows. When the adjustment was perfect, I stopped the clock at ten in the morning and we carried it in triumph to its usual abiding place, where, when I had tried the action to see that the tick was even, I once more stopped the pendulum and would have left it to the care of its owner. But Mr Parrish insisted that I should come in in the evening and start it myself, and further, that I should stay until midnight and see that the date did actually change at the correct moment. To which I agreed very readily; whereby I not only gained a supper that was a banquet compared with my customary diet and had the satisfaction of seeing the date change on the very stroke of midnight, but I received such commendations from my usually undemonstrative employer that I began seriously to consider the possibility of an increase in my wages in the not too distant future.

But, alas! the future had something very different in store for me.

CHAPTER EIGHT

Mr Parrish Remembers

For a month or two after the agreeable episode just recounted, the stream of my life flowed on tranquilly and perhaps rather monotonously. But I was quite happy. My position in Mr Parrish's establishment seemed fairly settled and I had the feeling that my employer set some value on me as a workman. Not, however, to the extent of increasing my salary, though of this I still cherished hopes. But I did not dare to raise the question; for at least I had an assured livelihood, if a rather meagre one, and so great was my horror of being thrown out of employment that I would have accepted the low wage indefinitely rather than risk my security. So I worked on contentedly, poor as a church mouse, but always hoping for better times.

But at last came the explosion which blew my security into atoms. It was a disastrous affair and foolish, too; and what made it worse was that it was my own hand that set the match to the gunpowder. Very vividly do I recall the circumstances, though, at first, they seemed trivial enough. A man from a tool-maker's had come into the workshop to inspect a new slide-rest that his firm had fitted to the lathe. When he had examined it and pronounced it satisfactory, he picked up the heavy bag that he had brought and was turning towards the door when Mr Parrish said:

"If you have got the account with you, I may as well settle up now."

The man produced the account from his pocket-book and handed it to Mr Parrish, who glanced at it and then, diving into his coat-tail pocket, brought out a leather wallet (which I instantly recognized as an old acquaintance) and, extracting from it a five-pound note, handed the latter to the man in exchange for the receipt and a few shillings change. As our visitor put away the note, Mr Parrish said to me:

"Take Mr Soames' bag, Polton, and carry it out to the cab."

I picked up the bag, which seemed to be filled with tool-makers' samples, and conveyed it out to the waiting "growler", where I stowed it on the front seat, and, waiting with the door open, saw Mr Soames safely into the vehicle and shut him in. Returning into the house, I encountered Mr Parrish, who was standing at the front door; and then it was that some demon of mischief impelled me to an act of the most perfectly asinine folly.

"I see, Sir," I said with a fatuous smirk, "that you still carry your wallet in your coat-tail pocket."

He halted suddenly and stared at me with a strange, startled expression that brought me to my senses with a jerk. But it was too late. I saw that the fat was in the fire, though I didn't guess how much fat there was or how big was the fire. After a prolonged stare, he commanded, gruffly:

"Come into my room and tell me what you mean."

I followed him in, miserably, and when he had shut the door, I explained:

"I was thinking, Sir, of what the inspector at the police station said to you about carrying your wallet in your tail pocket. Don't you remember, Sir?"

"Yes," he replied, glaring at me ferociously, "I remember. And I remember you, too, now that you have reminded me. I always thought that I had seen you before. So you are the young rascal who was found in possession of the stolen property."

"But I didn't steal it, Sir," I pleaded.

"Ha!" said he. "So you said at the time. Very well. That will do for the present."

I sneaked out of the room very crestfallen and apprehensive. "For the present!" What did he mean by that? Was there more trouble to come? I looked nervously in at the workshop, but as the other occupants had now gone to dinner, I took myself off and repaired to an *à-la-mode* beef shop in Oxford Market, where I fortified myself with a big basinful of the steaming compound and "topped up" with a halfpennyworth of apples from a stall in the market. Then I whiled away the remainder of the dinner hour rambling about the streets, trying to interest myself in shop windows, but unable to rid myself of the haunting dread of what loomed in the immediate future.

At length, as the last minutes of the dinner hour ran out, I crept back timorously, hoping to slink unnoticed along the passage to the workshop. But even as I entered, my forebodings were realized. For there was my employer, evidently waiting for me, and a glance at his face prepared me for instant dismissal. He motioned to me silently to follow him into his room, and I did so in the deepest dejection; but when I entered and found a third person in the room, my dejection gave place to something like terror. For that third person was Detective Sergeant Pitts.

He recognized me instantly, for he greeted me drily by name. Then, characteristically, he came straight to the point.

"Mr Parrish alleges that you have opened his cash drawer with a false key and have, from time to time, taken certain monies from it. Now, before you say anything, I must caution you that anything you may say will be taken down in writing and may be used in evidence against you. So be very careful. Do you wish to say anything?"

"Certainly I do," I replied, my indignation almost overcoming my alarm. "I say that I have no false key, that I have never touched the drawer except in Mr Parrish's presence, and that I have never taken any money whatsoever."

The sergeant made a note of my reply in a large black note-book and then asked:

"Is it true that you made a key to fit this drawer?"

"Yes, for Mr Parrish; and he has that key and the broken one from which it was copied. I made no other key."

"How did you make that key? By measurements only, or did you make a squeeze?"

"I made a squeeze from the broken key, and, as soon as the job was finished, I destroyed it."

"That's what he says," exclaimed Mr Parrish, "but it's a lie. He kept the squeeze and made another key from it."

The sergeant cast a slightly impatient glance at him and remarked, drily:

"We are taking his statement," and continued: "Now, Polton, Mr Parrish says that he marked some, or all, of the money in that drawer with a P scratched just behind the head. If you have got any money about you, perhaps you would like to show it to us."

"Like, indeed!" exclaimed Mr Parrish. "He'll have to be searched whether he likes it or not."

The sergeant looked at him angrily, but, as I proceeded to turn out my pockets and lay the contents on the table, he made no remark until Mr Parrish was about to pounce on the coins that I had laid down, when he said, brusquely:

"Keep your hands off that money, Mr Parrish. This is my affair."

Then he proceeded to examine the coins, one by one, laying them down again in two separate groups. Having finished, he looked at me steadily and said:

"Here, Polton, are five coins: three half-crowns and a shilling and a sixpence. All the half-crowns are marked with a P. The other coins are not marked. Can you explain how you came by those half-crowns?"

"Yes, Sir. I received them from Mr Parrish when he paid me my wages last Saturday. He gave me four half-crowns, two florins and a shilling; and he took the money from that drawer."

The sergeant looked at Mr Parrish. "Is that correct?" he asked.

"I paid him his wages – fifteen shillings – but I don't admit that those are the coins I gave him."

"But," the sergeant persisted, "did you take the money from that drawer?"

"Of course I did," snapped Parrish. "It's my petty-cash drawer."

"And did you examine the coins to see whether they were marked?"

"I expect I did, but I really don't remember."

"He did not," said I. "He just counted out the money and handed it to me."

The sergeant gazed at my employer with an expression of bewilderment.

"Well, of all – " he began, and then stopped and began again: "But what on earth was the use of marking the money and then paying it out in the ordinary way?"

The question stumped Mr Parrish for the moment. Then, having mumbled something about "a simple precaution", he returned to the subject of the squeeze and the key. But the sergeant cut him short.

"It's no use just making accusations without proof. You've got nothing to go on. The marked money is all bunkum, and as to the key, you are simply guessing. You've not made out any case at all."

"Oh, haven't I?" Parrish retorted. "What about that key and the lock that he repaired and the stolen money? I am going to prosecute him, and I call on you to arrest him now."

"I'm not going to arrest him," said the sergeant; "but if you still intend to prosecute, you'd better come along and settle the matter with the inspector at the station. You come, too, Polton, so that you can answer any questions."

Thus did history repeat itself Once more, after five years, did I journey to the same forbidding destination in company with the same accuser and the guardian of the law. When we arrived at the police station and were about to enter, we nearly collided with a smartly dressed gentleman who was hurrying out, and whom I recognized as my late benefactor, Mr Cohen. He recognized me at the same moment and stopped short with a look of surprise at the sergeant.

"Why, what's this, Polton?" he demanded. "What are you doing here?"

"He is accused by this gentleman," the sergeant explained, "of having stolen money from a drawer by means of a false key."

"Bah!" exclaimed Mr Cohen. "Nonsense. He is a most respectable lad. I know him well and can vouch for his excellent character."

"You don't know him as well as I do," said Mr Parrish, viciously.

Mr Cohen turned on him a look of extreme disfavour and then addressed the sergeant.

"If there is going to be a prosecution, Sergeant, I shall undertake the defence. But I should like to have a few words with Polton and hear his account of the affair before the charge is made."

To this Mr Parrish was disposed to object, muttering something about "collusion", but, as the inspector was engaged at the moment, the sergeant thrust my adviser and me into a small, empty room and shut the door. Then Mr Cohen began to ply me with questions, and so skilfully were they framed that in a few minutes he had elicited, not only the immediate circumstances, but also the material antecedents, including the incident of the wax squeeze and Mr Kennet's observations with the reflecting level. I had just finished my recital when the sergeant opened the door and invited us to step into the inspector's office.

Police officers appear to have astonishing memories. The inspector was the same one who had taken – or rather refused – the charge on my former visit, and I gathered that not only was his recognition of accused and accuser instantaneous, but that he even remembered the circumstances in detail. His mention of the fact did not appear to encourage Mr Parrish, who began the statement of his case in a rather diffident tone; but he soon warmed up, and finished upon a note of fierce denunciation. He made no reference to the marked coins, but the sergeant supplied the deficiency with a description of the incident to which the inspector listened with an appreciative grin.

"It comes to this, then," that officer summed up. "You have missed certain money from your cash-drawer and you suspect Polton of having stolen it because he is able to make a key."

"And a very good reason, too," Mr Parrish retorted, defiantly.

"You have no proof that he did actually make a key?"

"He must have done so, or he wouldn't have been able to steal the money."

The inspector exchanged glances of intelligence with the sergeant and then turned to my adviser.

"Now, Mr Cohen, you say you are acting for the accused. You have heard what Mr Parrish has said. Is there any answer to the charge?"

"There is a most complete and conclusive answer," Mr Cohen replied. "In the first place I can prove that Polton destroyed the wax squeeze immediately when he had finished the key. Further, I can prove that, while Polton was absent, trying the key in the lock, some other person abstracted a piece of the wax and made an impression on it with the broken key. He thought he was unobserved, but he was mistaken. Someone saw him take the wax and make the squeeze. Now, the person who made that squeeze was a member of Mr Parrish's household, and so would have had access to Mr Parrish's office in his absence."

"He wouldn't," Mr Parrish interposed. "I always lock my office when I go away from it."

"And when you are in it," the inspector asked, "where is the key?"

"In the door, of course," Mr Parrish replied impatiently.

"On the outside, where anyone could take it out quietly, make a squeeze and put it back. And somebody must have made a false key if the money was really stolen. The drawer couldn't have been robbed when you were in the office."

"That is exactly what I am saying," Mr Parrish protested. "This young rogue made two keys, one of the door and one of the cash-drawer."

The inspector took a deep breath and then looked at Mr Cohen.

"You say, Mr Cohen, that you can produce evidence. What sort of evidence?"

"Absolutely conclusive evidence, Sir," Mr Cohen replied. "The testimony of an eye-witness who saw Polton destroy his squeeze and saw the other person take a piece of the wax and make the impression. If this case goes into court, I shall call that witness and he will disclose the identity of that person. And then I presume that the police would take action against that person."

"Certainly," replied the inspector. "If Mr Parrish swears that money was stolen from that drawer and you prove that some person, living in the house, had made a squeeze of the drawer-key, we should, naturally, charge that person with having committed the robbery. Can you swear, Mr Parrish, that the money was really stolen and give particulars of the amounts?"

"Well," replied Mr Parrish, mightily flustered by these new developments, "to the best of my belief – but if there is going to be a lot of fuss and scandal, perhaps I had better let the matter drop and say no more about it."

"That won't do, Mr Parrish," my champion said, sharply. "You have accused a most respectable young man of a serious crime, and you have actually planted marked money on him and pretended that he stole it. Now, you have got, either to support that accusation – which you can't do, because it is false – or withdraw the charge unconditionally and acknowledge your mistake. If you do that, in writing, I am willing to let the matter drop, as you express it. Otherwise, I shall take such measures as may be necessary to establish my client's innocence."

The pretty obvious meaning of Mr Cohen's threat was evidently understood, for my crestfallen accuser turned in dismay to the inspector with a mumbled request for advice; to which the officer replied, briskly:

"Well. What's the difficulty? You've been guessing, and you've guessed wrong. Why not do the fair thing and admit your mistake like a man?"

In the end, Mr Parrish surrendered, though with a very bad grace; and when Mr Cohen had written out a short statement, he signed it, and Sergeant Pitts attested the signature and Mr Cohen bestowed the document in his wallet; which brought the proceedings to an end. Mr Parrish departed in dudgeon; and I – when I had expressed my profound gratitude to Mr Cohen for his timely help – followed him, in considerably better spirits than when I had arrived.

But as soon as I was outside the police station, the realities of my position came back to me. The greater peril of the false charge and possible conviction and imprisonment, I had escaped; but the other peril still hung over me. I had now to return to my place of employment, but I knew that there would be no more employment for me. Mr Parrish was an unreasonable, obstinate man, and evidently vindictive. No generous regret for the false accusation could I expect, but rather an exacerbation of his anger against me. He would never forgive the humiliation that Mr Cohen had inflicted on him.

My expectations were only too literally fulfilled. As I entered the house, I found him waiting for me in the hall with a handful of silver in his fist.

"Ha!" said he, "so you have had the impudence to come back. Well, I don't want you here. I've done with you. Here are your week's wages, and now you can take yourself off."

He handed me the money and pointed to the door, but I reminded him that my tools were in the workshop and requested permission to go and fetch them.

"Very well," said he, "you can take your tools, and I will come with you to see that you don't take anything else."

He escorted me to the workshop, where, as we entered, Kennet looked at us with undissembled curiosity, and Gus cast a furtive and rather nervous glance over his shoulder. Both had evidently gathered that there was trouble in the air.

"Now," said Mr Parrish, "look sharp. Get your things together and clear out."

As the order was given, in a tone of furious anger, Gus bent down over his bench and Kennet turned to watch us with a scowl on his face that suggested an inclination to take a hand in the proceedings. But if he had had any such intention, he thought better of it, though he continued to look at me, gloomily, as I packed my bag, until Mr Parrish noticed him and demanded, angrily:

"What are you staring at, Kennet? Mind your own business and get on with your work."

"Polton got the sack?" asked Kennet.

"Yes, he has," was the gruff reply.

"What for?" Kennet demanded with equal gruffness.

"That's no affair of yours," Parrish replied. "You attend to your own job."

"Well," said Kennet, "you are sending away a good workman, and I hope he'll get a better billet next time. So long, mate"; and with this he turned back sulkily to his lathe, while I, having now finished packing my bag, said "good-bye" to him and was forthwith shepherded out of the workshop.

As I took my way homeward – that is, towards Foubert's Place – I reflected on the disastrous change in my condition that a few foolish words had wrought. For I could not disguise from myself the fact that my position was even worse than it had been when poor Mr Abraham's death had sent me adrift. Then, I had a reasonable explanation of my being out of work, but now I should not dare to mention my last employer. I had been dismissed on suspicion of theft. It was a false suspicion and its falsity could be proved. But no stranger would go into that question. The practical effect was the same as if I had been guilty. I should have to evade any questions as to my last employment.

A review of my resources was not more encouraging. I had nine shillings left from my last wages and the fifteen shillings that Mr Parrish had just paid me, added to which was a small store in my money-box that I had managed to put by from week to week. I knew the amount exactly, and, casting up the entire sum of my wealth, found that the total was two pounds, three shillings and sixpence. On that I should have to subsist and pay my rent until I should obtain some fresh employment; and the ominous question as to how long it would last was one that I did not dare to consider.

When I had put away my tool-bag in the cupboard and bestowed the bulk of my money in the cash-box, I took a long drink from the water-jug to serve in lieu of tea and set forth towards Clerkenwell to use what was left of the day in taking up once more the too-familiar quest.

CHAPTER NINE

Storm and Sunshine

Over the events of the succeeding weeks I shall pass as lightly as possible. There is no temptation to linger or dwell in detail on these dismal recollections, which could be no more agreeable to read than to relate. Nevertheless, it is necessary that I should give at least a summary account of them, since they were directly connected with the most important event of my life.

But it was a miserable time, repeating in an intensified form all the distressing features of that wretched inter-regnum that followed Mr Abraham's death. For then I had at least begun my quest in hope, whereas now something like despair haunted me from the very beginning. I knew from the first how little chance I had of finding employment, especially since I could not venture to name my last employer; but that difficulty never arose, for no one ever entertained my application. The same old obstacle presented itself every time: I was not a qualified journeyman, but only a half-time apprentice.

Still I went on doggedly, day after day, trapesing the streets until I think I must have visited nearly every clock-maker in London and a number of optical-instrument makers as well; and as the days passed, I looked forward with ever-growing terror to the inevitable future towards which I was drifting. For my little store of money dwindled steadily. From the first I had cut my food down to an irreducible minimum.

Tea and butter I never tasted; but even a loaf of bread with an occasional portion of cheese, or a faggot or a polony, cost something; and there was the rent to pay at the end of every week. Each night, as I counted anxiously the shrinking remainder which stood between me and utter destitution, I saw the end drawing ever nearer and nearer.

Meanwhile, my distress of mind must have been aggravated by my bodily condition; for though the meagre scraps of food that I doled out to myself with miserly thrift were actually enough to support life, I was in a state of semi-starvation. The fact was obvious to me, not only from the slack way in which my clothes began to hang about me, but from the evident signs of bodily weakness. At first I had been able to tramp the streets for hours at a time without resting, but now I must needs seek, from time to time, some friendly doorstep or window-ledge to rest awhile before resuming my fruitless journeyings.

Occasionally, as I wandered through the streets, realizing the hopelessness of my quest, there passed through my mind vaguely the idea of seeking help from some of my friends: from Mr Beeby or Mr Cohen, or even Aunt Judy. But always I put it off as a desperate measure only to be considered when everything else had failed; and Aunt Judy I think I never considered at all. I had last written to her just after I had finished the calendar: a buoyant, hopeful letter, conveying to her the impression that a promising future was opening out to me, as I indeed believed. She would be quite happy about me, and I could not bear to think of the bitter disappointment and disillusionment that she would suffer if I were to disclose the dreadful reality. Besides, she and dear, honest Uncle Sam were but poor people, living decently, but with never a penny to spare. How could I burden them with my failure? It was not to be thought of.

But, in fact, as the time ran on, I seemed to become less capable of thought. My alarm at the approaching catastrophe gave place to a dull, fatalistic despair almost amounting to indifference. Even when I handed Mr Stokes my last half-crown for rent – in advance

– and knew that another week would see me without even a night's shelter, I seemed unable clearly to envisage the position. There still remained an uncounted handful of coppers. I was not yet penniless.

But there was something more in my condition than mere mental dullness. At intervals I became aware of it myself. Not only did my thoughts tend to ramble in a confused, dreamlike fashion, mingling objective realities with things imagined; I was conscious of bodily sensations that made me suspect the onset of definite illness: a constant, distressing headache, with attacks of shivering (though the weather was warm) and a feeling as if a stream of icy water were being sprayed on my back. And now the gnawing hunger from which I had suffered gave place to an intense repugnance to food. On principle, I invested the last but one of my pence in a polony. But I could not eat it; and when I had ineffectively nibbled at one end, I gave up the attempt and put it in my pocket for future use. But I had a craving for a drink of tea, and my last penny was spent at a coffee-shop, where I sat long and restfully in the old-fashioned "pew" with a big mug of the steaming liquor before me.

That is my last connected recollection of this day. Whither I went after leaving the coffee-shop I have no idea. Hour after hour I must have wandered aimlessly through the streets, for the night had fallen when I found myself sitting on the high step of a sheltered doorway with my aching head supported by my hands. A light rain was pattering down on the pavement, and no doubt it was to escape this that I had crept into the doorway. But I do not remember. Indeed, my mind must have been in a very confused state, for I seemed to wake up as from a dream or a spell of unconsciousness when a light shone on me and a voice addressed me.

"Now, young fellow, you can't sit there. You must move on."

I raised my head and received the full glare of the lantern in my face, which caused me instantly to close my eyes. There was a short pause, and then the voice resumed, persuasively:

"Come, now, my lad, up you get."

With the aid of my hands on the step, I managed to rise a little way, but then sank down again with my back against the door. There was another pause, during which the policeman – now faintly visible – stooped over me for a closer inspection. Then a second voice interposed:

"What's this? He can't be drunk, a kid like that."

"No, he isn't," the first officer replied. He grasped my wrist, gently, in a very large hand, and exclaimed: "God! The boy's red-hot. Just feel his wrist."

The other man did so and brought *his* lantern to bear on me. Then they both stood up and held a consultation of which I caught only a few stray phrases such as, "Yes, Margaret's is nearest," and, finally, "All right. Run along to the stand and fetch one. Four-wheeler, of course."

Here, one of the officers disappeared, and the other, leaning over me, asked in a kindly tone what my name was and where I lived. I managed to answer these questions, the replies to which the officer entered in a book, but the effort finished me, and I dropped forward again with my head in my hands. Presently a cab drew up opposite the doorway, and the two officers lifted me gently and helped me into it, when I saw by the light of its lamps that they were a sergeant and a constable. The latter got in with me and slammed the door with a bang that seemed like the blow of a hammer on my head, and the cab rattled away noisily, the jar of its iron tyres on the granite setts shaking me most abominably.

Of that journey I have but the haziest recollection. I know that I huddled in the corner with my teeth chattering, but I must have sunk into a sort of stupor, for I can recall nothing more than a muddled, dream-like, consciousness of lights and people, of being lifted about and generally discommoded, of having my clothes taken off, and, finally, of being washed by a white-capped woman with a large sponge – a proceeding that made my teeth chatter worse than ever.

Thenceforward time ceased to exist for me. I must have lain in a dull torpid condition with occasional intervals of more definite consciousness. I was dimly aware that I was lying in a bed in a large, light room in which there were other people, and which I recognized as a hospital ward. But mostly my mind was a blank, conscious only of extreme bodily discomfort and a dull headache that never left me a moment of ease.

How long I continued in this state, indifferent to, and hardly conscious of, my surroundings, but always restless, weary and suffering, I have no idea (excepting from what I was told afterwards). Days and nights passed uncounted and unperceived, and the memory of that period which remains is that of a vague, interminable dream.

The awakening came, I think, somewhat suddenly. At any rate, I remember a day when I, myself, was conscious of a change. The headache and the restlessness had gone, and with them the muddled, confused state of mind. I was now clearly aware of what was going on around me, though too listless to take particular notice, lying still with my eyes closed or half-closed, in a state of utter exhaustion, with a sensation of sinking through the bed. Vaguely, the idea that I was dying presented itself, but it merely floated through my mind without arousing any interest. The effort even of thinking was beyond my powers.

In the afternoon of this day the physician made his periodical visit. I was aware of droning voices and the tread of many feet as he and the little crowd of students moved on from bed to bed, now passing farther away and now coming nearer. Presently they reached my bed, and I opened my eyes sleepily to look at them. The physician was a short, pink-faced gentleman with upstanding silky white hair and bright blue eyes. At the moment he was examining the chart and case-paper and discussing them with a tall, handsome young man whom I recognized as one of the regular disturbers of my peace. I took no note of what they were saying until he handed the chart-board to a white-capped lady (another of the disturbers) with the remark:

"Well, Sister, the temperature is beginning to remit, but he doesn't seem to be getting any fatter."

"No, indeed," the sister replied. "He is an absolute skeleton, and he's most dreadfully weak. But he seems quite sensible today."

"H'm. Yes," said the physician. Then, addressing the students, he continued: "A rather difficult question arises. We are in a dilemma. If we feed him too soon we may aggravate the disease and send his temperature up; if we don't feed him soon enough we may – well, we may feed him too late. And in this case there is the complication that the patient was apparently in a state of semi-starvation when he was taken ill; so he had no physiological capital to start with. Now, what are we to do? Shall we take the opinion of the learned house physician?" He smiled up at the tall young gentleman and continued: "You've had him under observation, Thorndyke. Tell us what you'd do."

"I should take what seems to be the lesser risk," the house physician replied, promptly, "and begin feeding him at once."

"There!" chuckled the physician. "The oracle has spoken, and I think we agree. We usually do agree with Mr Thorndyke; and when we don't, we're usually wrong. Ha! ha! What? Very well, Thorndyke. He's your patient, so you can carry out your own prescription."

With this, the procession moved on to the next bed; and I closed my eyes and relapsed into my former state of dreamy half-consciousness. From this, however, I was presently aroused by a light touch on my shoulder and a feminine voice addressing me.

"Now, Number Six, wake up. I've brought you a little supper, and the doctor says you are to take the whole of it."

I opened my eyes and looked sleepily at the speaker, a pleasant-faced, middle-aged nurse who held in one hand a glass bowl, containing a substance that looked like pomade, and in the other a spoon; and with the latter she began to insinuate very small quantities of the pomade into my mouth, smilingly ignoring my feeble efforts to resist. For though the taste of the stuff was agreeable enough, I still had an intense repugnance to food and only wanted to be left alone. But she was very patient and very persistent, giving me little rests and then rousing me up and coaxing me to make another effort. And so, I suppose, the pomade was at last finished; but I don't know, for I must have fallen asleep and must have slept several hours, since it was night when I awoke and the ward was in semi-darkness. But the pomade had done its work. The dreadful sinking feeling had nearly gone and I felt sufficiently alive to look about me with a faintly-awakening interest; which I continued to do until the night sister espied me and presently bore down on me with a steaming bowl and a feeding cup.

"Well, Number Six," said she, "you've had quite a fine, long sleep, and now you are going to have some nice, hot broth; and perhaps, when you have taken it, you'll have another sleep." Which turned out to be the case, for though I recall emptying the feeding-cup, I remember nothing more until I awoke to find the sunlight streaming into the ward and the nurse and Mr Thorndyke standing beside my bed.

"This is better, Number Six," said the latter. "They tell me you have been sleeping like a dormouse. How do you feel this morning?"

I replied in a ridiculous whisper that I felt much better; at which he smiled, pleasantly, and remarked that it was the first time he had heard my voice, "if you can call it a voice," he added. Then he felt my pulse, took my temperature, and, having made a few notes on the case-paper, departed with another smile and a friendly nod.

I need not follow my progress in detail. It was uninterrupted, though very slow. By the end of the following week my temperature had settled down and I was well on my way to recovery. But I was desperately weak and wasted to a degree of emaciation that I should have supposed to be impossible in a living man. However, this seemed to be a passing phase, for now, so far from feeling any repugnance to food, I hailed the appetizing little meals that were brought to me with voracious joy.

As my condition improved, Mr Thorndyke's visits tended to grow longer. When the routine business had been dispatched, he would linger for a minute or two to exchange a few words with me (very few on my side and mostly playful or facetious on his) before passing on to the next bed; and whenever, during the day or night, he had occasion to pass through the ward, if I were awake, he would always greet me, at least, with a smile and a wave of the hand. Not that he specially singled me out for these attentions, for every patient was made to feel that the house physician was interested in him as a man and not merely as a "case".

Nevertheless, I think there was something about me that attracted his attention in a particular way, for on several occasions I noticed him looking me over in an appraising sort of fashion, and I thought that he seemed especially interested in my hands. And apparently I was right, as I learned one afternoon when, having finished his round, he came and sat down on the chair by my bedside to talk to me. Presently he picked up my right hand, and, holding it out before him, remarked:

"This is quite a lady-like hand, Polton" (he had dropped "Number Six"); "very delicate and soft. And yet it is a good, serviceable hand, and I notice that you use it as if you were accustomed to do skilled work with it. Perhaps I am wrong; but I have been wondering what your occupation is. You are too small for any of the heavy trades."

"I am a clock-maker, Sir," I replied, "but I have put in some time at cabinet-making and I have had a turn at making philosophical instruments, such as levels and theodolites. But clockmaking is my proper trade."

"Then," said he, "Providence must have foreseen that you were going to be a clock-maker and furnished you with exactly the right kind of hands. But you seem to have had a very varied experience, considering your age."

"I have, Sir, though it wasn't all of my own choosing. I had to take the job that offered itself, and when no job offered, it was a case of wearing out shoe-leather."

"Ha!" said he, "and I take it that you had been wearing out a good deal of shoe-leather at the time when you were taken ill."

"Yes, Sir. I had been having a very bad time."

I suppose I spoke somewhat dismally, for it had suddenly dawned on me that I should leave the hospital penniless and with worse prospects than ever. He looked at me thoughtfully, and, after a short pause, asked:

"Why were you not able to get work?"

I considered the question and found it difficult to answer; and yet I wanted to explain, for something told me that he would understand and sympathize with my difficulties, and we all like to pour our troubles into sympathetic ears.

"There were several reasons, Sir, but the principal one was that I wasn't able to finish my apprenticeship. But it's rather a long story to tell to a busy gentleman."

"I'm not a busy gentleman for the moment," said he with a smile. "I've finished my work for the present; and I shall be a very interested gentleman if you care to tell me the story. But perhaps you would rather not recall those bad times."

"Oh, it isn't that, Sir. I should like to tell you if it wouldn't weary you."

As he once more assured me of his interest in my adventures and misadventures, I began, shyly and awkwardly, to sketch out the history of my apprenticeship, with scrupulous care to keep it as short as possible. But there was no need. Not only did he listen with lively interest; but when I became unduly sketchy he interposed with questions to elicit fuller details, so that, becoming more at my ease, I told the little story of my life in a consecutive narrative, but still keeping to the more significant incidents. The last, disastrous, episode, however, I related at length – mentioning no names except that of Mr Cohen – as it seemed necessary to be circumstantial in order to make my innocence perfectly clear; and I was glad that I did so, for my listener followed that tragedy of errors with the closest attention.

"Well, Polton," he said when I had brought the narrative up to date, "you have had only a short life, but it has been a pretty full one – a little too full, at times. If experience makes men wise, you should be bursting with wisdom. But I do hope you have taken in your full cargo of that kind of experience."

He looked at his watch, and, as he rose, remarked that he must be getting back to duty; and having thanked me for "my most interesting story," walked quickly but silently out of the ward, leaving me with a curious sense of relief at having unburdened myself of my troubles to a confessor so kindly and sympathetic.

That, however, was not the last of our talks, for thenceforward he adopted the habit of making me little visits, sitting on the chair by my bedside and chatting to me quite familiarly without a trace of patronage. It was evident that my story had greatly interested him, for he occasionally put a question that showed a complete recollection of all that I had told him. But more commonly he drew me out on the subject of clocks and watches. He made me explain, with drawings, the construction and mode of working of a gravity escapement and the difference between a chronometer and a lever watch. Again, he was quite curious on the subject of locks and keys and of instruments such as theodolites, of which he had no experience; and though mechanism would seem to be rather outside the province of a doctor, I found him very quick in taking in mechanical ideas and quite keen on acquiring the little items of technical knowledge that I was able to impart.

But these talks, so delightful to me, came to a rather sudden end, at least for a time; for one afternoon, just as he was leaving me, he announced:

"By the way, Polton, you will be handed over to a new house physician tomorrow. My term of office has come to an end." Then, observing that I looked rather crestfallen, he continued: "However, we shan't lose sight of each other. I am taking charge of the museum and laboratory for a week or two while the curator is away, and, as the laboratory opens on the garden, where you will be taking the air when you can get about, I shall be able to keep an eye on you."

This was some consolation for my loss, and something to look forward to, and it begot in me a sudden eagerness to escape from bed and see what I could do in the way of walking. Apparently, I couldn't do much; for when the sister, in response to my entreaties, wrapped me in a dressing-gown, and, with a nurse's aid, helped me to totter to the nearest armchair, I sat down with alacrity, and, at the end of half an hour, was very glad to be conducted back to bed.

It was not a very encouraging start, but I soon improved on it. In a few days I was crawling about the ward unassisted, with frequent halts to rest in the armchair; and by degrees the rests grew shorter and less frequent, until I was able to pace up and down the ward quite briskly. And at last came the joyful day when the nurse produced my clothes (which appeared to have been cleaned since I last saw them) and helped me to put them on; and, it being a warm, sunny morning, the sister graciously acceded to my request that I might take a little turn in the garden.

That was a red-letter day for me. Even now I recall with pleasure the delightful feeling of novelty with which I took my journey downwards in the lift, swathed in a dressing-gown over my clothes and fortified by a light lunch (which I devoured, wolfishly), and the joy with which I greeted the sunlit trees and flower-beds as the nurse conducted me along a path and deposited me on a seat. But better still was the sight of a tall figure emerging from the hospital and advancing with long strides along the path. At the sight of him my heart leaped, and I watched him anxiously lest he should take another path and pass without seeing me. My eagerness surprised me a little at the time; and now, looking back, I ask myself how it had come about that Mr Thorndyke was to me so immeasurably different from all other men. Was it some prophetic sense which made me dimly aware of what was to be? Or could it be that I, an insignificant, ignorant lad, had somehow instinctively divined the intellectual and moral greatness of the man? I cannot tell. In a quiet, undemonstrative way he had been gracious, kindly and sympathetic; but beyond this there had seemed to be a sort of magnetism about him which attracted me, so that to the natural respect and admiration with which I regarded him was unaccountably added an actual personal devotion.

Long before he had drawn near, he saw me and came straight to my seat.

"Congratulations, Polton," he said, cheerfully, as he sat down beside me. "This looks like the beginning of the end. But we mustn't be impatient, you know. We must take things easily and not try to force the pace."

He stayed with me about five minutes, chatting pleasantly, but principally in a medical strain, advising me and explaining the dangers and pitfalls of convalescence from a severe and exhausting illness. Then he left me, to go about his business in the laboratory, and I followed him with my eyes as he entered the doorway of a range of low buildings. But in a few moments he reappeared, carrying a walking-stick, and, coming up to my seat, handed the stick to me.

"Here is a third leg for you, Polton," said he; "a very useful aid when the natural legs are weak and unsteady. You needn't return it. It is an ancient derelict that has been in the laboratory as long as I have known the place."

I thanked him, and, as he returned to the laboratory, I rose and took a little walk to try the stick, and very helpful I found it; but even if I had not, I should still have prized the simple ash staff for the sake of the giver, as I have prized it ever since. For I have it to this day; and the silver band that I put on it bears the date on which it was given.

A few days later Mr Thorndyke overtook me as I was hobbling along the path with the aid of my "third leg".

"Why, Polton," he exclaimed, "you are getting quite active and strong. I wonder if you would care to come and have a look at the laboratory."

I grasped eagerly at the offer, and we walked together to the building and entered the open doorway – left open, I presumed when I was inside, to let out some of the smell.

The premises consisted of the laboratory proper, a large room with a single long bench and a great number of shelves occupied by stoppered glass jars of all sizes, mostly filled with a clear liquid in which some very queer-looking objects were suspended (one, I was thrilled to observe, was a human hand). On the lower shelves were ranged great covered earthenware pots which I suspected to be the source of the curious, spirituous odour. Beyond the laboratory was a workroom furnished with a lathe, two benches and several racks of tools.

When he had shown me round, Mr Thorndyke seated me in a Windsor armchair close to the bench where he was working at the cutting, staining and mounting of microscopical sections for use in the medical school. When I had been watching him for some time, he looked round at me with a smile.

"I suspect, Polton," said he, "that you are itching to try your hand at section-mounting. Now, aren't you?"

I had to confess that I was; whereupon he, most good-naturedly, provided me with a glass bowl of water and a pile of watch-glasses and bade me go ahead, which I did with the delight of a child with a new toy. Having cut the sections on the microtome and floated them off into the bowl, I carried out the other processes in as close imitation of his methods as I could, until I had a dozen slides finished.

"Well, Polton," said he, "there isn't much mystery about it, you see. But you are pretty quick at learning – quicker than some of the students whom I have to teach."

He examined my slides with the microscope, and, to my joy, pronounced them good enough to go in with the rest; and he was just beginning to label them when I perceived, through the window, the nurse who had come to shepherd the patients in to dinner. So, with infinite regret, I tore myself away, but not until I had been rejoiced by an invitation to come again on the morrow.

The days that followed were among the happiest of my life. Every morning – and, later, every afternoon as well – I presented myself at the laboratory and was greeted with a friendly welcome. I was allowed to look on at, and even to help in, all kinds of curious, novel and fascinating operations. I assisted in the making of a plaster cast of a ricketty boy's deformed legs; in the injecting with carmine gelatine of the blood-vessels of a kidney; and in the cutting and mounting of a section of a tooth. Every day I had a new experience and learned something fresh; and in addition was permitted and encouraged to execute repairs in the workroom on various invalid instruments and appliances. It was a delightful time. The days slipped past in a dream of tranquil happiness.

I have said "the days," but I should rather have said the hours that I spent in the laboratory. They were hours of happiness unalloyed. But with my return to the ward came a reaction. Then I had to face the realities of life, to realize that a dark cloud was rising, ever growing darker and more threatening. For I was now convalescent; and this was a hospital, not an almshouse. My illness was over and it was nearly time for me to go. At any moment now I might get my discharge; and then – but I did not dare to think of what lay before me when I should go forth from the hospital door into the inhospitable streets.

At last the blow fell. I saw it coming when, instead of sending me out to the garden, the sister bade me stay by my bed when the physician was due to make his visit. So there I stood, watching the procession of students moving slowly round the ward with the feelings of a condemned man awaiting the approach of the executioner. Finally, it halted opposite my bed. The physician looked at me critically, spoke a few kindly words of congratulation, listened to the sister's report, and, taking the chart-board from her, wrote a few words on the case paper, returned the board to her and moved on to the next bed.

"When do I go out, Sister?" I asked, anxiously, as she replaced the board on its peg. She evidently caught and understood the note of anxiety, for she replied very gently, with a quick glance at my downcast face, "The day after tomorrow," and turned away to rejoin the procession.

So the brief interlude of comfort and happiness was over and once more I must go forth to wander, a wretched Ishmaelite, through the cheerless wilderness. What I should do when I found myself cast out into the street, I had no idea. Nor did I try to form any coherent plan. The utter hopelessness of my condition induced a sort of mental paralysis, and I could only roam about the garden (whither I had strayed when sentence had been pronounced) in a state of vague, chaotic misery. Even the appetizing little supper was swallowed untasted, and, for the first time since the dawn of my convalescence, my sleep was broken and troubled.

On the following morning I presented myself as usual at the laboratory. But its magic was gone. I pottered about in the workroom to finish a repairing job that I had on hand, but even that could not distract me from the thought that I was looking my last on this pleasant and friendly place. Presently, Mr Thorndyke came in to look at the instrument that I was repairing – it was a rocking microtome – but soon transferred his attention from the instrument to me.

"What's the matter, Polton?" he asked. "You are looking mighty glum. Have you got your discharge?"

"Yes, Sir," I replied. "I am going out tomorrow."

"Ha!" said he, "and from what you have told me, I take it that you have nowhere to go."

I admitted, gloomily, that this was the case.

"Very well," said he. "Now I have a little proposal that I want you to consider. Come and sit down in the laboratory and I'll tell you about it."

He sat me in a Windsor armchair, and, seating himself on the bench stool, continued: "I am intending to set up in practice; not in an ordinary medical practice, but in that branch of medicine that is connected with the law and is concerned with expert medical and scientific evidence. For the purposes of my practice I shall have to have a laboratory, somewhat like this, with a workshop attached; and I shall want an assistant to help me with the experimental work. That assistant will have to be a skilled mechanic, capable of making any special piece of apparatus that may be required, and generally handy and adaptable. Now, from what you have told me and what I have seen for myself, I judge that you would suit me perfectly. You have a working knowledge of three crafts, and I have seen that you are skilful, painstaking and quick to take an idea, so I should like to have you as my assistant. I can't offer much of a salary at first, as I shall be earning nothing, myself, for a time, but I could pay you a pound a week to begin with, and, as I should provide you with food and a good, big bed-sitting room, you could rub along until something better turned up. What do you say?"

I didn't say anything. I was speechless with emotion, with the sudden revulsion from black despair to almost delirious joy. My eyes filled and a lump seemed to rise in my throat.

Mr Thorndyke evidently saw how it was with me, and, by way of easing the situation, he resumed: "There is one other point. Mine will be a bachelor establishment. I want no servants; so that, if you come to me, you would have to render a certain amount of personal and domestic services. You would keep the little household in order and occasionally prepare a meal. In fact, you would be in the position of my servant as well as laboratory assistant. Would you object to that?"

Would I object! I could have fallen down that instant and kissed his boots. What I did say was that I should be proud to be his servant and only sorry that I was not more worthy of that honourable post.

"Then," said he, "the bargain is struck; and each of us must do his best to make it a good bargain for the other."

He then proceeded to arrange the details of my assumption of office, which included the transfer of five shillings "to chink in my pocket and pay the cabman," and, when all was settled, I went forth, at his advice, to take a final turn in the garden; which I did with a springy step and at a pace that made the other patients stare.

As I entered the ward, the sister came up to me with a rather troubled face.

"When you go out tomorrow, Number Six, what are you going to do? Have you any home to go to?"

"Yes, Sister," I replied, triumphantly. "Mr Thorndyke has just engaged me as his servant."

"Oh, I am *so* glad," she exclaimed. "I have been rather worried about you. But I am quite happy now, for I know that you will have the very best of masters."

She was a wise woman, was that sister.

I pass over the brief remainder of my stay in hospital. The hour of my discharge, once dreaded, but now hailed with joy, came in the middle of the forenoon; and, as my worldly goods were all on my person, no preparations were necessary. I made the round of the ward to say farewell to my fellow-patients, and, when the sister had given me a hearty handshake (I should have liked to kiss her), I was conducted by the nurse to the secretary's office and there formally discharged. Then, pocketing my discharge ticket, I made my way to the main entrance and presented myself at the porter's lodge.

"Ah!" said the porter when I had introduced myself, "so you are Mr Thorndyke's young man. Well, I've got to put you into a hansom and see that you know where to go. Do you?"

"Yes," I answered, producing the card that my master had given me and reading from it. "The address is 'Dr John Thorndyke, 5A King's Bench Walk, Inner Temple, London, EC.' "

"That's right," said he; "and remember that he's *Doctor* Thorndyke now. We call him Mister because that's the custom when a gentleman is on the junior staff, even if he is an MD. Here's a hansom coming in, so we shan't have to fetch one."

The cab came up the courtyard and discharged its passenger at the entrance, when the porter hailed the driver, and, having hustled me into the vehicle, sang out the address to which I was to be conveyed and waved his hand to me as we drove off, and I returned his salutation by raising my hat.

I enjoyed the journey amazingly, surveying the busy streets over the low doors with a new pleasure and thinking how cheerful and friendly they looked. I had never been in a hansom before and I suppose I never shall again. For the hansom is gone; and we have lost the most luxurious and convenient passenger vehicle ever devised by the wit of man.

That cabman knew his business. Londoner as I was, the intricacies of his route bewildered me completely; and when he came to the surface, as it were, in Chancery Lane, which I recognized, he almost immediately finished me off by crossing Fleet Street and passing through a great gateway into a narrow lane bordered by ancient timber houses. Half-way down this lane he turned into another, at the entrance to which I read the name, "Crown Office Row," and this ended in a great open square surrounded by tall houses. Here I was startled by a voice above my head demanding:

"You said Five A, didn't you?"

I looked up, and was astonished to behold a face looking down on me through a square opening in the roof; but I promptly answered "Yes," whereupon the face vanished and I saw and heard a lid shut down, and a few moments later the cab drew up opposite the portico of a house on the eastern side of the square. I hopped out, and, having verified the number, asked the cabman what there was to pay; to which he replied, concisely, "Two bob," and, leaning down, held out his hand. It seemed a lot of money, but, of course, he knew what his fare was, so, having handed up the exact amount, I turned away and stepped into the entry, on the jamb of which was painted: "First pair, Dr John Thorndyke."

The exact meaning of this inscription was not quite clear to me, but as the ground floor was assigned to another person, I decided to explore the staircase; and having ascended to the first-floor landing, was reassured by observing the name "Dr Thorndyke" painted in white lettering over a doorway, the massive, ironbound door of which was open, revealing an inner door garnished by a small and very tarnished brass knocker. On this I struck a single modest rap, when the door was opened by Dr Thorndyke, himself.

"Come in, Polton," said he, smiling on me very kindly and shaking my hand. "Come into your new home – which is my home, too; and I hope it will be a happy one for us both. But it will be what we make it. Perhaps, if your journey hasn't tired you, you would like me to show you over the premises."

I said that I was not tired at all, so he led me forth at once and we started to climb the stairs, of which there were four flights to the third-floor landing.

"I have brought you to the top floor," said The Doctor, "to introduce you to your own domain. The rest of the rooms you can explore at your leisure. This is your bedroom."

He threw open a door, and when I looked in I was struck dumb with astonishment and delight. It was beyond my wildest dreams – a fine, spacious room with two windows, furnished in a style of which I had no previous experience. A handsome carpet covered the floor, the bed surpassed even the hospital beds, there were a wardrobe, a chest of drawers, a set of bookshelves, a large table by one of the windows and a small one beside the bed, a fine easy chair and two other chairs. It was magnificent. I had thought that only noblemen lived in such rooms. And yet it was a very picture of homely comfort.

I was struggling to express my gratitude when The Doctor hustled me down to the second floor to inspect the future laboratory and workshop. At present they were just large, empty rooms, but the kitchen was fully furnished and in going order, with a gas-cooker and a dresser filled with china, and the empty larder was ready for use.

"Now," said The Doctor, "I must run off to the hospital in a few minutes, but there are one or two matters to settle. First, you will want some money to fit yourself out with clothes. I will advance you ten pounds for that purpose. Then, until we are settled down, you will have to get your meals at restaurants. I will give you a couple of pounds for those and any stores that you may lay in, and you will keep an account and let me know when you want any more money. And remember that you are a convalescent, and don't stint your diet. I think that is all for the present except the latch-keys, which I had better give you now."

He laid the money and the two keys on the table, and was just turning to go when it occurred to me to ask if I should get an evening meal prepared for him. He looked at me with a smile of surprise and replied:

"You're a very enterprising convalescent, Polton, but you mustn't try to do too much at first. No, thank you. I shall dine in the board-room tonight and get home about half-past nine."

When he had gone, I went out, and, having taken a substantial lunch at a restaurant near Temple Bar, proceeded to explore the neighbourhood with a view to household stores. Eventually I found in Fetter Lane enough suitable shops to enable me to get the kitchen and the larder provided for a start, and, having made my purchases, hurried home to await the delivery of the goods. Then I spent a delightful afternoon and evening rambling about the house, planning the workshop, paying repeated visits to my incomparable room, and inaugurating the kitchen by preparing myself an enormous high tea; after which, becoming extremely sleepy, I went down and paced up and down the Walk to keep myself awake.

When The Doctor came home I would have expounded my plans for the arrangement of the workshop. But he cut me short with the admonition that convalescents should be early birds, and sent me off to bed; where I sank at once into a delicious slumber and slept until it was broad daylight and a soft-toned bell informed me that it was seven o'clock.

This day is the last that I shall record; for it saw the final stage of that wonderful transformation that changed the old Nathaniel Polton, the wretched, friendless outcast, into the pampered favourite of Fortune.

When I had given The Doctor his breakfast (which he praised, warmly, but begged me to remember in future that he was only one man) and seen him launched on his way to the hospital, I consumed what he had left on the dish – one fried egg and a gammon rasher – and, having tidied up The Doctor's bedroom and my own, went forth to wind up the affairs of Polton, the destitute, and inaugurate Polton, the opulent; to "ring out the old and ring in the new". First, I visited a "gentlemen's outfitters", where I purchased a ready-made suit of a sober and genteel character (I heard the shopman whisper something about "medium boy's size") and other garments appropriate to it, including clerical grey socks, a pair of excellent shoes and a soft felt hat. The parcel being a large and heavy one I bought a strong rug-strap with which to carry it, and so was able, with an occasional rest, to convey it to Foubert's Place, where I proposed to settle any arrears of rent that Mr Stokes might claim. However, he claimed none, having let my room when I failed to return. But he had stored my property in an attic, from which he very kindly assisted me to fetch it, so that I had, presently, the satisfaction of seeing all my worldly goods piled up on the counter: the tool-chest that I had made in Mr Beeby's workshop, my whole collection of clock-maker's tools, and my beloved books, including Mr Denison's invaluable monograph. When they were all assembled, I went out and chartered a four-wheeled cab, in which I stowed them all – chest, tools, books, and the enormous parcel from the outfitters. Then I bade Mr Stokes a fond farewell, gave the cabman the address (at which he seemed surprised; and I am afraid that I *was* a rather shabby little ragamuffin) shut myself in the cab and started for home.

Home! I had not known the word since Aunt Judy and Uncle Sam had flitted away out of my ken. But now, as the cab rattled over the stones until it made my teeth chatter, I had before me the vision of that noble room in the Temple which was my very own, to have and to hold in perpetuity, and the gracious friend and master whose presence would have turned a hovel into a mansion.

As soon as we arrived, I conveyed my goods – in relays – upstairs; and when I had paid off the cabman, I proceeded to dispose of them. The tools I deposited in the future workshop as the first instalment of its furnishing, the books and parcel I carried up to my own apartment. And there the final scene was enacted. When I had arranged my little library lovingly in the bookshelves, I opened the parcel and laid out its incredible contents on the bed. For a while I was so overcome by their magnificence that I could only gloat over them in ecstasy. I had never had such clothes before, and I felt almost shy at their splendour. However, they were mine, and I was going to wear them; and so reflecting, I proceeded boldly to divest myself of the threadbare, frayed and faded habiliments that had served me so long until I had stripped to the uttermost rag (and rag is the proper word). Then I inducted myself cautiously into the new garments, finishing up (in some discomfort) with a snowy and rather stiff collar, a silk neck-tie, and the sober but elegant black coat.

For quite a long time I stood before the mirror in the wardrobe door surveying, with something of amused surprise and a certain sense of unreality, the trimly-dressed gentleman who confronted me. At length, I turned away with a sigh of satisfaction, and, having carefully put away the discarded clothing for use in the workshop, went down to await The Doctor's return.

And here I think I had better stop, leaving Dr Jervis to relate the sequel. Gladly would I go on – having now got into my stride – to tell of my happy companionship with my beloved master, and how he and I fitted out the workshop, and then, working on our joiner's bench, gradually furnished the laboratory with benches and shelves. But I had better not. My tale is told; and now I must lay down my pen and hold my peace. Yet still I love to look back on that wonderful morning in the hospital laboratory when a few magical words banished in an instant the night of my adversity and ushered in the dawn.

But it was not only the dawn; it was the sunrise. And the sun has never set. A benevolent Joshua has ordained that I shall live the days of my life in perpetual sunshine; and that Joshua's name is John Thorndyke.

PART TWO

THE CASE OF MOXDALE DECEASED

Narrated by Christopher Jervis, MD

CHAPTER TEN

Fire!

To an old Londoner, the aspect of the town in the small hours of the morning, in "the middle watch" as those dark hours are called in the language of the mariner, is not without its attractions. For however much he may love his fellow-creatures, it is restful, at least for a time, to take their society in infinitesimal doses, or even to dispense with it entirely, and to take one's way through the empty and silent streets free to pursue one's own thoughts undistracted by the din and hurly-burly that prevail in the daylight hours.

Thus I reflected as I turned out of Marylebone Station at about half-past two in the morning, and, crossing the wide, deserted road, bore away south-east in the direction of the Temple. Through what side streets I passed I cannot remember, and in fact never knew, for, in the manner of the born-and-bred Londoner, I simply walked towards my destination without consciously considering my route. And as I walked in a silence on which my own footfalls made an almost startling impression, I looked about me with something like curiosity and listened for the occasional far-off sounds which told of some belated car or lorry wending its solitary way through some distant street.

I was approaching the neighbourhood of Soho and passing through a narrow street lined by old and rather squalid houses, all dark and silent, when my ear caught a sound which, though faint and far-away, instantly attracted my attention: the clang of a bell, not rung, but struck with a hammer and repeating the single note in a quick succession of strokes – the warning bell of a fire-engine. I listened with mild interest – it was too far off to concern me – and compared the sound with that of the fire-engines of my young days. It was more distinctive, but less exciting. The bell gave its message plainly enough, but it lacked that quality of urgency and speed that was conveyed by the rattle of iron tyres on the stones and the sound of galloping horses.

Ding, ding, ding, ding, ding. The sound was more distinct. Then the engine must be coming my way; and even as I noted the fact, the clang of another bell rang out from the opposite direction, and suddenly I became aware of a faintly pungent smell in the air. Then, as I turned a corner, I met a thin cloud of smoke that was drifting up the street and noticed a glow in the sky over the house-tops; and presently, reaching another corner, came into full view of the burning house, though it was still some distance away, near the farther end of the street.

I watched it with some surprise as I walked quickly towards it, for there seemed to be something unusual in its appearance. I had not seen many burning houses but none that I had seen had looked quite like this one. There was a furious intensity in the way that it flared up that impressed me as abnormal. From the chimneys, flames shot up like the jets from a gas-blowpipe, and the windows emitted tongues of fire that looked as if they were being blown out by bellows. And the progress of the fire was frightfully rapid, for even in the short time that it took me to walk the length of the street there was an evident change. Glowing spots began to appear in the roof, flames poured out of the attic windows, and smoke and flame issued from the ground floor, which seemed to be some kind of shop.

No crowd had yet collected, but just a handful of chance wayfarers like myself and a few policemen, who stood a little distance away from the house, looking on the scene of destruction and listening anxiously to the sounds of the approaching engines, now quite near and coming from several different directions.

"It's a devil of a blaze," I remarked to one of the constables. "What is it? An oil-shop?"

"It's worse than that, Sir," he replied. "It's a film dealer's. The whole place chock full of celluloid films. It's to be hoped that there isn't anybody in the house, but I'm rather afraid there is. The caretaker of the offices next door says that there is a gentleman who has rooms on the first floor. Poor look-out for him if he is in there now. He will be burned to a cinder by this time."

At this moment the first of the engines swung round the corner and swept up to the house with noiseless speed, discharging its brass-helmeted crew, who began immediately to prepare for action: opening the waterplugs, rolling out lengths of hose, and starting the pumps. In a minute or two, four other engines arrived, accompanied by a motor fire-escape; but the latter, when its crew had glanced at the front of the house, was trundled some distance up the street out of the way of the engines. There was obviously no present use for it, nor did there seem to be much left for the engines to do, for, almost at the moment when the first jet of water was directed at the flaming window-space, the roof fell in with a crash and a roar, a volume of flame and sparks leaped up into the sky, and through the holes which had once been windows an uninterrupted sheet of fire could be seen from the top of the house to the bottom. Evidently, the roof, in its fall, had carried away what had been left of the floors, and the house was now no more than an empty shell with a mass of flaming debris at its base.

Whether the jets of water that were directed in through the window-holes had any effect, or whether the highly inflammable material had by this time all been burnt, I could not judge, but, after the fall of the roof, the fire began almost suddenly to die down, and a good deal of the firemen's attention became occupied by the adjoining house, which had already suffered some injury from the fire and now seemed likely to suffer more from the water. But in this I was not greatly interested, and, as the more spectacular phase of the disaster seemed to have come to an end, I extricated myself from the small crowd that had now collected and resumed my progress towards the Temple and the much-desired bed that awaited me there.

To a man who has turned in at past four o'clock in the morning, competition with the lark is not practicable. It was getting on for eleven when I emerged from my bedroom and descended the stairs towards the breakfast-room, becoming agreeably conscious of a subtle aroma which memory associated with bacon and coffee.

"I heard you getting up, Sir," said Polton with a last, satisfied glance at the breakfast-table, "and I heard you come in last night, or rather this morning, so I have cooked an extra rasher. You did make a night of it, Sir."

"Yes," I admitted, "it was rather a late business, and what made me still later was a house on fire somewhere near Soho which I stopped for a while to watch. A most tremendous blaze. A policeman told me that it was a celluloid film warehouse. so you can imagine how it flared up."

I produced this item of news designedly, knowing that it would be of interest; for Polton, the most gentle and humane of men, had an almost morbid love of the horrible and the tragic. As I spoke, his eyes glistened, and he commented with a sort of ghoulish relish:

"Celluloid films! And a whole warehouse full of them, too! It must have been a fine sight. I've never seen a house on fire – not properly on fire; only just smoke and sparks. Was there a fire-escape?"

"Yes, but there was nothing for it to do. The house was like a furnace."

"But the people inside, Sir. Did they manage to get out in time?"

"I am not certain that there was anybody in the house. I heard something about a gentleman who had rooms there, but there was no sign of him. It is not certain that he was there, but if he was, he is there still. We shall know when the firemen and salvage men are able to examine the ruins."

"Ha!" said Polton, "there won't be much of him left. Where did you say the place was, Sir?"

"I can't tell you the name of the street, but it was just off Old Compton Street. You will probably see some notice of the fire in the morning paper."

Thereupon, Polton turned away as if to go in search of the paper, but at the door he paused and looked back at me.

"Speaking of burning houses, Sir," said he, "Mr Stalker called about half an hour ago. I told him how things were, so he said he would probably look in again in an hour's time. If he does, will you see him downstairs or shall I bring him up?"

"Oh, bring him up here. We don't make a stranger of Mr Stalker."

"Yes, Sir. Perhaps he has come to see you about this very fire."

"He could hardly have got any particulars yet," said I. "Besides, fire insurance is not in our line of business."

"No, Sir," Polton admitted; "but it may be about the gentleman who had the rooms. A charred body might be in your line if they happen to know that there is one among the ruins."

I did not think it very likely, for there had hardly been time to ascertain whether the ruins did or did not contain any human remains. Nevertheless, Polton's guess turned out to be right; for when Stalker (having declined a cup of coffee and then explained, according to his invariable custom, that he happened to be passing this way and thought he might as well just look in) came to the point, it appeared that his visit was concerned with the fire in Soho.

"But, my dear Stalker," I protested, "we don't know anything about fires."

"I know," he replied with an affable smile. "The number of things that you and Thorndyke don't know anything about would fill an encyclopaedia. Still, there are some things that you do know. Perhaps you have forgotten that fire at Brattle's oil-shop, but I haven't. You spotted something that the fire experts had overlooked."

"Thorndyke did. I didn't until he pointed it out."

"I don't care which of you spotted it," said he. "I only know that, between you, you saved us two or three thousand pounds."

I remembered the case quite well, and the recollection of it seemed to justify Stalker's attitude.

"What do you want us to do?" I asked.

"I want you just to keep an eye on the case. The question of fire-raising will be dealt with by the Brigade men and the Salvage Corps. They are experts and they have their own methods. You have different methods and you bring a different sort of expert eye to bear on the matter."

"I wonder," said I, "why you are so Nosey-Parkerish about this fire. There hasn't been time for you to get any particulars."

"Indeed!" said he. "We don't all stay in bed until eleven o'clock. While you were slumbering I was getting a report and making enquiries."

"Ha!" I retorted. "And while you were slumbering I was watching your precious house burning; and I must say that it did you credit."

Here, in response to his look of surprise, I gave him a brief account of my morning's adventure.

"Very well," said he when I had finished. "Then you know the facts and you can understand my position. Here is a house, full of inflammable material, which unaccountably bursts into flames at three o'clock in the morning. That house was either unoccupied or had a single occupant who was presumably in bed and asleep, as he apparently made no attempt to escape."

I offered a vague suggestion of some failure of the electric installation such as a short circuit or other accident, but he shook his head.

"I know that such things are actually possible," said he, "but it doesn't do to accept them too readily. A man who has been in this business as long as I have acquires a sort of intuitive perception of what is and what is not a normal case; and I have the feeling that there is something a little queer about this fire. I had the same feeling about that oil-shop case, which is why I asked Thorndyke to look into it. And then there are rumours of a man who was sleeping in the house. You heard those yourself. Now, if that man's body turns up in the debris, there is the possibility of a further claim, as there was in the oil-shop case."

"But, my dear Stalker!" I exclaimed, grinning in his face. "This is foresight with a vengeance. This fire may have been an incendiary fire. There may have been a man sleeping in the house and he may have got burned to death; and that man may have insured his life in your Society. How does that work out by the ordinary laws of chance. Pretty long odds, I think."

"Not so long as you fancy," he replied. "Persons who lose their lives in incendiary fires have a tendency to be insured. The connection between the fire and the death may not be a chance connection. Still, I will admit that, beyond a mere suspicion that there may be something wrong about this fire, I have nothing to go on. I am asking you to watch the case *ex abundantia cautelæ,* as you lawyers say. And the watching must be done now while the evidence is available. It's no use waiting until the ruins have been cleared away and the body – if there is one – buried."

"No," I agreed; "Thorndyke will be with you in that. I will give him your instructions when I see him at lunch-time, and you can take it that he won't lose any time in collecting the facts. But you had better give us something in writing, as we shall have to get authority to inspect the ruins and to examine the body if there is one to examine."

"Yes," said Stalker, "I'll do that now. I have some of our letter-paper in my case."

He fished out a sheet, and, having written a formal request to Thorndyke to make such investigations as might be necessary in the interests of the Griffin Assurance Company, handed it to me and took his departure. As his footsteps died away on the stairs, Polton emerged from the adjacent laboratory and came in to clear away the breakfast-things. As he put them together on the tray he announced:

"I've read the account of the fire, Sir, in the paper, but there isn't much more than you told me. Only the address – Billington Street, Soho."

"And now," said I, "you would like to go and have a look at it, I suppose?"

"Well," he admitted, "it would be interesting after having heard about it from you. But you see, Sir, there's lunch to be got ready. The Doctor had his breakfast a bit earlier than you did, and not quite so much of it."

"Never mind about lunch," said I. "William can see to that." (William, I may explain, was a youth who had lately been introduced to assist Polton and relieve him of his domestic duties; and a very capable under-study he had proved. Nevertheless, Polton clung tenaciously to what he considered his privilege of attending personally to "The Doctor's" wants, which, in effect, included mine.) "You see, Polton," I added by way of overcoming his scruples, "one of us ought to go, and I don't want to. But The Doctor will want to make an inspection at the earliest possible moment and he will want to know how soon that will be. At present, the ruins can't have cooled down enough for a detailed inspection to be possible, but you could find out from the man in charge how things are and when we could make our visit. We shall want to see the place before it has been considerably disturbed, and, if there are any human remains, we shall want to know where the mortuary is."

On this Polton brightened up considerably. "Of course, Sir," said he, "if I could be of any use, I should like to go; and I think William will be able to manage, as it is only a cold lunch."

With this he retired, and a few minutes later I saw him from the window hurrying along Crown Office Row, carefully dressed and carrying a fine, silver-topped cane and looking more like a dignitary of the Church than a skilled artificer.

When Thorndyke came in, I gave him an account of Stalker's visit as well as of my own adventure.

"I don't quite see," I added, "what we can do for him or why he is in such a twitter about this fire."

"No," he replied. "But Stalker is enormously impressed by our one or two successes and is inclined to over-estimate our powers. Still, there seem to be some suspicious features in the case, and I notice, on the placards, a rumour that a man was burned to death in the fire. If that is so, the affair will need looking into more narrowly. But we shall hear more about that when Polton comes back."

We did. For when, just as we had finished lunch, our deputy returned, he was able to give us all the news up to the latest developments. He had been fortunate enough to meet Detective Sergeant Wills, who was watching the case for the police, and had learned from him that a body had been discovered among the debris, but that there was some mystery about its identity, as the tenant of the rooms was known to be away from home on a visit to Ireland. But it was not a mere matter of hearsay, for Polton had actually seen the body brought out on a stretcher and had followed it to the mortuary.

"You couldn't see what its condition was, I suppose?" said I.

"No, Sir," he replied, regretfully. "Unfortunately, it was covered up with a waterproof sheet."

"And as to the state of the ruins; did you find out how soon an examination of them will be possible?"

"Yes, Sir. I explained matters to the Fire Brigade officer and asked him when you would be able to make your inspection. Of course, everything is too hot to handle just now. They had the greatest difficulty in getting at the corpse; but the officer thought that by tomorrow morning they will be able to get to work, and he suggested that you might come along in the forenoon."

"Yes," said Thorndyke, "that will do. We needn't be there very early, as the heavier material – joists and beams and the debris of the roof – will have to be cleared away before we shall be able to see anything. We had better make our visit to the mortuary first. It is possible that we may learn more from the body than from the ruins. At any rate, it is within our province, which the ruins are not."

"Judging from what I saw," said I, "there will be mighty little for anyone to learn from the ruins. When the roof fell, it seemed to go right through to the basement."

"Will you want anything got ready, Sir?" Polton asked, a little anxiously.

Thorndyke apparently noted the wistful tone, for he replied:

"I shall want you to come along with us, Polton; and you had better bring a small camera with the adjustable stand. We shall probably want photographs of the body, and it may be in an awkward position."

"Yes, Sir," said Polton. "I will bring the extension as well; and I will put out the things that you are likely to want for your research-case."

With this, he retired in undissembled glee, leaving us to discuss our arrangements.

"You will want authorities to examine the body and the ruins," said I. "Shall I see to them? I have nothing special to do this afternoon."

"If you would, Jervis, it would be a great help," he replied. "I have some work which I should like to finish up, so as to leave tomorrow fairly free. We don't know how much time our examinations may take."

"No," said I, "especially as you seem to be taking the case quite seriously."

"But, my dear fellow," said he, "we must. There may be nothing in it at all, but, in any case, we have got to satisfy Stalker and do our duty as medico-legal advisers to *The Griffin*."

With this he rose and went forth about his business, while I, having taken possession of Stalker's letter, set out in quest of the necessary authorities.

CHAPTER ELEVEN

The Ruins

In the medico-legal mind the idea of horror, I suppose, hardly has a place. It is not only that sensibilities tend to become dulled by repeated impacts, but that the emotions are, as it were, insulated by the concentration of attention on technical matters. Speaking, however, dispassionately, I must admit that the body which had been disinterred from the ruins of the burned house was about as horrible an object as I had ever seen. Even the coroner's officer, whose emotional epidermis might well have grown fairly tough, looked at that corpse with an undisguised shudder, while as to Polton, he was positively appalled. As he stood by the table and stared with bulging eyes at the dreadful thing, I surmised that he was enjoying the thrill of his life. He was in a very ecstasy of horror.

To both these observers, I think, Thorndyke's proceedings imparted an added touch of gruesomeness; for my colleague – as I have hinted – saw in that hideous object nothing but a technical problem, and he proceeded in the most impassive and matter-of-fact way to examine it feature by feature and note down his observations as if he were drawing up an inventory. I need not enter into details as to its appearance. It will easily be imagined that a body which had been exposed to such intense heat that not only was most of its flesh reduced to mere animal charcoal, but the very bones, in places, were incinerated to chalky whiteness, was not a pleasant object to look on. But I think that what most appalled both Polton and the officer was the strange posture that it had assumed: a posture suggesting some sort of struggle or as if the man had been writhing in agony or shrinking from a threatened attack. The body and limbs were contorted in the strangest manner, the arms crooked, the hands thrust forward, and the skeleton fingers bent like hooks.

"Good Lord, Sir!" Polton whispered, "how the poor creature must have suffered! And it almost looks as if someone had been holding him down."

"It really does," the coroner's officer agreed; "as if somebody was attacking him and wouldn't let him escape."

"It does look rather horrid," I admitted, "but I don't think you need worry too much about the position of the limbs. This contortion is almost certainly due to shrinkage of the muscles after death as the heat dried them. What do you think, Thorndyke?"

"Yes," he agreed. "It is not possible to draw any conclusions from the posture of a body that has been burned to the extent that this has, and burned so unequally. You notice that, whereas the feet are practically incinerated, there are actually traces of the clothing on the chest; apparently a suit of pyjamas, to judge by what is left of the buttons."

At this moment the door of the mortuary opened to admit a newcomer, in whom we recognized a Dr Robertson, the divisional surgeon and an old acquaintance of us both.

"I see," he remarked, as Thorndyke laid down his tape measure to shake hands, "that you are making your examination with your usual thoroughness."

"Well," Thorndyke replied, "the relevant facts must be ascertained now or never. They may be of no importance, but one can't tell that in advance."

"Yes," said Robertson, "that is a sound principle. In this case, I don't much think they are. I mean data in proof of identity, which are what you seem to be collecting. The identity of this man seems to be established by the known circumstances, though not so very clearly, I must admit."

"That seems a little obscure," Thorndyke remarked. "Either the man's identity is known, or it isn't."

The divisional surgeon smiled. "You are a devil for accuracy, Thorndyke," said he, "but you are quite right. We aren't here to make guesses. But the facts as to the identity appear to be pretty simple. From the statement of Mr Green, the lessee of the house, it seems that the first-floor rooms were let to a man named Gustavus Haire, who lived in them, and he was the only person resident in the house; so that, when the business premises closed down for the day and the employees went home, he had the place to himself."

"Then," said Thorndyke, "do we take it that this is the body of Mr Gustavus Haire?"

"No," replied Robertson, "that is where the obscurity comes in. Mr Haire has − fortunately for him − gone on a business visit to Dublin, but, as Mr Green informs us, during his absence he allowed a cousin of his, a Mr Cecil Moxdale, to occupy the rooms, or at least to use them to sleep in to save the expense of an hotel. The difficulty is that Moxdale was not known personally to Mr Green, or to anybody else, for that matter. At present, he is little more than a name. But, of course, Haire will be able to give all the necessary particulars when he comes back from Ireland."

"Yes," Thorndyke agreed, "but meanwhile there will be no harm in noting the facts relevant to the question of identity. The man may have made a will, or there may be other reasons for establishing proof of his identity independently of Haire's statements. I have made notes of the principal data, but I am not very happy about the measurements. The contorted state of the body makes them a little uncertain. I suggest that you and Jervis take a set of measurements each, independently, and that we compare them afterwards."

Robertson grinned at me, but he took the tape measure without demur and proceeded quite carefully to take the principal dimensions of the contorted body and the twisted limbs, and, when he had finished, I repeated the measurements, noting them down in my pocket-book. Then we compared our respective findings – which were in substantial agreement – and Thorndyke copied them all down in his note-book.

"When you came in, Robertson," said he, "we were discussing the posture of the body, and we had concluded that the contortion was due to shrinkage and had no significance. Do you agree?"

"I think so. It is not an unusual condition, and I don't see what significance it could have. The cause of death is practically established by the circumstances. But it certainly is a queer posture. The head especially. The man looks as if he had been hanged."

"He does," Thorndyke agreed, "and I want you to take a careful look at the neck. I noticed Jervis looking at it with a good deal of interest. Has my learned friend formed any opinion?"

"The neck is certainly dislocated," I replied, "and the odontoid process is broken. I noted that, but I put it down to the effects of shrinkage of the neck muscles, and possibly to some disturbance when the body was moved."

Robertson stooped over the body and examined the exposed neck-bones narrowly, testing the head for mobility and finding it quite stiff and rigid.

"Well," said he, "the neck is undoubtedly broken, but I am inclined to agree with Jervis, excepting that, as the neck is perfectly rigid, I don't think that the dislocation could have been produced by the moving of the body. I should say that it is the result of shrinkage; in fact, I don't see how else it could have been caused, having regard to the circumstances in which the body was found."

Thorndyke looked dissatisfied. "It always seems to me," said he, "that when one is examining a particular fact, it is best to forget the circumstances; to consider the fact without prejudice and without connection with anything else, and then, as a separate proceeding, to relate it to the circumstances."

The divisional surgeon chuckled. "This," said he, "is what the Master instils into his pupils. And quite right, too. It is sound doctrine. But still, you know, we must be reasonable. When we find the body of a man among the debris of a house which has been burned out, and the evidence shows that the man was the only occupant of that house, it seems a little pedantic to enquire elaborately whether he may not have died from the effects of manual strangulation or homicidal hanging."

"My point," Thorndyke rejoined, as a parting shot, "is that our function is to ascertain the objective facts, leaving their interpretation to the coroner and his jury. Looking at that odontoid process, I find that the appearance of the fragments where the break took place is more consistent with the fracture having occurred during life than after death and during the subsequent shrinkage. I admit that I do not see how the fracture can have happened in the known – or assumed – circumstances, and I further admit that the appearances are not at all decisive."

I took another careful look at the fractured bone and was disposed to agree with Thorndyke; but I had also to agree with Robertson when he closed the discussion with the remark:

"Well, Thorndyke, you may be right, but in any case the point seems to be of only academic interest. The man was alone in the house, so he couldn't have died from homicide; and I have never heard of anyone committing suicide by dislocating his neck."

Nevertheless, he joined us in a very thorough examination of the body for any other traces of injury (of which I need hardly say there were none) and for any distinctive appearances which might help to determine the identity in case the question should arise. I noticed him closely examining the teeth, and as they had already attracted my attention, I asked:

"What do you make of those teeth? Is that roughening and pitting of the enamel due to the heat, or to some peculiarity of the teeth, themselves?"

"Just what I was wondering," he replied. "I think it must be the result of the fire, for I don't recognize it as a condition that I have ever seen on living teeth. What do you think, Thorndyke?"

"I am in the same position as yourself," was the reply. "I don't recognize the condition. It is not disease, for the teeth are quite sound and strong. On the other hand, I don't quite understand how that pitting could have been produced by the heat. So I have just noted the appearance in case it should have any significance later."

"Well," said Robertson, "if Thorndyke is reduced to an open verdict, I suppose we may follow suit," and with this we returned to the general examination. When we had finished, he helped us to lift the stretcher, on which the body had been left, from the table to the floor to enable Polton to expose the photographs that Thorndyke required as records, and, when these had been taken, our business at the mortuary was finished.

"I suppose," said Robertson, "you are going to have a look at the ruins, now. It seems a trifle off the medico-legal track, but you may possibly pick up some information there. I take it that you are acting for the insurance company?"

"Yes," replied Thorndyke, "on instructions. As you say, it seems rather outside our province, as the company appears to be interested only in the house. But they asked me to watch the case, and I am doing so."

"You are indeed," Robertson exclaimed. "All that elaborate examination of the body seems to be completely irrelevant, if the question is only, how did the house catch fire? You carry thoroughness to the verge of fanaticism."

Thorndyke smiled. "Not fanaticism," said he; "merely experience, which bids us gather the rosebuds while we may. The question of today is not necessarily the question of tomorrow. At present we are concerned with the house; but there was a dead body in it. A month hence that body may be the problem, but by then it will be underground."

Robertson grinned at me. " 'Twas ever thus," he chuckled. "You can't get a rise out of Thorndyke – for the reason, I suppose, that he is always right. Well, I wish you luck in your explorations and hope to meet you both at the inquest."

With this, he took his departure, and, as Polton had now got his apparatus packed up, we followed him and made our way to what the papers described as "the Scene of the Conflagration".

It was a rather melancholy scene, with a tinge of squalor. The street was still wet and muddy, but a small crowd stood patiently, regardless of the puddles, staring up at the dismal shell with its scorched walls and gaping windows – the windows that I had seen belch forth flames but which now showed only the cold light of day. A rough hoarding had been put up to enclose the ground floor, and at the wicket of this a Salvage Corps officer stood on guard. To him Thorndyke addressed himself, producing his authority to inspect the ruins.

"Well, Sir," said the officer, "you'll find it a rough job, with mighty little to see and plenty to fall over. And it isn't over-safe. There's some stuff overhead that may come down at any moment. Still, if you want to look the place over, I can show you the way down."

"Your people, I suppose," said Thorndyke, "have made a pretty thorough inspection. Has anything been discovered that throws any light on the cause or origin of the fire?"

The officer shook his head. "No, Sir," he replied. "Not a trace. There wouldn't be. The house was burned right out from the ground upwards. It might have been lighted in a dozen places at once and there would be nothing to show it. There isn't even part of a floor left. Do you think it is worth while to take the risk of going down?"

"I think I should like to see what it looks like," said Thorndyke, adding, with a glance at me, "but there is no need for you and Polton to risk getting a brick or a chimney-pot on your heads."

Of course, I refused to be left out of the adventure, while, as to Polton, wild horses would not have held him back.

"Very well, gentlemen," said the officer, "you know your own business," and with this he opened the wicket and let us through to the brink of a yawning chasm which had once been the cellars. The remains of the charred beams had been mostly hauled up out of the way, but the floor of the cellars was still hidden by mountainous heaps of bricks, tiles, masses of charred wood and all-pervading white ash, amidst which three men in leather, brass-bound helmets were working with forks and shovels and with their thickly-gloved hands, removing the larger debris such as bricks, tiles, and fragments of boards and joists, while a couple of large sieves stood ready for the more minute examination of the dust and small residue.

We made our way cautiously down the ladder, becoming aware of a very uncomfortable degree of warmth as we descended and noting the steam that still rose from the wet rubbish. One of the men stopped his work to look at us and offer a word of warning.

"You'd better be careful where you are treading," said he. "Some of this stuff is still red underneath, and your boots aren't as thick as mine. You'd do best to stay on the ladder. You can see all there is to see from there, which isn't much. And mind you don't touch the walls with your hands."

His advice seemed so reasonable that we adopted it, and seated ourselves on the rungs of the ladder and looked about the dismal cavern as well as we could through the clouds of dust and steam.

"I see," said Thorndyke, addressing the shadowy figure nearest to us, "that you have a couple of sieves. Does that mean that you are going to sift all the small stuff?"

"Yes," was the reply. "We are going to do this job a bit more thoroughly than usual on account of the dead man who was found here. The police want to find out all they can about him, and I think the insurance people have been asking questions. You see, the dead man seems to have been a stranger, and he hasn't been properly identified yet. And I think that the tenant of the house isn't quite satisfied that everything was according to Cocker."

"And I suppose," said Thorndyke, "that whatever is found will be kept carefully and produced at the inquest?"

"Yes. Everything that is recovered will be kept for the police to see. The larger stuff will be put into a box by itself, and the smaller things which may be important for purposes of identification are to be sifted out and put into a separate box so that they don't get mixed up with the other things and lost sight of But our instructions are that nothing is to be thrown away until the police have seen it."

"Then," Thorndyke suggested, "I presume that some police officer is watching the case. Do you happen to know who he is?"

"We got our instructions from a detective sergeant name of Wills, I think – but an inspector from Scotland Yard looked in for a few minutes this morning; a very pleasant-spoken gentleman he was. Looked more like a dissenting minister than a police officer."

"That sounds rather like Blandy," I remarked; and Thorndyke agreed that the description seemed to fit our old acquaintance. And so it turned out; for when, having finished our survey of the cellars, we retired up the ladder and came out of the wicket, we found Sergeant Wills and Inspector Blandy in conference with the officer who had admitted us. On observing us, Blandy removed his hat with a flourish and made demonstrations of joy.

"Well, now," he exclaimed, "this is very pleasant. Dr Jervis, too, and Mr Polton *with* photographic apparatus. Quite encouraging. No doubt there will be some crumbs of expert information which a simple police officer may pick up."

Thorndyke smiled a little wearily. Like me, he found Blandy's fulsome manner rather tiresome. But he replied amiably enough:

"I am sure, Inspector, we shall try to be mutually helpful, as we always do. But at present I suspect that we are in much the same position: just observers waiting to see whether anything significant comes into sight."

"That is exactly my position," Blandy admitted. "Here is a rather queer-looking fire and a dead man in the ruins. Nothing

definitely suspicious, but there are possibilities. There always are
when you find a dead body in a burned house. You have had a look
at the ruins, Sir. Did you find anything suggestive in them?"

"Nothing whatever," Thorndyke replied; "nor do I think
anyone else will. The most blatant evidences of fire-raising would
have been obliterated by such total destruction. But my inspection
was merely formal. I have no expert knowledge of fires, but, as I
am watching the case for the Griffin Company, I thought it best
to view the ruins."

"Then," said Blandy with a slightly disappointed air, "you are
interested only in the house, not in the body?"

"Officially, that is so; but, as the body is a factor in the case, I
have made an examination of it, with Dr Robertson, and if you
want copies of the photographs that Polton has just taken at the
mortuary, I will let you have them."

"But how good of you!" exclaimed Blandy.

"Certainly, Doctor, I should like to have them. You see," he
added, "the fact that this dead man was not the ordinary resident
makes one want to know all about him and how he came to be
sleeping in that house. I shall be most grateful for the photographs;
and if there is anything that I can do – "

"There is," Thorndyke interrupted. "I learn that you are, very
wisely, making a thorough examination of the debris and passing
the ashes through a sieve."

"I am," said Blandy, "and what is more, the sergeant and I
propose to superintend the sifting. Nothing from a pin upwards
will be thrown away until it has been thoroughly examined. I
suppose you would like to see the things that we recover."

"Yes," replied Thorndyke, "when you have finished with them,
you might pass them on to me."

Blandy regarded Thorndyke with a benevolent and slightly foxy
smile, and, after a moment's pause, asked deferentially:

"Was there anything in particular that you had in your mind,
Doctor? I mean, any particular kind of article?"

"No," Thorndyke replied. "I am in the same position as you are. There are all sorts of possibilities in the case. The body tells us practically nothing, so we can only pick up any stray facts that may be available, as you appear to be doing."

This brought the interview to an end. Blandy and the sergeant disappeared through the wicket, and we went on our way homewards to see what luck Polton would have with his photographs.

Chapter Twelve

Light on the Mystery

For the reader of this narrative, the inquest on the body that had been recovered from the burnt house will serve, as it did to me, to present the known facts of the case in a coherent and related group – a condition which had been made possible by the stable and mummified state of the corpse. For, as the body was now virtually incorruptible, it had been practicable to postpone the inquiry until the circumstances had been investigated by the police and the principal facts ascertained, at least sufficiently for the purpose of an inquest.

When we arrived, the preliminaries had just been completed; the jury, having viewed the body, had taken their places and the coroner was about to open the proceedings. I need not report his brief address, which merely indicated the matters to be inquired into, but will proceed to the evidence. The first witness was Mr Henry Budge, and he deposed as follows:–

"On the 19th of April, about a quarter to three in the morning, I started with my neighbour, James Place, to walk home from the house of a friend in Noel Street, where we had been spending the previous evening playing cards. My way home to Macclesfield Street lay through Billington Street, and Mr Place walked that way with me. All the houses that we passed were in darkness with the exception of one in Billington Street in which we noticed a light showing through the Venetian blinds of two of the windows. Mr

Place pointed them out to me, remarking that we were not the only late birds. That would be about three o'clock."

"Was the light like ordinary lamp, or electric light?" the coroner asked.

"No. It looked more like fire-light – rather red in colour and not very bright. Only just enough to make the windows visible."

"Will you look at this photograph of the house, in which the windows are marked with numbers, and tell us which were the ones that were lighted up?"

The witness looked at the photograph and replied that the lighted windows were those marked 8 and 9, adding that the one marked 7 seemed to be quite dark.

"That," said the coroner, "is important as showing that the fire broke out in the bed-sitting room on the first floor. Number seven is the window of the store or workroom. Yes?"

"Well, we didn't take any particular notice. We just walked on until we came to Little Pulteney Street, where Place lives, and there we stopped at a corner talking about the evening's play. Presently, Place began to sniff, and then I noticed a smell as if there was a chimney on fire. We both crossed the road and looked up over the tops of the houses, and then we could see smoke drifting across and we could just make out the chimney that it seemed to be coming from. We watched it for a few minutes, and then we saw some sparks rising and what looked like a reddish glow on the smoke. That made us both think of the house with the lighted window, and we started to walk back to have another look. By the time we got into Billington Street we could see the chimney quite plain with lots of sparks flying out of it, so we hurried along until we came opposite the house, and then there was no mistake about it. All three windows on the first floor were brightly lighted up, and in one of them the Venetian blinds had caught; and now small flames began to show from the top of the chimney. We consulted as to what we should do, and decided that Place should run off and find a policeman while I tried to knock up the people of the house. So Place ran off, and I crossed the road to the front door of the house at the side of the shop."

"And did you make a considerable noise?"

"I am afraid I didn't. There was no proper knocker, only one of these new things fixed to the letter-box. I struck that as hard as I could and I pressed the electric bell, but I couldn't tell whether it sounded or not. So I kept on with the silly little knocker."

"Did you hear any sounds of any kind from within the house?"

"Not a sign, though I listened at the letter-box."

"How long were you there alone?"

"Three or four minutes, I should think. Perhaps a little more. Then Place came running back with a policeman, who told me to go on knocking and ringing while he and Place roused up the people in the houses next door. But by this time the house was fairly alight, flames coming out of all three first-floor windows and a light beginning to show in the windows of the floor above. And then it got too hot for me to stay at the door, and I had to back away across the street."

"Yes," said the coroner, glancing at the jury, "I think the witness has given us a very clear and vivid description of the way and the time at which the fire broke out. The rest of the story can be taken up by other witnesses when we have heard Mr Place."

The evidence of James Place, given quite briefly, merely confirmed and repeated that of Mr Budge, with the addition of his description of his meeting with the policeman. Then the latter, Edwin Pearson by name, was called and, having been sworn, deposed that on the 19th of April at about 3.14 a.m. he was accosted at the corner of Meard Street, Soho, by the last witness, who informed him that there was a house on fire in Billington Street. He immediately ran off with Place to the nearest fire alarm and sent off the warning. That was at 3.16 a.m. by his watch. Then he and the last witness hurried off to Billington Street, where they found the house alight as Mr Budge had described it, and had endeavoured to rouse the inmates of the burning house and the two adjoining houses, and were still doing so when the first of the engines arrived. That would be about 3.24 a.m.

Here the narrative passed to the officer in charge of the engine which had been the first on the scene; and, when he had been sworn, the coroner remarked:

"You realize that this is an inquiry into the death of the man whose body was found in the burnt house. The information that we want is that which is relevant to that death. Otherwise, the burning of the house is not specially our concern."

"I understand that," replied the witness – whose name had been given as George Bell. "The principal fact bearing on the death of deceased is the extraordinary rapidity with which the fire spread, which is accounted for by the highly inflammable nature of the material that the house contained. If deceased was asleep when the fire broke out, he might have been suffocated by the fumes without waking up. A mass of burning cellulose would give off volumes of poisonous gas."

"You have made an examination of the ruins. Did you find any evidence as to how the fire started?"

"No. The ruins were carefully examined by me and by several other officers, but no clue to the origin of the fire could be discovered by any of us. There was nothing to go on. Apparently, the fire started in the first-floor rooms, and it would have been there that the clues would be found. But those rooms were completely destroyed. Even the floors had been carried away by the fall of the roof, so that there was nothing left to examine."

"Does it appear to you that there is anything abnormal about this fire?"

"No. All fires are, in a sense, abnormal. The only unusual feature in this case is the great quantity of inflammable material in the house. But the existence of that was known."

"You find nothing to suggest a suspicion of fire-raising? The time, for instance, at which it broke out?"

"As to the time, there is nothing remarkable or unusual in that. The beginning of a fire may be something which makes no show at first: a heap of soot behind a stove or a spark on some material which will smoulder but not burst into flame. It may go on smouldering for quite a long time before it reaches some material that is really inflammable. A spark on brown paper, for instance, might smoulder slowly for an hour or more; then, if the glowing part spread and came into contact with a celluloid film, there would be a burst of flame and the fire would be started; and in such a house as this, the place might be well alight in a matter of minutes."

"Then you have no suspicion of incendiarism?"

"No, there is nothing positive to suggest it. Of course, it can't be excluded. There is simply no evidence either way."

"In what way might the fire have originated?"

The witness raised his eyebrows in mild protest but he answered the rather comprehensive question without comment.

"There are a good many possibilities. It might have been started by the act of some person. That is possible in this case, as there was a person in the house, but there is no evidence that he started the fire. Then there is the electric wiring. Something might have occurred to occasion a short circuit – a mouse or a cockroach connecting two wires. It is extremely uncommon with modern wiring, and in this case, as the fuses were destroyed, we can't tell whether it happened or not. And then there is the possibility of spontaneous combustion. That does occur occasionally. A heap of engineer's cotton waste soaked with oil will sometimes start burning by itself. So will a big bin of sawdust or a large mass of saltpetre. But none of these things are known to have been in this house."

"As to human agency. Suppose this person had been smoking in bed?"

"Well, that is a dangerous habit; but, after all, it would be only guess-work in this case. I have no evidence that the man was smoking in bed. If there is such evidence, then the fire might have been started in that way, though, even then, it would not be a certainty."

This concluded Mr Bell's evidence, and, when he had been allowed to retire, the coroner commented:

"As you will have observed, members of the jury, the expert evidence is to the effect that the cause of the fire is unknown; that is to say that none of the recognized signs of fire-raising were found. But possibly we may get some light on the matter from consideration of the circumstances. Perhaps we had better hear what Mr Green can tell us before we take the medical evidence."

Accordingly, Mr Walter Green was called, and, having been sworn, deposed:

"I am the lessee of the premises in which the fire occurred, and I carried on in them the business of a dealer in films of all kinds: kine films, X-ray films and the ordinary films for use in cameras. I do not manufacture but I am the agent for several manufacturers; and I also deal to some extent in projectors and cameras, both kine and ordinary. I always kept a large stock of films. Some were kept in the ground-floor shop for immediate sale, and the reserve stock was stored in the rooms on the second and third floors."

"Were these films inflammable?"

"Nearly all of them were highly inflammable."

"Then this must have been a very dangerous house. Did you take any special precautions against fire?"

"Yes. The store-rooms were always kept locked, and the rule was that they were only to be entered by daylight and that no smoking was allowed in them. We were naturally very careful."

"And were the premises insured?"

"Yes, both the building and the contents were fully insured. Of course, the rate of insurance was high in view of the special risk."

"How many persons were ordinarily resident in the house?"

"Only one. Formerly the premises used to be left at night entirely unoccupied, but, as there was more room than we needed, I decided to let the first floor. I would sooner have let it for use as offices, but my present tenant, Mr Gustavus Haire, applied for it as a residential flat, and I let it to him, and he has resided in it for the last six months."

"Was he in residence at the time of the fire?"

"No. Fortunately for him, he was absent on a visit to Ireland at the time. The gentleman who met his death in the fire was a relative of Mr Haire's to whom he had lent the flat while he was away."

"We will come to the question of deceased presently, but first we might have a few particulars about Mr Haire; as to his occupation, for instance."

"I really don't know very much about him. He seems to be connected with the film and camera trade, mostly, I think, as a traveller and agent for some of the wholesale firms. But he does some sort of dealing on his own account, and he seems to be something of a mechanic. He has done some repairs on projectors for me, and once he mended up a gramophone motor that I bought second hand. And he does a little manufacturing, if you can call it by that name: he makes certain kinds of cements and varnishes. I don't know exactly how much or what he does with them, but I presume that he sells them, as I can't think of any use that he could have for the quantities that he makes."

"Did he carry on this industry on your premises?"

"Yes, in the small room that adjoined the bedroom, which he also used as a workroom for his mechanical jobs. There was a cupboard in it in which he used to keep his stocks of varnish and the solvents for making them – mostly acetone and amyl acetate."

"Aren't those solvents rather inflammable?"

"They are very inflammable; and the varnish is still worse, as the basis is cellulose."

"You say that you don't know how much of this stuff he used to make in that room. Haven't you any idea?"

"I can't suggest a quantity, but I know that he must have made a good deal of it, because he used to buy some, at least, of his material from me. It consisted mostly of worn-out or damaged films, and I have sold him quite a lot from time to time. But I believe he had other sources of supply."

"And you say he used to store all this inflammable material – the celluloid, the solvents and the varnish – in that small room?"

"Yes; but I think that when the little room got full up, he used to overflow into the bedroom – in fact, I know he did, for I saw a row of bottles of varnish on the bedroom mantelpiece, one of them a Winchester quart."

"Then you have been into Mr Haire's rooms? Perhaps you could give us a general idea as to their arrangement and what was in them."

"I have only been in them once or twice, and I didn't take very much notice of them, as I just went in to talk over some matters which we had been discussing. There were two rooms; a small one – that would have the window marked 7 in the photograph. It was used as a workroom and partly as a store for the cements and varnishes. It contained a smallish deal table which had a vice fixed to it and served as a workbench. It was littered with tools and bits of scrap of various kinds and there was a gas-ring on a sheet of iron. Besides the table, there was a stool and a good-sized cupboard, rather shallow and fitted with five or six shelves which seemed to be filled principally with bottles.

"The other room was quite a fair size – about twenty feet long and twelve feet wide. It was used as a bed-sitting room and was quite comfortably furnished. The bed was at the end opposite window number 9, with the dressing-table and washstand near it. At the other end was a mahogany table, a small sideboard, a set of book-shelves, three single chairs, an easy chair by the fireplace, and a grandfather clock against the wall in the corner. There was some sort of carpet on the floor and a rug before the fireplace. That is all I remember about the furniture of the room; but what dwells in my memory is the appalling untidiness of the place. The floor was littered with newspapers and magazines, the mantelpiece and the sideboard were filled up with bottles and boxes and pipes and all sorts of rubbish, and there were brown-paper parcels all over the place: stacked along the walls and round the clock and even under the bed."

"Do you know what was in those parcels?"

"I don't know, but I strongly suspect that they contained his stock of films. I recognized one as a parcel that he had had from me."

The coroner looked at the witness with a frown of astonishment.

"It seems incredible," he exclaimed. "These rooms must have been even more dangerous than the rest of the house."

"Much more," the witness agreed; "for, in the business premises, the films were at least securely packed. We didn't keep them loose in paper parcels."

"No. It is perfectly astonishing. This man, Haire, might as well have been living and sleeping in a powder magazine. No wonder that the fire started in his flat. The necessary conditions seem to have been perfect for the start of a fire. But still we have no evidence as to what actually started it. I suppose, Mr Green, you have no suggestion to offer on that question?"

"Of course, I have no certain knowledge, though I have a very definite suspicion. But a suspicion is not evidence."

"No, but I suppose that you had something to go on. Let us hear what you suspect and why you suspect it."

"My opinion is based on a conversation that I had with Mr Haire shortly before he went away. It occurred in a little restaurant in Wardour Street where we both used to go for lunch. He was telling me about his proposed visit to Dublin. He said he was not sure how long he might be away, but he thought it would be as well for him to leave me his address in case anyone should call on any matter that might seem urgent. So he wrote down the address of the firm on whom he would be calling and gave it to me, and I then said, jestingly, that, as there would be no one in the house while he was away, I hoped he would deposit his jewellery and plate and other valuable property in the bank before he left.

"He smiled and promised that he would, but then he remarked that, in fact, the house would probably not be empty, as he had agreed to let a cousin of his have the use of the rooms to sleep in while he was away. I was not very pleased to hear this, and I remarked that I should not much care to hand the keys of any rooms of mine to another person. He agreed with me, and admitted that he would rather have avoided the arrangement; 'but,' he said, 'what could I do? The man is my cousin and quite a decent fellow. He happens to be coming up to town just at the time when I shall be away, and it will be a great convenience to him to have a place where he can turn in and save the expense of an hotel. He may not use the rooms after all, but if he does, I don't expect that you will see much of him, as he will only be coming to the rooms to sleep. His days will be occupied in various business calls. I must admit,' he added, 'that I wish him at Halifax, but he asked me to let him have the use of the rooms, and I didn't feel that I could refuse.'

" 'Well,' I said, 'I should have refused. But he is your cousin, so I suppose you know all about him.'

" 'Oh, yes,' he replied; 'he is quite a responsible sort of man; and I have cautioned him to be careful.'

"That struck me as a rather curious remark, so I said:

" 'How do you mean? What did you caution him about?' and he replied:

" 'Oh, I just cautioned him not to do himself too well in the matter of drinks in the evening, and I made him promise not to smoke in bed.'

" 'Does he usually smoke in bed?' I asked; and he replied:

" 'I think he likes to take a book to bed with him and have a read and a smoke before going to sleep. But he has promised solemnly that he won't.'

" 'Well,' I said, 'I hope he won't. It is a shockingly dangerous habit. He might easily drop off to sleep and let his cigarette fall on the bed-clothes.'

" 'He doesn't smoke cigarettes in bed,' said Haire. 'He smokes a pipe; his favourite is a big French clay bowl in the form of a death's head with glass eyes and a cherry-wood stem. He loves that pipe. But you need not worry; he has sworn not to smoke in bed.'

"I was not very happy about the affair, but I didn't like to make a fuss. So I made no further objection."

"I think," said the coroner, "that you ought to have forbidden him to lend the rooms. However, you didn't. Did you learn what this man's name was?"

"Yes, I asked Mr Haire, in case I should see the man and have occasion to speak to him. His name was Moxdale – Cecil Moxdale."

"Then we may take it that the body which is the subject of this inquiry is that of Cecil Moxdale. Did you ever see him?"

"I think I saw him once. That would be just before six in the evening of the 14th of April. I was standing inside the doorway of my premises when Mr Haire passed with another man, whom I assumed to be Mr Moxdale from his resemblance to Mr Haire. The two men went to the street door which is the entrance to Mr Haire's staircase and entered together."

"Could you give us any description of Moxdale?"

"He was a biggish man – about five feet nine or ten – with dark hair and a rather full dark moustache. That is all I noticed. I only took a passing glance a him."

"From what you said just now," the coroner suggested, "I suppose we may assume that you connect the outbreak of the fire with this unfortunate man?"

"I do," the witness replied. "I have no doubt that he lit up his pipe notwithstanding his promise, and set his bedclothes on fire. That would account for everything, if you remember that there were a number of parcels under the bed which were almost certainly filled with inflammable films."

"Yes," the coroner agreed. "Of course, it is only a surmise, but it is certainly a very probable one. And that, I suppose, Mr Green, is all that you have to tell us."

"Yes, Sir," was the reply, "that is about all I know of the case."

The coroner glanced at the jury and asked if there were any questions, and, when the foreman replied that there were none, the witness was allowed to retire when the depositions had been read and signed.

There was a short pause, during which the coroner glanced at the depositions and, apparently, reflected on the last witness' evidence.

"I think," he said at length, "that, before going further into the details of this deplorable affair, we had better hear what the doctors have to tell us. It may seem, having regard to the circumstances in which deceased met his death and the condition of the body, that the taking of medical evidence is more or less of a formality; but, still, it is necessary that we should have a definite statement as to the cause of death. We will begin with the evidence of the divisional surgeon, Dr William Robertson."

As his name was mentioned, our colleague rose and stepped up to the table, where the coroner's officer placed a chair for him.

CHAPTER THIRTEEN

The Facts and the Verdict

"You have, I believe," said the coroner when the preliminary questions had been answered, "made an examination of the body which is now lying in the mortuary?"

"Yes, I examined that body very thoroughly. It appears to be that of a strongly-built man about five feet ten inches in height. His age was rather difficult to judge, and I cannot say more than that he was apparently between forty and fifty, but even that is not a very reliable estimate. The body had been exposed to such intense heat that the soft tissues were completely carbonized, and, in some parts, entirely burned away. Of the feet, for instance, there was nothing left but white incinerated bone."

"The jury, when viewing the body, were greatly impressed by the strange posture in which it lay. Do you attach any significance to that?"

"No. The distortion of the trunk and limbs was due to the shrinkage of the soft parts under the effects of intense heat. Such distortion is not unusual in bodies which have been burned."

"Can you make any statement as to the cause of death?"

"My examination disclosed nothing on which an opinion could be based. The condition of the body was such as to obliterate any signs that there might have been. I assume that deceased died from the effects of the poisonous fumes given off by the burning celluloid – that he was, in fact, suffocated. But that is not properly a medical opinion. There is, however, one point which I ought to mention. The neck was dislocated and the little bone called the odontoid process was broken."

"You mean, in effect," said the coroner, "that the neck was broken. But surely a broken neck would seem to be a sufficient cause of death."

"It would be in ordinary circumstances; but in this case I think it is to be explained by the shrinkage. My view is that the contraction of the muscles and the soft structures generally displaced the bones and broke off the odontoid process."

"Can you say, positively, that the dislocation was produced in that way?"

"No. That is my opinion, but I may be wrong. Dr Thorndyke, who examined the body at the same time as I did, took a different view."

"We shall hear Dr Thorndyke's views presently. But doesn't it seem to you a rather important point?"

"No. There doesn't seem to me to be much in it. The man was alone in the house and must, in any case, have met his death by accident. In the circumstances, it doesn't seem to matter much what the exact, immediate cause of death may have been."

The coroner looked a little dissatisfied with this answer, but he made no comment, proceeding at once to the next point.

"You have given us a general description of the man. Did you discover anything that would assist in establishing his identity?"

"Nothing beyond the measurements and the fact that he had a fairly good set of natural teeth. The measurements and the general description would be useful for identification if there were any known person with whom they could be compared. They are not very specific characters, but if there is any missing person who might be the deceased, they might settle definitely whether this body could, or could not, be that of the missing person."

"Yes," said the coroner, "but that is of more interest to the police than to us. Is there anything further that you have to tell us?"

"No," replied the witness, "I think that is all that I have to say."

Thereupon, when the depositions had been read and signed the witness retired and his place was taken by Thorndyke.

"You examined this body at the same time as Dr Robertson, I think?" the coroner suggested.

"Yes, we made the examination together, and we compared the results so far as the measurements were concerned."

"You were, of course, unable to make any suggestion as to the identity of deceased?"

"Yes. Identity is a matter of comparison, and there was no known person with whom to compare the body. But I secured, and made notes of, all available data for identification if they should be needed at any future time."

"It was stated by the last witness that there was a dislocation of the neck with a fracture of the odontoid process. Will you explain that to the jury and give us your views as to its significance in this case?"

"The odontoid process is a small peg of bone which rises from the second vertebra, or neck-bone, and forms a pivot on which the head turns. When the neck is dislocated, the displacement usually occurs between the first and the second vertebra, and then, in most cases, the odontoid process is broken. In the case of deceased, the first and second vertebrae were separated and the odontoid process was broken. That is to say that deceased had a dislocated neck, or, as it is commonly expressed, a broken neck."

"In your opinion, was the neck broken before or after death?"

"I should say that it was broken before death; that, in fact, the dislocation of the neck was the immediate cause of death."

"Do you say positively that it was so?"

"No. I merely formed that opinion from consideration of the appearances of the structures. The broken surfaces of the odontoid process had been exposed to the fire for some appreciable time, which suggested that the fracture had occurred before the shrinkage. And then it appeared to me that the force required to break the process was greater than the shrinkage would account for. Still, it is only an opinion. Dr Robertson attributed the fracture to the shrinkage, and he is as likely to be right as I am."

"Supposing death to have been caused by the dislocation, what significance would you attach to that circumstance?"

"None at all, if the facts are as stated. If the man was alone in the house when the fire broke out, the exact cause of death would be a matter of no importance."

"Can you suggest any way in which the neck might have been broken in the circumstances which are believed to have existed?"

"There are many possible ways. For instance, if the man was asleep and was suddenly aroused by the fire, he might have scrambled out of bed, entangled the bedclothes, and fallen on his head. Or again, he might have escaped from the bedroom and fallen down the stairs. The body was found in the cellar. There is no evidence as to where the man was when death took place."

"At any rate, you do not consider the broken neck in any way incompatible with accidental death?"

"Not in the least; and, as I said before, Dr Robertson's explanation may be the correct one, after all."

"Would you agree that, for the purposes of this inquiry, the question as to which of you is right is of no importance?"

"According to my present knowledge and belief, I should say that it is of no importance at all."

This was the sum of Thorndyke's evidence, and, when he had signed the depositions and returned to his seat, the name of Inspector Blandy was called; whereupon that officer advanced to the table and greeted the coroner and the jury with his habitual benevolent smile. He polished off the preliminaries with the readiness born of long experience and then, having, by the coroner's invitation, seated himself, he awaited the interrogation.

"I believe, Inspector," the coroner began, "that the police are making certain investigations regarding the death of the man who is the subject of this inquiry. Having heard the evidence of the other witnesses, can you give us any additional facts?"

"Nothing very material," Blandy replied. "The inquiries which we are making are simply precautionary. A dead man has been found in the ruins of a burnt house, and we want to know who that man was and how he came to be in that house, since he was admittedly not the tenant of the premises. As far as our inquiries have gone, they have seemed to confirm the statement of Mr Green that the man was the one referred to by Mr Haire as Cecil Moxdale. But our inquiries are not yet complete."

"That," said the coroner, "is a general statement. Could you give us the actual facts on which your conclusions are based?"

"The only facts bearing on the identity of deceased have been obtained by an examination of various things found among the ashes of the burned house. The search was made with the greatest care, particularly that for the smaller objects which might have a more personal character. When the larger objects had been removed, the fine ash was all passed through sieves so that nothing should be overlooked. But everything that was found has been preserved for further examination if it should be necessary."

"You must have got a rather miscellaneous collection," the coroner remarked. "Have you examined the whole lot?"

"No. We have concentrated on the small personal articles, and these seem to have yielded all the information that we are likely to get, and have practically settled the question of identity. We found, for instance, a pair of cuff-links of steel, chromium plated, on which the initials CM were engraved. We also found a clay pipe-bowl in the form of a death's head which had once had glass eyes and still had the remains of the glass fused in the eye-sockets. This had the initials CM scratched deeply on the under-surface of the bowl."

"That was a very significant discovery," the coroner remarked, "having regard to what Mr Green told us. Yes?"

"There was also a stainless-steel plate which seemed to have belonged to an attache-case or a suit-case and which had the initials CM engraved on it, and a gold watch, of which the case was partly fused, but on which we could plainly make out the initials GH."

"GH," the coroner repeated. "That, then, would be Mr Haire's watch. Isn't that rather odd?"

"I think not, sir," replied Blandy. "These were Mr Haire's rooms, and they naturally contained articles belonging to him. Probably he locked up this valuable watch before going on his travels."

"Did you find any other things belonging to him?"

"Nothing at all significant. There was a vice and some tools and the remains of an eight-day clock which apparently belonged to him, and there were some other articles that might have been his, but they were mixed up with the remains of projectors and various things which had probably come from the shop or the stores above. But the small personal articles were the really important ones. I have brought those that I mentioned for your inspection."

Here he produced from his attache-case a small glass-topped box in which the links, the steel nameplate, the death's-head pipe-bowl, and the half-fused gold watch were displayed on a bed of cotton wool, and handed it to the coroner, who, when he had inspected it, passed it to the foreman of the jury.

While the latter and his colleagues were poring over the box, the coroner opened a fresh line of inquiry.

"Have you tried to get into touch with Mr Haire?" he asked.

"Yes," was the reply, "and I am still trying, unsuccessfully up to the present. The address that Mr Haire gave to Mr Green was that of Brady & Co., a firm of retail dealers in photographic materials and appliances. As soon as I got it from Mr Green, I communicated with the Dublin police, giving them the principal facts and asking them to find Mr Haire, if they could, and pass on to him the information about the fire and also to find out from him who the man was whose body had been found in the burnt house.

"The information that I have received from them is to the effect that they called on Bradys about mid-day on the 19th, but Mr Haire had already left. They learned that he had made a business call on Bradys on the morning of the 16th, having arrived in Dublin the previous night. He called again on the 18th, and then said that he was going on to Cork, and possibly from there to Belfast. In the interval, it seemed that he had made several calls on firms engaged in the photographic trade, but Bradys had the impression that he had left Dublin on the evening of the 18th.

"That is all that I have been able to discover so far, but there should be no great difficulty in tracing Mr Haire; and even if it should not be possible, he will probably be returning from Ireland quite soon, and then he will be able to give us all the particulars that we want about this man, Cecil Moxdale − if that is his name."

"Yes," said the coroner, "but it will be too late for this inquiry. However, there doesn't seem to be any great mystery about the affair. The man's name was given to us by Mr Green, and the identity seems to be confirmed by the initials on the articles which were recovered from the ruins; particularly the pipe, which had been described to us by Mr Green as belonging to Cecil Moxdale. We know practically nothing about the man; but still we know enough for the purpose of this inquiry. It might be expedient to adjourn the proceedings until fuller particulars are available, but I hardly think it is necessary. I suppose, Inspector, you have nothing further to tell us?"

"No, sir," replied Blandy. "I have told you all that I know about the affair."

"Then," said the coroner, "that completes the evidence; and I think, members of the jury, that there is enough to enable you to decide on your verdict."

He paused for a moment, and then proceeded to read the depositions and secure the signature, and, when this had been done and Blandy had retired to his seat, he opened his brief summing up of the evidence.

"There is little that I need say to you, members of the jury," he began. "You have heard the evidence, all of which has been quite simple and all of which points plainly to the same conclusion. You have to answer four questions: Who was deceased, and where, when, and by what means did he come by his death?

"As to the first question, who was he? The evidence that we have heard tells us no more than that his name was Cecil Moxdale and that he was a cousin of Mr Gustavus Haire. That is not much, but, still, it identifies him as a particular individual. As to the conclusiveness of the evidence on this point, that is for you to judge. To me, the identity seems to be quite clearly established.

"As to the time and place of his death, it is certain that it occurred in the early morning on the 19th of April in the house known as 34, Billington Street, Soho. But the question as to how he came by his death is not quite so clear. There is some conflict of opinion on the part of the two medical witnesses respecting the immediate cause of death. But that need not trouble us; for they are agreed that, whatever might have been the immediate cause of death, the ultimate cause — with which we are concerned — was some accident arising out of the fire. There appears to be no doubt that deceased was alone in the house at the time when the fire broke out; and, that being so, his death could only have been due to some misadventure for which no one other than himself could have been responsible.

"There is, indeed, some evidence that he may, himself, have been responsible both for the outbreak of the fire and for his own death. There is a suggestion that he may, in spite of his promise to Mr Haire, have indulged in the dangerous practice of smoking in bed. But there is no positive evidence that he did, and we must not form our conclusions on guesses or inferences.

"That is all that I need say; and with that I shall leave you to consider your verdict."

There was, as the coroner had justly remarked, very little to consider. The facts seemed quite plain and the conclusion perfectly obvious. And that was evidently the view of the jury, for they gave the matter but a few minutes' consideration, and then returned the verdict to the effect that "the deceased, Cecil Moxdale, had met his death by misadventure due to the burning of the house in which he was sleeping".

"Yes," the coroner agreed, "that is the obvious conclusion. I shall record a verdict of Death by Misadventure."

On this, the Court rose; and, after a few words with the coroner and Robertson, Thorndyke and I, accompanied by Polton (who had been specially invited to attend), took our departure and shaped a course for King's Bench Walk.

CHAPTER FOURTEEN

A Visit From Inspector Blandy

With the close of the inquest, our connection with the case of the burnt house in Billington Street and Cecil Moxdale, deceased, seemed to have come to an end. No points of doubt or interest had arisen, or seemed likely to arise hereafter. We appeared to have heard the last of the case, and, when Thorndyke's notes and Polton's photographs had been filed, we wrote it off as finished with. At least, I did. But later events suggested that Thorndyke had kept it in mind as a case in which further developments were not entirely impossible.

My view of the case was apparently shared by Stalker; for when, being in the City on other business, we dropped in at his office, he expressed himself to that effect.

"An unsatisfactory affair from our point of view," he commented, "but there was nothing that we could really boggle at. Of course, when an entire insured stock is destroyed, you have to be wary. A trader who has a redundant or obsolete or damaged stock can make a big profit by burning the whole lot out and recovering the full value from the insurance society. But there doesn't seem to be anything of that kind. Green appears to be perfectly straight. He has given us every facility for checking the value of the stock, and we find it all correct."

"I suppose," said I, "you couldn't have raised the question of negligence in allowing a casual stranger to occupy a bedroom in his box of fireworks. He knew that Moxdale wasn't a very safe tenant."

"There is no evidence," Thorndyke reminded me, "that Moxdale set fire to the house. He probably did, but that is a mere guess on our part."

"Exactly," Stalker agreed, "and even if he did, he certainly did not do it consciously or intentionally. And, by the way, speaking of this man Moxdale, it happens, oddly enough, that his life was insured in this office. So he has let us in for two payments."

"Anything considerable?" Thorndyke asked.

"No. Only a thousand."

"Have you paid the claim?"

"Not yet; in fact, no claim has been made up to the present, and it isn't our business to hunt up the claimants. But we shall have to pay, for I suppose that even you could not make out a case of suicide."

"No," Thorndyke admitted, "I think we can exclude suicide. At any rate, there was nothing to suggest it. You accept the identity?"

"There doesn't seem to be much doubt," replied Stalker, "but the next of kin, or whoever makes the claim, will have to confirm the statements of Green and Haire. But I don't think there is anything in the question of identity. Do you?"

"So far as I know, the question was fairly well settled at the inquest, and I don't think it could be contested unless some positive evidence to the contrary should be produced. But we have to bear in mind that the identity was based on the statement of Walter Green and that his evidence was hearsay evidence."

"Yes," said Stalker, "I will bear that in mind when the claim is put in, if it ever is. If no claim is made, the question will not be of any interest to me."

So that was the position. Stalker was not interested and, consequently, we, as his agents, had no further interest in the case; and, so far as I was concerned, it had passed into complete oblivion when my recollection of it was revived by Thorndyke. It was at breakfast time a week or two after our conversation with Stalker that my colleague,, who was, according to his habit, glancing over the legal notices in *The Times,* looked up at me and remarked:

"Here is a coincidence in a small way. I don't remember having ever met with the name of Moxdale until we attended the late inquest. It certainly is not a common name."

"No," I agreed, "I don't think I ever heard it excepting in connection with Cecil Moxdale deceased. But what is the coincidence?"

"Here is another Moxdale, also deceased," he replied, handing me the paper and indicating the paragraph. It was an ordinary solicitor's notice beginning, "Re. Harold Moxdale deceased who died on the 30th of April 1936" and calling on creditors and others to make their claims by a certain specified date; of no interest to me apart from the mere coincidence of the name. Nor did Thorndyke make any further comment, though I observed that he cut out the notice, and, having fixed it with a dab of paste to a sheet of paper, added it to the collection of notes forming the Moxdale dossier. Then, once more, the "case" seemed to have sunk into oblivion.

But a few days later it was revived by no less a person than Inspector Blandy; and the manner of its revival was characteristic of that extremely politic gentleman. It was about half-past eight one evening when, after an early dinner, Thorndyke, Polton and I were holding a sort of committee meeting to review and reclassify the great collection of microscope slides of hairs, fibres and other "comparison specimens" which had accumulated in the course of years. We had just finished the first of the new cabinets and were labelling the drawers when an unfamiliar knock, of an almost apologetic softness, was executed on the small brass knocker of the inner door.

"Confound it!" I exclaimed, impatiently. "We ought to have shut the oak. Who the deuce can it be?"

The question was answered by Polton, who, as he opened the door and peered out, stepped back and announced:

"Inspector Blandy."

We both stood up, and Thorndyke, with his customary suavity, advanced to greet the visitor and offer him a chair.

"Pray, gentlemen," exclaimed Blandy, casting an inquisitive glance over the collection on the table, "do not let me disturb you, though, to be sure, I can see that I am disturbing you. But the disturbance need be only of the briefest. I have come – very improperly, without an appointment – merely to tender apologies and to make all too tardy amends. When I have done that, I can go, and leave you to pursue your investigations."

"They are not investigations," said Thorndyke. "We are just going over our stock of test specimens and re-arranging them. But what do you mean by apologies and reparations? We have no grievance against you."

"You are kind enough to say so," replied Blandy, "but I am, nevertheless, a defaulter. I made a promise and have not kept it. *Mea culpa.*" He tapped his chest lightly with his knuckles and continued: "When I had the pleasure of meeting you in the ruins of the burned house I promised to let you have an opportunity of examining the various objects that were retrieved from the debris. This evening, it suddenly dawned on me that I never did so. I was horrified, and, in my impulsive way, I hurried, without reflection, to seek your forgiveness and to make such amends as were possible."

"I don't think, Blandy," said Thorndyke, "that the trifling omission mattered. We seemed to have all the information that we wanted."

"So we did, but perhaps we were wrong. At any rate, I have now brought the things for you to see, if they are still of any interest. It is rather late, I must admit."

"Yes, by Jove!" I agreed. "It is the day after the fair. But what things have you brought, and where are they?"

"The exhibits which you saw at the inquest, I have here in my attache-case. If you would like me to leave them with you for examination at your leisure, I can do so, but we shall want them back. The other things are in a box in my car, and, as we have finished with them, you can dispose of them as you please when you have examined them, if you think the examination worth while."

"I take it," said Thorndyke, "that you have been through them pretty thoroughly. Did you find anything in any way significant?"

The inspector regarded Thorndyke with his queer, benevolent smile as he replied: "Not significant to me; but who knows what I may have overlooked? I could not bring to bear on them either your intellect, your encyclopaedic knowledge, or your unrivalled means of research." Here he waved his hand towards the table and seemed to bestow a silent benediction on the microscopes and the trays of slides. "Perhaps," he concluded, "these simple things might have for you some message which they have withheld from me."

As I listened to Blandy's discourse, I found myself speculating on the actual purpose of his visit. He could not have come to talk this balderdash or to deliver the box of trash that he had brought with him. What object, I wondered, lay behind his manoeuvres? Probably it would transpire presently; but, meanwhile, I thought it as well to give him a lead.

"It is very good of you, Blandy," said I, "to have brought us these things to look at, but I don't quite see why you did it. Our interest in the affair ended with the inquest, and I take it that yours did too. Or didn't it?"

"It did not," he replied. "We were then making certain inquiries through the Irish police, and we have not yet obtained the information that we were seeking. The case is still incomplete."

"Do you mean," Thorndyke asked, "that Mr Haire has not been able to tell you all that you wanted to know?"

"We have not been able to get into touch with Mr Haire; which is a rather remarkable fact, and becomes still more remarkable as the time passes and we get no news of him."

"In effect, then," said Thorndyke, "Mr Haire has disappeared. Have you taken any special measures to trace him?"

"We have taken such measures as were possible," replied Blandy. "But we are in a difficult position. We have no reliable description of the man, and, if we had, we could hardly proceed as if we were trying to trace a 'wanted' man. It is curious that he should not have turned up in his usual places of resort, but there is nothing incriminating in the fact. We have no reason to suppose that he is keeping out of sight. There is nothing against him. No one could suspect him of having had any hand in starting the fire, as he was not there and another man was. But still, it is a little mysterious. It makes one wonder whether there could have been something that we overlooked."

"Yes," Thorndyke agreed, "there does certainly seem to be something a little queer about the affair. As I understand it, Haire went away with the stated intention of making a short visit to Dublin. He was known to have arrived there on a certain day and to have made two calls at a business house. He is said to have announced his intention to go on to Belfast, but it is not known whether he did, in fact, go there. Nothing at all is known as to his movements after he had left the dealer's premises. From that moment, no one, so far as we know, ever saw him again. Isn't that the position?"

"That is the position exactly, Sir," replied Blandy, "and a very curious position it is if we remember that Haire was a man engaged in business in London and having a set of rooms there containing his household goods and personal effects."

"Before the fire," I remarked. "There wasn't much left of either after the flare up. He hadn't any home then to come back to."

"But, Sir," Blandy objected, "what reason is there for supposing that he knew anything about the fire? He was somewhere in Ireland when it happened. But a fire in a London by-street isn't likely to be reported in the Irish papers."

"No," I admitted, "that is true; and it only makes the affair still more queer."

There was a short silence. Then Thorndyke raised a fresh question.

"By the way, Inspector," said he, "there was a legal notice in *The Times* a few days ago referring to a certain Moxdale deceased. Did you happen to observe it?"

"Yes, my attention was called to it by one of my colleagues, and, on the chance that there might be some connection with the other Moxdale deceased, I called on the solicitors to make a few enquiries. They are quite a respectable firm – Horne, Croner, and Horne of Lincoln's Inn – and they were as helpful as they could be, but they didn't know much about the parties. The testator, Harold Moxdale, was an old gentleman, practically a stranger to them, and the other parties were nothing more than names. However, I learned that the principal beneficiary was the testator's nephew, Cecil Moxdale, and that, if he had not had the misfortune to be burned, he would have inherited a sum of about four thousand pounds."

"It is possible," I suggested, "that it may not be the same Cecil Moxdale. You say that they did not know anything about him. Did you try to fix the identity?"

"It wasn't necessary," replied Blandy, "for the next beneficiary was another nephew named Gustavus Haire; and as we knew that Haire and Moxdale were cousins, that settled the identity."

As Blandy gave this explanation, his habitual smile became tinged with a suggestion of foxiness, and I noticed that he was furtively watching Thorndyke to see how he took it. But there was no need, for my colleague made no secret of his interest.

"Did you learn whether these two bequests were in any way mutually dependent?" he asked.

Blandy beamed on him almost affectionately. It was evident that Thorndyke's "reactions" were those that had been desired.

"A very pertinent question, Sir," he replied.

"Yes, the two bequests were mutually contingent. The entire sum to be divided between the two nephews was about six thousand pounds. Of this, four thousand went to Cecil and two thousand to Gustavus. But it was provided that if either of them should predecease the testator, the whole amount should go to the survivor."

"My word, Blandy!" I exclaimed. "This puts quite a new complexion on the affair. As Harold Moxdale died, if I remember rightly, on the 30th of April, and Cecil died on the 19th of the same month, it follows that the fire in Billington Street was worth four thousand pounds to Mr Gustavus Haire. A decidedly illuminating fact."

Blandy turned his benign smile on me. "Do you find it illuminating, Sir?" said he. "If you do, I wish you would reflect a few stray beams on me."

Thorndyke chuckled, softly. "I am afraid, Jervis," said he, "that the inspector is right. This new fact is profoundly interesting – even rather startling. But it throws no light whatever on the problem."

"It establishes a motive," I retorted.

"But what is the use of that?" he demanded. "You, as a lawyer, know that proof of a motive to do some act is no evidence, by itself, that the person who had the motive did the act. Haire, as you imply, had a motive for making away with Moxdale. But before you could even suggest that he did actually make away with him, you would have to prove that he had the opportunity and the intention; and even that would carry you no farther than suspicion. To support a charge, there would have to be some positive evidence that the act was committed."

"Exactly, Sir," said Blandy; "and the position is that we have not a particle of evidence that Haire had any intention of murdering his cousin, and there is clear evidence that he had no opportunity. When the fire broke out, he was in Ireland and had been there five days. That is, for practical purposes, an absolutely conclusive alibi."

"But," I persisted, "aren't there such things as time-fuses or other timing appliances?"

Blandy shook his head. "Not in a case like this," he replied. "Of course, we have considered that question, but there is nothing in it. In the case of a man who wants to set fire to a lock-up shop or empty premises, it is possible to use some such appliance – a time-fuse, or a candle set on some inflammable material, or an alarm clock – to give him time to show himself a few miles away and establish an alibi; and even then the firemen usually spot it. But here you have a flat, with somebody living in it, and the owner of that flat on the other side of the Irish Channel, where he had arrived five days before the fire broke out.

"No, Sir, I don't think Mr Haire is under any suspicion of having raised the fire. The thing is a physical impossibility. And I don't know of any other respect in which he is under suspicion. It is odd that we can't discover his whereabouts, but there is really nothing suspicious in it. There is no reason why he should let anyone know where he is."

I did not contest this, though my feeling was that Haire was purposely keeping out of sight, and I suspected that Blandy secretly took the same view. But the inspector was such an exceedingly downy bird that it was advisable not to say too much. However, I now understood – or thought I did – why he had made this pretext to call on us; he was at a dead end and hoped to interest Thorndyke in the case and thereby get a lead of some kind. And now, having sprung his mine, he reverted to the ostensible object of his visit.

"As to this salvage stuff," said he. "Would you like me to leave these small things for you to look over?"

I expected Thorndyke to decline the offer, for there was no mystery about the things, and they were no affair of ours in any case. But, to my surprise, he accepted, and, having checked the list, signed the receipt which Blandy had written out.

"And as to the stuff in the box; perhaps Mr Polton might show my man where to put it."

At this, Polton, who had been calmly examining and sorting the test-slides during the discussion (to which I have no doubt he had given close attention), rose and suggested that the box should be deposited in the laboratory in the first place; and when Thorndyke had agreed, he departed to superintend the removal.

"I am afraid," said Blandy, "that you will find nothing but rubbish in that box. That, at least, is what it appeared like to me. But, having studied some of your cases, I have been deeply impressed by your power of extracting information from the most unpromising material, and it is possible that these things may mean more to you than they do to me."

"It is not very likely," Thorndyke replied. "You appear to have extracted from them all the information that one could expect. They have conveyed to you the fact that Cecil Moxdale was apparently the occupant of the rooms at the time of the fire, and that is probably all that they had to tell."

"It is all they had to tell me," said Blandy, rising and picking up his attache-case, "and it is not all that I want to know. There is still the problem of how the fire started, and they throw no light on that at all."

"You have got the clay pipe," I suggested. "Doesn't that tell the story?"

He smiled at me with amiable reproach as he replied: "We don't want the material for plausible guesses. We want facts, or at least a leading hint of some kind, and I still have hopes that you may hit on something suggestive."

"You are more optimistic than I am," replied Thorndyke; "but I shall look over the material that you have brought, and, if it should yield any facts that are not already known to you, I promise to let you have them without delay."

Blandy brightened up appreciably at this, and, as he turned to depart, he expressed his gratitude in characteristic terms.

"That, Sir, is most generous of you. It sends me on my way rejoicing in the consciousness that my puny intelligence is to be reinforced by your powerful intellect and your encyclopaedic knowledge. I thank you, gentlemen, for your kindly reception of an intruder and a disturber of your erudite activities, and I wish you a very good evening."

With this, the inspector took his departure, leaving us both a little overpowered by his magniloquence and me a little surprised by Thorndyke's promise which had evoked it.

CHAPTER FIFTEEN

Polton on the War Path

As the inspector's footsteps died away on the stairs, we looked at one another and smiled.

"That was a fine peroration, even for Blandy," I remarked. "But haven't you rather misled the poor man? He is evidently under the delusion that he has harnessed you firmly to his chariot."

"I only promised to look over his salvage; which I am quite ready to do for my own satisfaction."

"I don't quite see why. You are not likely to learn anything from it; and even if you were, this affair is not our concern."

"I don't know that we can say that," he replied. "But we needn't argue the point. I don't mind admitting that mere professional curiosity is a sufficient motive to induce me to keep an eye on the case."

"Well, that would be good news for Blandy, for it is obvious that he is completely stumped; and so am I, for that matter, assuming that there is anything abnormal about the case. I don't feel convinced that there is."

"Exactly," said Thorndyke; "that is Blandy's difficulty. It is a very odd and puzzling case. Taking the group of circumstances as a whole, it seems impossible to accept it as perfectly normal; but yet, when one examines the factors separately, there is not one of them at which one can cavil."

"I am not sure that I follow that," said I. "Why can we not accept the circumstances as normal? I should like to hear you state the case as it presents itself to you."

"Well," he replied, "let us first take the facts as a whole. Here is a house which, in some unknown way, catches fire in the small hours of the morning. In the debris of that house is found the body of a man who has apparently been burned to death."

"Yes," I agreed, with a grin, "the body certainly had that appearance."

"It transpires later," Thorndyke continued, disregarding my comment, "that the death of that man, A, benefits another man, B, to the extent of four thousand pounds. But the premises in which the fire occurred belong to and are controlled by B; and they had been lent by B to A for his occupation while B should be absent in Ireland. The event by which the benefit accrues to B – the death of Harold Moxdale – has occurred quite a short time after the fire. Finally, the tenant, B, who had ostensibly gone away from his residence to make a short visit to Ireland, has never returned to that residence or made any communication to his landlord – has, in fact, disappeared."

"Blandy doesn't admit that Haire has disappeared," I objected.

"We mustn't take Blandy's statements too literally. In spite of his disclaimers, it is evident that he is hot on the trail of Mr Gustavus Haire; and the fact is that, in the ordinary sense of the word, Haire has disappeared. He has absented himself from his ordinary places of resort, he has communicated with nobody, and he has left no traces by which the police could discover his whereabouts.

"But now take the facts separately. The origin of the fire is a mystery, but there is not a particle of evidence of incendiarism. The only person who could have been suspected had been overseas several days before the fire broke out."

"Do you consider that his absence at the time puts him quite outside the picture? I mean, don't you think that the fire could have been started by some sort of timing apparatus?"

"Theoretically, I have no doubt that it could. But it would have had to be a rather elaborate apparatus. The common alarm clock would not have served. But really the question seems to be of only academic interest for two reasons. First, the fire experts were on the look-out for some fire-raising appliance and found no trace of any; second, the presence of Moxdale in the rooms seems to exclude the possibility of any such appliance having been used, and, third, even the appliance that you are postulating would not have served its purpose with anything like calculable certainty."

"You mean that it might not have worked, after all?"

"No. What I mean is that it could not have been adjusted to the actual purpose, which would have been to cause the death of the man. It would have been useless to fire the house unless it were certain that the man would be in it at the time and that he would not be able to escape. But neither of these things could be foreseen with any degree of certainty. No, Jervis, I think that, on our present knowledge, we must agree with Blandy and the others that no suspicion of arson stands against Gustavus Haire."

"That is what he says, but it is obvious he does suspect Haire."

"I was speaking in terms of evidence," Thorndyke rejoined. "Blandy admits that he has nothing against Haire and therefore cannot treat the disappearance as a flight. If he met Haire, he couldn't detain him or charge him with any unlawful act. But he feels – and I think quite rightly – that Haire's disappearance is a mystery that needs to be explained.

"Blandy, in fact, is impressed by the case as a whole; by the appearance of a connected series of events with the suggestion of a purpose behind it. He won't accept those events as normal events, brought about merely by chance; but he sees no way of challenging them so as to start an inquiry. That is why he came to us. He hopes that we may be able to give him some kind of leading fact."

"And so you are proposing to go over the box of rubbish that he has brought on the chance that you may find the leading fact among it?"

"I think we may as well look over it," he replied. "It is wildly improbable that it will yield any information, but you never know. We have, on more than one occasion, picked up a useful hint from a most unlikely source. Shall we go up and see what sort of rubbish the box contains?"

We ascended to the laboratory floor, where we found Polton looking with undissembled distaste at a large packing-case filled to the brim with miscellaneous oddments, mostly metallic, and all covered with a coating of white ash.

"Looks as if Mr Blandy has turned out a dustbin," Polton commented, "and passed the contents on to us. A rare job it was getting it up the stairs. Shall I put the whole of the stuff out on the bench?"

"You may as well," replied Thorndyke, "though I think Blandy might have weeded some of it out. Door-handles and hinges are not likely to yield much information."

Accordingly, we all set to work transferring the salvage to the large bench, which Polton had tidily covered with newspaper, sorting it out to some extent as we did so, and making a preliminary inspection. But it was a hopeless-looking collection, for the little information that it conveyed we possessed already.

We knew about the tools from the little workshop, the projectors and the remains of gramophones and kinematograph cameras, and, as to the buttons, studs, keys, pen-knives, and other small personal objects, they were quite characterless and could tell us nothing.

Nevertheless, Thorndyke glanced at each item as he picked it out of its dusty bed and laid it in its appointed place on the bench, and even Polton began presently to develop an interest in the proceedings.

But it was evidently a merely professional interest, concerning itself exclusively with the detached fragments of the gramophone motors and other mechanical remains and particularly with the battered carcase of the grandfather clock, and I strongly suspected that he was simply on the look-out for usable bits of scrap.

Voicing my suspicion, I suggested: "This ought to be quite a little windfall for you, Polton. A lot of this clockwork seems to be quite sound – I mean as to the separate parts."

He laid down the clock (as tenderly as if it had been in going order) and regarded me with a cunning and crinkly smile.

"It's an ill wind, Sir, that blows nobody good. My reserve stock of gear-wheels and barrels and other spare parts will be all the richer for Mr Blandy's salvage. And you can't have too many spares; you never know when one of them may be the very one that you want. But might I suggest that, as this is a rather dirty job, you let me finish setting the things out and come and look over them at your leisure in the morning, when I have been through them with a dusting-brush."

As I found the business not only dirty but rather boresome – and in my private opinion perfectly futile – I caught at the suggestion readily, and Thorndyke and I then retired to the sitting-room to resume our operations on the test-slides, after cleansing our hands.

"We seem to have been ejected," I remarked as we sat down to the table. "Perhaps our presence hindered the collection of scrap."

Thorndyke smiled. "That is possible," said he. "But I thought that I detected an awakening interest in the inspection. At any rate, it will be as well to let him sort out the oddments before we go through them. He is a good observer, and he might notice things that we should overlook and draw our attention to them."

"You don't really expect to get any information out of that stuff, do you?" I asked.

"No," he replied. "The inspection is little more than a formality, principally to satisfy Blandy. Still, Jervis, we have our principles, and one of them – and a very important one – is to examine everything, no matter how insignificant. This won't be the first rubbish-heap that we have inspected; and it may be that we shall learn something from it, after all."

Thorndyke's suggestion of "an awakening interest" on Polton's part was curiously confirmed on the following day and thereafter.

For, whereas I made my perfunctory inspection of the rubbish and forthwith – literally – washed my hands of it, and even Thorndyke looked it over with little enthusiasm, Polton seemed to give it a quite extraordinary amount of attention.

By degrees, he got all the mechanical oddments sorted out into classified heaps, and once I found him with a small sieve, carefully sifting the ash and dirt from the bottom of the box. And his interest was not confined to the contents of that unclean receptacle; for, having been shown the gold watch which the inspector had left with us, he skilfully prised it open and examined its interior through his eyeglass with the most intense concentration.

Moreover, I began to notice something new and unusual in his manner and appearance: a suggestion of suppressed excitement and a something secret and conspiratorial in his bearing. I mentioned the matter to Thorndyke, but, needless to say, he had noticed it and was waiting calmly for the explanation to transpire. We both suspected that Polton had made some sort of discovery, and we both felt some surprise that he had not communicated it at once.

And then, at last, came the disclosure; and most astonishing it was. It occurred a few mornings after Blandy's visit, when Thorndyke and I, happening to go up to the laboratory, found our friend at the bench, poring over one of the heaps of mechanical fragments with a pair of watch-maker's tweezers in his hand.

"Well, Polton," I remarked, "I should think that you have squeezed the inspector's treasures nearly dry."

He looked up at me with his queer, crinkly smile and replied: "I am rather afraid that I have, Sir."

"And now, I suppose, you know all about it?"

"I wouldn't say that, Sir, but I know a good deal more than when I started. But I don't know all that I want to know."

"Well," I said, "at any rate, you can tell us who set fire to that house."

"Yes, Sir," he replied, "I think I can tell you that, without being too positive."

I stared at him in astonishment, and so did Thorndyke. For Polton was no jester, and, in any case, was much too well-mannered to let off jokes at his principals.

"Then," said I, "tell us. Who do you say it was?"

"I say that it was Mr Haire," he replied with quiet conviction.

"But, my dear Polton," I exclaimed. "Mr Haire was in Dublin when the fire broke out, and had been there five days. You heard the inspector say that it was impossible to suspect him."

"It isn't impossible for me," said Polton. "He could have done it quite well if he had the necessary means. And I am pretty sure that he had the means."

"What means had he?" I demanded.

"Well, Sir," he replied, "he had an eight-day long-case clock."

Of course, we knew that. The clock had been mentioned at the inquest. Nevertheless, Polton's simple statement impinged on me with a quite startling effect, as if some entirely new fact had emerged. Apparently it impressed Thorndyke in the same way, for he drew a stool up to the bench and sat down beside our mysterious little friend. "Now, Polton," said he, "there is something more than that. Tell us all about it."

Polton crinkled nervously as he pondered the question.

"It is rather a long and complicated story," he said, at length. "But I had better begin with the essential facts. This clock of Mr Haire's was not quite an ordinary clock. It had a calendar movement of a very unusual kind, quite different from the simple date disc which most of these old clocks have. I know all about that movement because it happens that I invented it and fitted it to a clock; and I am practically certain that this is the very clock.

"However, that doesn't matter for the moment, but I must tell you how I came to make it and how it worked. In those days, I was half-way through my time as apprentice, and I was doing some work for a gentleman who made philosophical instruments – his name was Parrish.

"Now, Mr Parrish had a clock of this kind – what they call a 'grandfather' nowadays – and it had the usual disc date in the dial.

But that was no use to him because he was rather near-sighted. What he wanted was a calendar that would show the day of the week as well as the date, and in good big characters that he could read when he was sitting at his writing-table; and he asked me if I could make one. Well, of course, there was no difficulty. The simple calendar work that is sometimes fitted to watches would have done perfectly. But he wouldn't have it because it works rather gradually. It takes a few minutes at least to make the change."

"But," said I, "surely that is of no consequence."

"Not the slightest, Sir. The change occurs in the night when nobody can see it, and the correct date is shown in the morning. But Mr Parrish was a rather precise, pernickety gentleman, and he insisted that the change ought to be made in an instant at the very moment of midnight, when the date does really change. So I had to set my wits to work to see what could be done; and at last I managed to design a movement that changed instantaneously.

"It was quite a simple affair. There was a long spindle, or arbor, on which were two drums, one having the days of the week in half-inch letters on it and the other carrying a ribbon with the thirty-one numbers painted the same size. I need not go into full details, but I must explain the action, because that is what matters in this case. There was a twenty-four hour wheel – we will call it the day-wheel – which took off from the hour-wheel, and this carried a snail which turned with it."

"You don't mean an actual snail, I presume," said I.

"No, Sir. What clock-makers call a snail is a flat disc with the edge cut out to a spiral shape, the shape of one of those flat water-snails. Resting against the edge of the snail by means of a projecting pin was a light steel bar with two pallets on it, and there was a seven-toothed star-wheel with long, thin teeth, one of which was always resting on the pallets. I may say that the whole movement excepting the day-wheel was driven by a separate little weight, so as to save the power of the clock.

"And now let me explain how it worked. The day-wheel, driven by the clock, made a complete turn in twenty-four hours, and it carried the snail round with it. But as the snail turned, its spiral edge gradually pushed the pallet-bar away. A tooth of the star-wheel was resting on the upper pallet; but when the snail had nearly completed its turn, it had pushed the bar so far away that the tooth slipped off the upper pallet on to the lower one – which was quite close underneath. Then the snail turned a little more and the pin came to the end of the spiral – what we call 'the step' – and slipped off, and the pallet-bar dropped back and let the tooth of the star-wheel slip off the lower pallet. Then the star-wheel began to turn until the next tooth was stopped by the upper pallet; and so it made a seventh of a turn, and, as it carried the two drums round with it, each of those made the seventh of a turn and changed the date in less than a second. Is that clear, Sir?"

"Quite clear," replied Thorndyke (speaking for himself), "so far as the mechanism goes, but not so clear as to your deductions from it. I can see that this quite innocent calendar movement could be easily converted into a fire-raising appliance. But you seem to suggest that it was actually so converted. Have you any evidence that it was?"

"I have, Sir," replied Polton. "What I have described is the calendar work just as I made it. There is no doubt about that, because when I took off the copper dial, there was the day-wheel with the snail on it still in place. Perhaps you noticed it."

"I did, but I thought it was part of some kind of striking-work."

"No, Sir. The striking-work had been removed to make room for the calendar-work. Well, there was the day-wheel and the snail, and I have found the pallet-bar and the star-wheel and some of the other parts, so it is certain that the calendar movement was there. But there was something else. Somebody had made an addition to it, for I found another snail and another pallet-bar almost exactly like those of the calendar. But there was this difference: the day-snail had marked on it twelve lines, each denoting two hours; but this second snail had seven lines marked on it, and those seven lines couldn't have meant anything but seven days."

"That is a reasonable assumption," said Thorndyke.

"I think, Sir, that it is rather more than an assumption. If you remember that the star-wheel and the spindle that carried the two drums made one complete revolution in seven days, you will see that, if this snail had been fixed on to the spindle, it would also have made a revolution in seven days. But do you see what follows from that?"

"I don't," said I, "so you may as well explain."

"Well, the day-snail turned once a day and, at the end of its turn, it suddenly let the pin drop into the step, released the star-wheel and changed the date in an instant. But this second snail would take a week to turn, and, at the end of the week, the pin would drop into the step, and in an instant something would happen. The question is, what was it that would have happened?"

"Yes," Thorndyke agreed, "that is the question, and first, can you think of any normal and innocent purpose that the snail might have served?"

"No, Sir. I have considered that question, and I can't find any answer. It couldn't have been anything connected with the calendar, because the weeks aren't shown on a calendar. There's no need. When Sunday comes round, you know that it is a week since last Sunday; and no one wants to number the weeks."

"It is conceivable," I suggested, "that someone might have had some reason for keeping count of the weeks, though it does seem unlikely. But could this addition be connected with the phases of the moon? They are sometimes shown on clocks."

"They are, usually, on these old clocks," replied Polton, "but this movement would have been of no use for that purpose. The moon doesn't jump from one phase to the next. It moves gradually; and the moon-disc on a clock shows the changes from day to day. Besides, this snail would have been unnecessary. A moon-disc could have been taken directly off the spindle and moved forward one tooth at each change of date. No, Sir, I can think of no use for that snail but to do some particular thing at a given time on a given day. And that is precisely what I think it was made for."

I could see that Thorndyke was deeply impressed by this statement, and so was I. But there were one or two difficulties, and I proceeded to point them out. "You speak, Polton, of doing something at a given time on a given day. But your calendar gave no choice of time. It changed on the stroke of midnight. But this fire broke out at three o'clock in the morning."

"The calendar changed at midnight," replied Polton, "because it was set to that time. But it could have been set to any other time. The snail was not fixed immovably on the pivot. It was held fast by a set-screw, but if you loosened the screw, you could turn the snail and set it to discharge at any time you pleased."

"And what about the other snail?" Thorndyke asked.

"That was made in exactly the same way. It had a thick collet and a small set-screw. So you see, Sir, the movement was easily controllable. Supposing you wanted it to discharge at three o'clock in the morning in five days' time; first you set the hands of the clock to three hours after midnight, then you set the day-snail so that the step was just opposite the pin, and you set the week-snail so that the pin was five marks from the step.

"Then both the snails would be in the correct position by the day-wheel, and at three in the morning on the fifth day both snails would discharge together and whatever you had arranged to happen at that time would happen to the moment.

"And you notice, Sir, that until it did happen, there would be nothing unusual to be seen or heard. To a stranger in the room, there would appear to be nothing but an ordinary grandfather clock with a calendar – unless the little windows for the calendar had been stopped up, as I expect they had been."

Here Thorndyke anticipated a question that I had been about to put; for I had noticed that Polton had described the mechanism, but had not produced the parts for our inspection, excepting the carcase of the clock, which was on the bench.

"I understand that you have the two snails and pallet-bars?"

"Yes, Sir, and I can show them to you if you wish. But I have been making a model to show how the mechanism worked, and I thought it best for the purposes of evidence, to make it with the actual parts. It isn't quite finished yet, but if you would like to see it – "

"No," replied Thorndyke, instantly realizing, with his invariable tact and sympathy, that Polton wished to spring his creation on us complete, "we will wait until the model is finished. But to what extent does it consist of the actual parts?"

"As far as the calendar goes, Sir, almost entirely. The day-wheel was on the clock-plate where you saw it. Then I found the snail and the spindle with the star-wheel still fixed to it. That is practically the whole of it excepting the wooden drums, which, of course, have gone.

"As to the week-mechanism, I have got the snail and the pallet-bar only. There may not have been much else, as the week-snail could have been set on the spindle and would then have turned with the star-wheel."

"There would have had to be a second star-wheel, I suppose," Thorndyke suggested.

"Not necessarily, Sir. If it was required for only a single discharge, a pivoted lever, or something that would drop right out when the pallet released it, would do. I have found one or two wheels that might have been used, but they may have come from the gramophone motors or the projectors, so one can't be sure."

"Then," said I, "you can't say exactly what the week-mechanism was like, or that your model will be a perfect reproduction of it?"

"No, Sir," he replied, regretfully. "But I don't think that really matters. If I produce a model, made from the parts found in the ruins, that would be capable of starting a fire, that will dispose of the question of possibility."

"Yes," said Thorndyke, "I think we must admit that. When will your model be ready for a demonstration?"

"I can promise to have it ready by tomorrow evening," was the reply.

"And would you be willing that Inspector Blandy should be present at the demonstration?"

The answer was most emphatically in the affirmative; and the gratified crinkle with which the permission was given suggested keen satisfaction at the chance of giving the inspector a shock.

So the matter was left; and Thorndyke and I retired, leaving our ingenious friend to a despairing search among the rubbish for yet further traces of the sinister mechanism.

CHAPTER SIXTEEN

Polton Astonishes the Inspector

Polton's revelation gave us both a good deal of material for thought, and, naturally, thought generated discussion.

"How does Polton's discovery impress you?" I asked. "Is it a real one, do you think, or is it possible that he has only found a mare's nest?"

"We must wait until we have seen the model," Thorndyke replied. "But I attach great weight to his opinions for several reasons."

"As, for instance – ?"

"Well, first there is Polton himself. He is a profound mechanician, with the true mechanician's insight and imagination. He reads a certain function into the machine which he has mentally reconstructed, and he is probably right. Then there is the matter which we were discussing recently: the puzzling, contradictory nature of the case. We agreed that the whole group of events looks abnormal; that it suggests a connected group of events, intentionally brought about, with an unlawful purpose behind it, but there is not a particle of positive evidence connecting anyone with those events in the character of agent. The crux of the matter has been from the first the impossibility of connecting Haire with the outbreak of the fire. His alibi seemed to be unchallengeable; for not only was he far away, days before the fire broke out; not only was there no trace of any fire-raising appliance; but the presence of the other man in the rooms seemed to exclude the possibility of any such appliance having been used.

"But if Polton's discovery turns out to be a real one, all these difficulties disappear. The impossible has become possible and even probable. It has become possible for Haire to have raised the fire while he was hundreds of miles away; and the appliance used was so ordinary in appearance that it would have passed unnoticed by the man who was living in the rooms. If Polton is right, he has supplied the missing link which brings the whole case together."

"You speak of probability," I objected. "Aren't you putting it too high? At the most, Polton can prove that the mechanism could have been used for fire-raising; but what is the evidence that it was actually so used?"

"There is no direct evidence," Thorndyke admitted. "But consider all the circumstances. The fire, itself, looked like the work of an incendiary, and all the other facts supported that view. The fatal objection was the apparent physical impossibility of the fire having been purposely raised. But Polton's discovery – if we accept it provisionally – removes the impossibility. Here is a mechanism which could have been used to raise the fire, and for which no other use can be discovered. That, I say, establishes a probability that it was so used; and that probability would remain even if it could be proved that the mechanism had some legitimate function."

"Perhaps you are right," said I. "At any rate, I think Blandy will agree with you. Is he coming to the demonstration?"

"Yes. I notified him and invited him to come. I couldn't do less; and, in fact, though I have no great love for the man, I respect his abilities. He will be here punctually at eight o'clock tonight."

In effect, the inspector was more than punctual, for he turned up, in a state of undisguised excitement, at half-past seven. I need not repeat his adulatory greeting of my colleague nor the latter's disclaimer of any merit in the matter. But I noted that he appeared to be genuinely grateful for Thorndyke's help and much more frank and open in his manner than he had usually been.

As the demonstration had been arranged for eight, we occupied the interval by giving him a general outline of the mechanism while he fortified himself with a glass of sherry (which Thorndyke had, in some way, ascertained to be his particular weakness) and listened with intense attention. At eight o'clock, exactly, by Polton's newly-completed regulator, the creator of that incomparable time-keeper appeared and announced that the model was ready for inspection, and we all, thereupon, followed him up to the laboratory floor.

As we entered the big workroom, Blandy cast an inquisitive glance round at the appliances and apparatus that filled the shelves and occupied the benches; then he espied the model, and, approaching it, gazed at it with devouring attention.

It was certainly an impressive object, and at the first glance I found it a little confusing, and not exactly what I had expected; but as the demonstration proceeded, these difficulties disappeared.

"Before I start the movement," Polton began, "I had better explain one or two things. This is a demonstration model, and it differs in some respects from the actual mechanism. That mechanism was attached to an eight-day clock, and it moved once in twenty-four hours. This one moves once in an abbreviated day of thirty seconds."

"Good gracious!" exclaimed Blandy. "How marvellous are the powers of the horologist! But I am glad that it is only a temporary arrangement. At that rate, we should all be old men in about twenty minutes."

"Well, Sir," said Polton, with an apologetic and crinkly smile, "you wouldn't want to stand here for five days to see it work. But the calendar movement is exactly the same as that in Mr Haire's clock; in fact, it is made from the actual parts that I found in your box, excepting the two wooden drums and the ratchet pulley that carries the cord and weight. Those I had to supply; but the spindle that carries the drums, I found with the star-wheel on it.

"As we haven't got the clock, I have made a simple little clock to turn the snail, like those that are used to turn an equatorial telescope. You can ignore that. But the rest of the movement is driven by this little weight, just as the original was. Then, as to the addition that someone had made to the calendar, I have fixed the week-snail to the end of the spindle. I don't suppose that is how it was done, but that doesn't matter. This shows how the snail and pallet-bar worked, which is the important point."

"And what is that contraption in the bowl?" asked Blandy.

"That," Polton replied a little evasively, "you can disregard for the moment. It is a purely conjectural arrangement for starting the fire. I don't suggest that it is like the one that was used. It is merely to demonstrate the possibility."

"Exactly," said Blandy. "The possibility is the point that matters."

"Well," Polton continued, "that is all that I need explain. I have fitted the little clock with a dial and one hand so that you can follow the time, and, of course, the day of the week and the day of the month are shown on the two drums. And now we can set it going. You see that the day-drum shows Sunday and the date-drum shows the first, and the hand on the dial shows just after three o'clock; so it has just turned three o'clock on Sunday morning. And, if you look at the week-snail, you will see that it is set to discharge on the fifth day – that is, at three o'clock on Friday morning. And now here goes."

He pulled up the little weight by its cord and released some sort of stop. Forthwith the little conical pendulum began to gyrate rapidly, and the single hand to travel round the dial, while Polton watched it ecstatically and chanted out the events as they occurred.

"Six a.m., nine a.m., twelve noon, three p.m., six p.m., nine p.m., midnight."

Here he paused with his eye on the dial, and we all watched expectantly as the hand moved swiftly towards the figure three. As it approached there was a soft click accompanied by a slight movement of the two drums. Then the hand reached the figure and there was another click; and, immediately, the two drums turned, and Sunday, the first, became Monday, the second.

So the rather weird-looking machine went on. The little pendulum gyrated madly, the hand moved rapidly round the dial, and at each alternate three o'clock there came the soft click, and then the two drums moved together and showed a new day. Meanwhile, Polton continued to chant out his announcements – rather unnecessarily, as I thought, for the thing was obvious enough.

"Tuesday, the third; Wednesday, the fourth; Thursday, the fifth, six a.m., nine a.m., noon, three p.m., six p.m., nine p.m., midnight – now, look out for Friday morning."

I think we were all as excited as he was, and we gazed at the dial with the most intense expectancy as the hand approached the figure, and the first warning click sounded. Then the hand reached the hour mark, and, immediately, there was a double click, followed by a faint whirring sound; and suddenly a cloud of white smoke shot up from the bowl and was instantly followed by a sheet of flame.

"My word!" exclaimed Blandy, "there's no nonsense about that. Would you mind showing us how that was done, Mr Polton?"

"It was quite a simple and crude affair," Polton replied, apologetically, "but, you see, I am not a chemist."

"The simpler, the better," said Blandy, "for it was quite effectual. I wish you had shown it to us before you let it off."

"That's all right, Sir," said Polton. "I've got another ready to show you, but I thought I would like you to see how it worked before I gave you the details."

"Quite right, too, Polton," said I. "The conjurer should always do the trick first, and not spoil the effect by giving the explanation in advance. But we want to see how it was done, now."

With a crinkly smile of satisfaction, Polton went to a cupboard, from which he brought out a second enamelled iron bowl, and, with the greatest care, carried it across to the bench.

"It is quite a primitive arrangement, you see," said he. "I have just put a few celluloid films in the bowl, and on the top one I have put a ring of this powder, which is a mixture of loaf sugar and chlorate of potash, both finely powdered and thoroughly stirred together. In the middle of the ring is this little wide-mouthed bottle, containing a small quantity of strong sulphuric acid. Now, as soon as any of the acid touches the mixture, it will burst into flame; so all that is necessary to start the fire is to capsize the bottle and spill the acid on the chlorate mixture.

"You see how I did that. When the escapement discharged, it released this small wheel, which was driven by a separate spring, and the wheel then began to spin and wind up this thin cord, the other end of which was attached to this spindle carrying this long wire lever. As soon as the cord tightened up, it carried the lever across the bowl until it struck the little bottle and knocked it over. You notice that I stood the bottle inside an iron washer so that it couldn't slide, but must fall over when it was struck."

"A most remarkable monument of human ingenuity," commented Blandy, beaming benevolently on our gratified artificer. "I regard you, Mr Polton, with respectful astonishment as a worker of mechanical miracles. Would it be possible to repeat the experiment for the benefit of the less gifted observer?"

Polton was only too delighted to repeat his triumph. Removing the first bowl, in which the fire had now died out, he replaced it with the second one and then proceeded to wind up the separate spring.

"There is no need to set it to the exact day," said he, "as it is only the ignition that you want to see. I will give you notice when it is ready to discharge; and you had better not stand too close to the bowl in case the acid should fly about. Now, there are two days to run; that is one minute."

We gathered round the bowl as near as was safe, and I noticed with interest the perfect simplicity of the arrangement and its infallible efficiency – so characteristic of Polton. In a couple of minutes the warning was given to "look out" and we all stepped back a pace. Then we heard the double click, and the cord – actually bookbinder's thread – which had fallen back when the spring had been rewound – began to tighten. As soon as it was at full tension the spindle of the long wire lever began to turn, carrying the latter at increasing speed towards the bowl. Passing the rim, it skimmed across until it met the bottle, and, giving it a little tap, neatly capsized it. Instantly, a cloud of white smoke shot up; the powder disappeared and a tongue of flame arose from the heap of films at the bottom of the bowl.

Blandy watched them with a smile of concentrated benevolence until the flame had died out. Then he turned to Polton with a ceremonious bow.

"Sir," said he, "you are a benefactor to humanity, an unraveller of criminal mysteries. I am infinitely obliged to you. Now I know how the fire in Billington Street arose, and who is responsible for the lamented death of the unfortunate gentleman whose body we found."

Polton received these tributes with his characteristic smile, but entered a modest disclaimer.

"I don't suggest, Sir, that this is exactly the method that was used."

"No," said Blandy, "but that is of no consequence. You have demonstrated the possibility and the existence of the means. That is enough for our purposes. But as to the details; have you formed any opinion on the methods by which the fire was communicated to the room from its starting-point?"

"Yes, Sir," Polton replied; "I have considered the matter and thought out a possible plan, which I feel sure must be more or less right. From Mr Green's evidence at the inquest we learned that the whole room was littered with parcels filled with used films; and it appeared that these parcels were stacked all round the walls, and even piled round the clock and under the bed. It looked as if those parcels, stacked round and apparently in contact, formed a sort of train from the clock round the room to the heap under the bed.

"Now, I think that the means of communication was celluloid varnish. We know that there was a lot of it about the room, including a row of bottles on the mantelpiece. This varnish is extremely inflammable. If some of it got spilt on the floor, alight, it would run about, carrying the flame with it and lighting up the films as it went. I think that is the way the fire was led away from the clock. You probably know, Sir, that the cases of these tall clocks are open at the bottom. The plinth doesn't make a watertight contact with the floor; and, even if it did, it would be easy to raise it an eighth of an inch with little wedges. My idea is that the stuff for starting the fire was in the bottom of the clock-case. It must have been; for we know that the mechanism was inside the clock, and there couldn't have been anything showing outside. I think that the bottom of the clock was filled with loose films, but underneath them were two or three bottles of celluloid varnish, loosely corked, and on top, the arrangement that you have just seen, or some other.

"When the escapement tipped the bottle over – or started the fire in some other way – the films would be set alight, and the flames would either crack the varnish-bottles right away or heat the varnish and blow out the corks. In any case, there would be lighted varnish running about inside the clock, and it would soon run out under the plinth, stream over the floor of the room and set fire to the parcels of films; and when one parcel was set alight, the fire would spread from that to the next, and so all over the room. That is my idea as to the general arrangement. Of course, I may be quite wrong."

"I don't think you are, Polton," said Thorndyke, "at least in principle. But, to come to details; wouldn't your suggested arrangement take up a good deal of space? Wouldn't it interfere with the pendulum and the weights?"

"I think there would be plenty of room, Sir," replied Polton. "Take the pendulum first. Now, these tall-case clocks are usually about six feet high, sometimes a little more. The pendulum is about forty-five inches over all and suspended from near the top. That brings the rating-nut to about twenty-four inches above the floor level – a clear two feet to spare for the films and the apparatus. Then as to the weights; there was only one weight, as the striking-gear had been taken away. It is a rule that the weight ought not to touch the floor even when the clock is quite run down. But supposing it did; there would be about four feet from the bottom of the weight to the floor when the clock was fully wound – and we can assume that it was fully wound when the firing mechanism was started. As the fall per day would be not more than seven inches, the weight would be thirteen inches from the floor at the end of the fifth day, or at three a.m. on the fifth day, twenty inches.

"That leaves plenty of room in any case. But you have to remember that the weight, falling straight down, occupies a space of not more than four inches square. All round that space there would be the full two feet or even more at the sides, keeping clear of the pendulum. I don't think, Sir, that the question of space raises any difficulty."

"I agree with you, Polton," said Thorndyke. "You have disposed of my objection completely. What do you say, Inspector?"

The inspector smiled benignly and shook his head.

"What can I say?" he asked. "I am rendered almost speechless by the contemplation of such erudition, such insight, and such power of mental synthesis. I feel a mere dilettante."

Thorndyke smiled appreciatively. "We are all gratified," said he, "by your recognition of Mr Polton's merits. But, compliments apart, how does his scheme strike you?"

"It strikes me," replied Blandy, subsiding into a normal manner (excepting his smile, which was of the kind that "won't come off"), "as supplying an explanation that is not only plausible but is probably the true explanation. Mr Polton has shown that our belief that it was impossible for Mr Haire to have raised the fire was a mistaken belief, that the raising of the fire was perfectly possible, that the means and appliances necessary for raising it were there, and that those means and appliances could have no other purpose. From which we are entitled to infer that those means were so used, and that the fire was actually raised, and was raised by Mr Gustavus Haire."

"Yes," Thorndyke agreed, "I think that is the position; and with that we retire, temporarily, at any rate, and the initiative passes to you. Mr Haire is a presumptive fire-raiser. But he is your Haire, and it is for you to catch him, if you can."

CHAPTER SEVENTEEN

Further Surprises

The air of finality with which Thorndyke had, so to speak, handed the baby back to Inspector Blandy might have been deceptive; but I don't think it even deceived the inspector. Certainly it did not deceive me. Never had I known Thorndyke to resign from an unsolved problem, and I felt pretty certain that he was at least keeping this particular problem in view, and, in his queer, secretive way, trying over the various possible solutions in his mind.

This being so, I made no pretence of having dismissed the case, but took every opportunity of discussing it, not only with Thorndyke but especially with Polton, who was the actual fountain of information. And there were, about this time, abundant opportunities for discussion, for we were still engaged, in our spare time, in the great work of rearranging and weeding out our large collection of microscopical slides for which Polton had recently made a new set of cabinets. Naturally, that artist assisted us in sorting out the specimens, and it was in the intervals of these activities that I endeavoured to fill in the blanks of my knowledge of the case.

"I have been thinking," I remarked on one of these occasions, "of what you told us, Polton, about that clock of Mr Haire's. You are of opinion that it is actually the clock to which you fitted the calendar for Mr Parrish. I don't know that it is a point of any importance, but I should like to know what convinces you that this is the identical clock, and not one which might have been copied from yours, or invented independently."

"My principal reason for believing that it is the same clock is that it is made from the same kind of oddments of material that I used. For instance, I made the pallet-bar from an old hack-saw blade which I happened to have by me. It was not specially suitable, and an ordinary clock-maker would almost certainly have used a strip of brass. But the pallet-bar of this clock has been made from a hack-saw blade."

He paused and seemed to reflect for a while. Then he continued:

"But there is another point; and the more I have thought about it the more it has impressed me. Mr Parrish had a nephew who lived with him and worked as a pupil in the workshop; a lad of about my own age or a little younger. Now this lad's name was Haire, and he was always called Gus. I supposed at the time that Gus stood for Augustus, but when I heard at the inquest the name of Gustavus Haire, I wondered if it might happen to be the same person. You can't judge by a mere similarity of names, since there are so many people of the same name. But when I saw this clock, I thought at once of Gus Haire. For he was in the workshop when I made the calendar, and he watched me as I was working on it and got me to explain all about it; though the principle on which it worked was obvious enough to any mechanic."

"Should you describe Gus Haire as a mechanic?" I asked.

"Yes, of a sort," Polton replied. "He was a poor workman, but he was equal to a simple job like the making of this calendar, especially when he had been shown; and certainly to the addition that had been made to it."

"And what sort of fellow was he – morally, I mean."

Polton took time to consider this question. At length he replied:

"It is not for me to judge any man's character, and I didn't know very much about him. But I do know this as a fact: that on a certain occasion when I was making a new key for Mr Parrish's cash drawer to replace one which was broken, Gus pinched a piece of my moulding wax and took a squeeze of the broken key; and that, later, Mr Parrish accused me of having opened that drawer with a false key and taken money from it. Now, I don't know that Gus made a false key and I don't know that any money was actually stolen; but when a man takes a squeeze of the key of another man's cash drawer, he lays himself open to a reasonable suspicion of an unlawful intention."

"Yes, indeed," said I. "A decidedly fishy proceeding; and from what you have just told us, it looks as if you were right – as if the clock were the original clock and Mr Gustavus Haire the original Gus, though it is not quite clear how Mr Parrish's clock came into his possession."

"I don't think, Sir," said he, "that it is difficult to imagine. Mr Parrish was his uncle, and, as he was an old man even then, he must be dead long since. The clock must have gone to someone, and why not to his nephew?"

"Yes," I agreed, "that is reasonable enough. However, we don't know for certain, and, after all, I don't see that the identity of either the clock or the man is of much importance. What do you think, Thorndyke?"

My colleague removed his eye from the microscope, and, laying the slide in its tray, considered the question. At length he replied:

"The importance of the point depends on how much Polton remembers. Blandy's difficulty at the moment is that he has no description of Gustavus Haire sufficiently definite for purposes of identification. Now, can we supply that deficiency? What do you say, Polton? Do you think that if you were to meet Gus Haire after all these years you would recognize him?"

"I think I should, Sir," was the reply. And then he added as an afterthought: "I certainly should if he hadn't lost his teeth."

"His teeth!" I exclaimed. "Was there anything very distinctive about his teeth?"

"Distinctive isn't the word, Sir," he replied. "They were most extraordinary teeth. I have never seen anything like them. They looked as if they were made of tortoiseshell."

"You don't mean that they were decayed?"

"Lord, no, Sir. They were sound enough; good strong teeth and rather large. But they were such a queer colour. All mottled over with brown spots. And those spots wouldn't come off. He tried all sorts of things to get rid of them – Armenian bole, charcoal, even jeweller's red stuff – but it was no use. Nothing would shift those spots."

"Well," I said, "if those teeth are still extant, they would be a godsend to Blandy, for a written description would enable a stranger to identify the man."

"I doubt if it would, Sir," Polton remarked with a significant smile. "Gus was extremely sensitive about those teeth, and showed them as little as possible when he talked or smiled. In those days he couldn't produce much in the way of a moustache, but I expect he does now, and I'll warrant he doesn't crop it too close."

"That is so," Thorndyke confirmed. "The only description of Haire that the police have, as I understand, is that given by Mr Green and that of the man who interviewed Haire in Dublin. Green's description is very vague and sketchy, while the Dublin man hardly remembered him at all except by name, and that only because he had kept the card which Haire had presented. But both of these men mentioned that Haire wore a full, drooping moustache."

"Still," I persisted, "the teeth are a very distinctive feature, and it would seem only fair to Blandy to give him the information."

"Perhaps it might be as well," Thorndyke agreed. Then, returning to the subject of Polton's old acquaintance, he asked:

"You say that Gus lived with his uncle. Why was that? Was he an orphan?"

"Oh, no, Sir. Only his people lived in the country, not very far away, for he used to go down and stay with them occasionally at weekends. It was somewhere in Essex. I have forgotten the name of the place, but it was a small town near the river."

"It wouldn't be Maldon?" Thorndyke suggested.

"That's the place, Sir. Yes, I remember now." He stopped suddenly and, gazing at his principal with an expression of astonishment, exclaimed: "Now, I wonder, Sir, how you knew that he lived at Maldon."

Thorndyke chuckled. "But, my dear Polton, I didn't know. I was only making a suggestion. Maldon happens to agree with your description."

Polton shook his head and crinkled sceptically. "It isn't the only waterside town in Essex," he remarked, and added: "No, Sir. It's my belief that you knew that he lived at Maldon, though how you knew I can't imagine."

I was disposed to agree with Polton. There was something a little suspicious in the way in which Thorndyke had dropped pat on the right place. But further questions on my part elicited nothing but an exasperating grin and the advice to me to turn the problem over in my mind and consider any peculiarities that distinguished Maldon from other Essex towns; advice that I acted upon at intervals during the next few days with disappointingly negative results.

Nevertheless, Polton's conviction turned out to be justified. I realized it when, one morning about a week later, I found Polton laying the breakfast-table and placing the "catch" from the letter-box beside our respective plates. As I entered the room, he looked at me with a most portentous crinkle and pointed mysteriously to a small package which he had just deposited by my colleague's plate. I stooped over it to examine the typewritten address, but at first failed to discover anything significant about it; then, suddenly, my eye caught the postmark, and I understood. That package had been posted at Maldon.

"The Doctor is a most tantalizing person, Sir," Polton exclaimed. "I don't mind admitting that I am bursting with curiosity as to what is in that package. But I suppose we shall find out presently."

Once more he was right; in fact, the revelation came that very evening. We were working our way through the great collection of test specimens, examining and discussing each slide, when Thorndyke looked up from the microscope and electrified Polton and me by saying:

"By the way, I have got a specimen of another kind that I should like to take your opinion on. I'll show it to you."

He rose and stepped across the room to a cabinet, from which he took a small cardboard box of the kind that dentists use for the packing of dental plates. Opening this, he took from it the wax model of an upper denture, complete with teeth, and laid it on the table.

There was a moment's silence as we both gazed at it in astonishment and Thorndyke regarded us with a quizzical smile. Then Polton, whose eyes seemed ready to drop out, exclaimed:

"God bless my soul! Why, they are Mr Haire's teeth!"

Thorndyke nodded. "Good!" said he. "You recognize these teeth as being similar to those of Gus Haire?"

"They aren't similar," said Polton; "they are identically the same. Of course, I know that they can't actually be his teeth, but they are absolutely the same in appearance: the same white, chalky patches, the same brown stains, and the same little blackish-brown specks. I recognized them in a moment, and I have never seen anything like them before or since. Now, I wonder how you got hold of them."

"Yes," said I, "that is what I have been wondering. Perhaps the time has come for the explanation of the mystery."

"There is not much mystery," he replied. "These teeth are examples of the rare and curious condition known as "mottled teeth"; of which perhaps the most striking feature is the very local distribution. It is known in many different places, and has been studied very thoroughly in the United States, but wherever it is met with it is confined to a quite small area, though within that area it affects a very large proportion of the inhabitants; so large that it is almost universal. Now, in this country, the most typically endemic area is Maldon; and, naturally, when Polton described Gus Haire's teeth and told us that Gus was a native of Essex, I thought at once of Maldon."

"I wonder, Sir," said Polton, "what there is about Maldon that affects people's teeth in this way. Has it been explained?"

"Yes," Thorndyke replied. "It has been found that wherever mottled teeth occur, the water from springs and wells contains an abnormal amount of fluorine, and the quantity of the fluorine seems to be directly related to the intensity of the mottling. Mr Ainsworth, whose admirable paper in the British Dental Journal is the source of my information on the subject, collected samples of water from various localities in Essex and analysis of these confirmed the findings of the other investigators. That from Maldon contained the very large amount of five parts per million."

"And how did you get this specimen?" I asked.

"I got into touch with a dental surgeon who practises in Maldon and explained what I wanted. He was most kind and helpful, and, as he has taken an interest in mottled teeth and carefully preserved all his extractions, he was able to supply me not only with this model to produce in court if necessary, but with a few spare teeth for experiments such as section-cutting."

"You seem to have taken a lot of trouble," I remarked, "but I don't quite see why."

"It was just a matter of verification," he replied. Polton's description was clear enough for us as we know Polton; but for the purposes of evidence, the actual identification on comparison is infinitely preferable. Now we may say definitely that Gus Haire's teeth were true mottled teeth; and if Gus Haire and Gustavus Haire are one and the same person, as they appear to be, then we can say that Mr Haire has mottled teeth."

"But," I objected, "does it matter to us what his teeth are like?"

"Ah!" said he, "that remains to be seen. But if it should turn out that it does matter, we have the fact."

"And are we going to pass the fact on to Blandy? It seems to be more his concern than ours."

"I think," he replied, "that, as a matter of principle, we ought to, though I agree with Polton that the information will not be of much value to him. Perhaps we might invite him to drop in and see the specimen and take Polton's depositions. Will you communicate with him?"

I undertook to convey the invitation; and when the specimen had been put away in the cabinet, we dismissed the subject of mottled teeth and returned to our task of revision.

But that invitation was never sent; for, on the following morning, the inspector forestalled it by ringing us up on the telephone to ask for an interview, he having, as he informed us, some new and important facts which he would like to discuss with us. Accordingly, with Thorndyke's concurrence, I made an appointment for that evening, which happened to be free of other engagements.

It was natural that I should speculate with some interest on the nature of the new facts that Blandy had acquired. I even attempted to discuss the matter with Thorndyke, but he, I need not say, elected to postpone discussion until we had heard the facts. Polton, on the other hand, was in a twitter of curiosity, and I could see that he had made up his mind by hook or by crook to be present at the interview; to which end, as the hour of the appointment drew near, he first placed an easy-chair for the inspector, flanked by a small table furnished with a decanter of sherry and a box of cigarettes, and then covered the main table with a portentous array of microscopes, slide-trays, and cabinets. Having made these arrangements, he seated himself opposite a microscope and looked at his watch; and I noticed thereafter that the watch got a good deal more attention than the microscope.

At length, punctually to the minute, the inspector's modest rat-tat sounded on the knocker, and Polton, as if actuated by a hidden spring, shot up from his chair like a jack-in-the-box and tripped across to the door. Throwing it open, with a flourish, he announced "Inspector Blandy"; whereupon Thorndyke and I rose to receive our guest, and, having installed him in his chair, filled his glass and opened the cigarette-box while Polton stole back to his seat and glued his eye to the microscope.

My first glance at the inspector as he entered assured me that he expected to spring a surprise on us. But I didn't intend to let him have it all his own way. As he sipped his sherry and selected a cigarette from the box, I anticipated his offensive and took the initiative.

"Well, Blandy, I suppose we may assume that you have caught your Haire?"

"I deprecate the word 'caught' as applied to Mr Haire," he answered, beaming on me, "but, in fact, we have not yet had the pleasure of meeting him. It is difficult to trace a man of whom one has no definite description."

"Ah!" said I, "that is where we are going to help you. We can produce the magic touchstone which would identify the man instantly."

Here I took the denture-box from the table, where it had been placed in readiness, and, having taken out the model, handed it to him. He regarded it for a while with an indulgent smile and then looked enquiringly at me.

"This is a very singular thing, Dr Jervis," said he. "Apparently a dentist's casting-model. But the teeth look like natural teeth."

"They look to me like deuced unnatural teeth," said I, "but, such as they are, they happen to be an exact facsimile of Mr Haire's teeth."

Blandy was visibly impressed, and he examined the model with a new interest.

"I am absolutely astounded," said he; "not so much at the strange appearance of the teeth, though they are odd enough, as by your apparently unbounded resources. May I ask how you made this extraordinary discovery?"

Thorndyke gave him a brief account of the investigation which Polton confirmed and amplified, to which he listened with respectful attention.

"Well," he commented, "it is a remarkable discovery and would be a valuable one if the identity had to be proved. In the existing circumstances it is not of much value, for Mr Haire is known to wear a moustache, and we may take it that his facial expression is not at all like that of the Cheshire Cat. And you can't stop a stranger in the street and ask him to show you his teeth."

He handed the model back to me, and, having refreshed himself with a sip of wine, opened the subject of his visit.

"Speaking of identity, I have learned some new facts concerning the body which was found in Mr Haire's house. I got my information from a rather unexpected source. Now, I wonder whether you can guess the name of my informant."

Naturally, I could not, and, as Thorndyke refused to hazard a guess, the inspector disclosed his secret with the air of a conjuror producing a goldfish from a hatbox.

"My informant," said he, "is Mr Cecil Moxdale."

"What!" I exclaimed, "the dead man!"

"The dead man," he repeated; "thereby refuting the common belief that dead men tell no tales."

"This is most extraordinary," said I, "though, as a matter of fact, the body was never really identified. But why did Moxdale not come forward sooner?"

"It seems," replied Blandy, "that he was travelling in the South of France at the time of the fire and, naturally, heard nothing about it. He has only just returned, and, in fact, would not have come back so soon but for the circumstance that he happened to see a copy of *The Times* in which the legal notice appeared in connection with his uncle's death."

"Then I take it," said Thorndyke, "that he made his first appearance at the solicitor's office."

"Exactly," replied Blandy; "and there he learned about his supposed death, and the solicitors communicated with me. I had left them my address and asked them to advise me in the case of any new developments."

There was a short pause, during which we all considered this "new development." Then Thorndyke commented:

"The reappearance of Moxdale furnishes conclusive negative evidence as to the identity of the body. Could he give any positive evidence?"

"Nothing that you could call evidence," replied Blandy. "Of course, he knows nothing. But he has done a bit of guessing; and there may be something in what he says."

"As to the identity of the body?" Thorndyke asked.

"Yes. He thinks it possible that the dead man may have been a man named O'Grady. The relations between Haire and O'Grady seem to have been rather peculiar; intimate but not friendly. In fact, Haire appears to have had an intense dislike for the other man, but yet they seem to have associated pretty constantly, and Moxdale has a strong impression that O'Grady used to "touch" Haire for a loan now and again, if they were really loans. Moxdale suspects that they were not; in short, to put it bluntly he suspects that Haire was being blackmailed by O'Grady."

"No details, I suppose?"

"No. It is only a suspicion. Moxdale doesn't know anything and he doesn't want to say too much; naturally, as Haire is his cousin."

"But how does this bear on the identity of the body?"

"Doesn't it seem to you to have a bearing? The blackmailing, I mean, if it can be established. Blackmailers have a way of dying rather suddenly."

"But," I objected, "it hasn't been established. It is only a suspicion, and a rather vague one at that."

"True," he admitted, "and very justly observed. Yet we may bear the suspicion in mind, especially as we have a fact which, taken in connection with that suspicion, has a very direct bearing on the identity of the body. Moxdale tells me that O'Grady had an appointment with Haire at his, Haire's, rooms in the forenoon of the fourteenth of April; the very day on which Haire must have started for Dublin. He knows this for a fact, as he heard O'Grady make the appointment. Now, that appointment, at that place and on that date, strikes me as rather significant."

"Apparently, Moxdale finds it significant, too," said I. "The suggestion seems to be that Haire murdered O'Grady and went away, leaving his corpse in the rooms."

"Moxdale didn't put it that way," said Blandy.

"He suggested that O'Grady might have had the use of the rooms while Haire was away. But that is mere speculation, and he probably doesn't believe it himself. Your suggestion is the one that naturally occurs to us; and if it is correct, we can understand why Haire is keeping out of sight. Don't you think so?"

The question was addressed to Thorndyke with a persuasive smile. But my colleague did not seem to be impressed.

"The figure of O'Grady," he said, "seems to be rather shadowy and elusive, as in fact, does the whole story. But perhaps Moxdale gave you a more circumstantial account of the affair."

"No, he did not," replied Blandy. "But my talk with him was rather hurried and incomplete. I dropped in on him without an appointment and found him just starting out to keep an engagement, so I only had a few minutes with him. But he voluntarily suggested a further meeting to go into matters in more detail; and I then ventured to ask if he would object to your being present at the interview, as you represent the insurance people, and he had no objection at all.

"Now, how would you like me to bring him along here so that you could hear his account in detail and put such questions as you might think necessary to elucidate it? I should be glad if you would let me, as you know so much about the case. What do you say?"

Thorndyke was evidently pleased at the proposal and made no secret of the fact, for he replied:

"It is very good of you, Blandy, to make this suggestion. I shall be delighted to meet Mr Moxdale and see if we can clear up the mystery of that body. Does your invitation include Jervis?"

"Of course it does," Blandy replied, heartily, "as he is a party to the inquiry; and Mr Polton, too, for that matter, seeing that he discovered the crucial fact. But, you understand that Moxdale knows nothing about that."

"No," said Thorndyke; "but if it should seem expedient for the purposes of the examination to let him know that the fire was raised by Haire, do you agree to my telling him?"

The inspector looked a little dubious.

"We don't want to make any unnecessary confidences," said he. "But, still, I think I had better leave it to your discretion to tell him anything that may help the inquiry."

Thorndyke thanked him for the concession, and, when one of two dates had been agreed on for the interview, the inspector took his leave, wreathed in smiles and evidently well satisfied with the evening's work.

CHAPTER EIGHTEEN
Thorndyke Administers a Shock

"I wonder, Sir," said Polton, as the hour approached for the arrival of our two visitors, "how we had better arrange the room. Don't want it to look too much like a committee meeting. But there's rather a lot of us for a confidential talk."

"It isn't so particularly confidential," I replied. "If there are any secrets to be revealed, they are not Moxdale's. He didn't pose as a dead man. The deception was Haire's."

"That's true, Sir," Polton rejoined with evident relief. "Still, I think I won't make myself too conspicuous, as he may regard me as an outsider."

The plan that he adopted seemed to me to have exactly the opposite effect to that intended, for, having arranged four chairs around the fireplace with a couple of small tables for wine and cigars, he placed a microscope and some trays of slides on the large table, drew up a chair and prepared to look preoccupied.

At eight o'clock precisely our visitors arrived, and, as I admitted them, I glanced with natural curiosity at "the deceased", and was impressed rather favourably by his appearance. He was a good-looking man, about five feet nine or ten in height, broad-shouldered, well set-up, and apparently strong and athletic; with a pleasant, intelligent face, neither dark nor fair, a closely-cropped dark moustache and clear grey eyes. He greeted me with a friendly smile, but I could see that, in spite of Polton's artful plans, he was a little taken aback by the size of the party, and especially by the apparition of Polton, himself, seated necromantically behind his microscope.

But Thorndyke soon put him at his ease, and, when the introductions had been effected (including "Mr Polton, our technical adviser"), we took our seats and opened the proceedings with informal and slightly frivolous conversation.

"We should seem to be quite old acquaintances, Mr Moxdale," said Thorndyke, "seeing that I have had the honour of testifying to a coroner's jury as to the cause of your death. But that sort of acquaintance ship is rather one-sided."

"Yes," Moxdale agreed, "it is a queer position. I come back to England to find myself the late Mr Moxdale and have to introduce myself as a resurrected corpse. It is really quite embarrassing."

"It must be," Thorndyke agreed, "and not to you alone; for, since you have resigned from the role of the deceased, you have put on us the responsibility of finding a name for your understudy. But the inspector tells us that you can give us some help in our search."

"Well," said Moxdale, "it is only a guess, and I may be all abroad. But there was someone in that house when it was burned, and, as I was not that someone, I naturally ask myself who he could have been. I happen to know of one person who might have been there, and I don't know of any other. That's the position. Perhaps there isn't much in it, after all."

"A vulgar saying," Blandy remarked, "has it that half a loaf is better than no bread. A possible person is at least something to start on. But we should like to know as much as we can about that person. What can you tell us?"

"Ah!" said Moxdale, "there is the difficulty. I really know nothing about Mr O'Grady. He is little more than a name to me, and only a surname at that. I can't even tell you his Christian name."

"That makes things a bit difficult," said Blandy, "seeing that we have got to trace him and find out whether he is still in existence.

But at any rate, you have seen him and can tell us what he was like."

"Yes, I have seen him – once, as I told you – and my recollection of him is that he was a strongly-built man about five feet nine or ten inches high, medium complexion, grey eyes, dark hair and moustache and no beard. When I saw him, he was wearing a black jacket, striped trousers, grey overcoat, and a light-brown soft felt hat."

"That is quite a useful description," said Blandy, "for excluding the wrong man, but not so useful for identifying the right one. It would apply to a good many other men; and the clothes were not a permanent feature. You told me about your meeting with him. Perhaps you wouldn't mind repeating the account for Dr Thorndyke's benefit."

"It was a chance meeting," said Moxdale. "I happened to be in the neighbourhood of Soho one day about lunch-time and it occurred to me to drop in at a restaurant that Haire had introduced me to; Moroni's in Wardour Street. I walked down to the further end of the room and was just looking for a vacant table when I caught sight of Haire, himself, apparently lunching with a man who was a stranger to me. As Haire had seen me, I went up to him and shook hands, and then, as I didn't know his friend, was going off to another table when he said:

" 'Don't go away, Cecil. Come and take a chair at this table and let me introduce you to my friend, O'Grady. You've heard me speak of him and he has heard me speak of you.'

"Accordingly, as O'Grady stood up and offered his hand, I shook it and sat down at the table and ordered my lunch; and in the interval before it arrived we chatted about nothing in particular, especially O'Grady, who was very fluent and had a rather pleasant, taking manner. By the time my food was brought, they had finished their lunch, and, having got their bills from the waiter, settled up with him. Then O'Grady said:

" 'Don't let me break up this merry party, but Time and Tide, you know – I must be running away. I am glad to have had the pleasure of meeting you, Moxdale, and turning a mere name into a person.'

"With this he got up and put on his overcoat and hat – I noticed the hat particularly because it was rather a queer colour – and when he had shaken hands with me, he said to Haire, just as he was turning to go:

" 'Don't forget our little business on Thursday. I shall call for you at eleven o'clock to the tick, and I shall bring the stuff with me. Better make a note of the time. So long'; and with a smile and a wave of the hand to me, he bustled away.

"When he had gone, I remarked to Haire that O'Grady seemed to be rather a pleasant, taking sort of fellow. He smiled grimly and replied:

" 'Yes, he is a plausible rascal, but if you should happen to meet him again, I advise you to keep your pockets buttoned. He is remarkably plausible.'

"I tried to get him to amplify this statement, but he didn't seem disposed to pursue the subject and presently he looked at his watch and then he, too, took his departure. That is the whole story, and there isn't much in it excepting the date of the appointment. The Thursday referred to would be the fourteenth of April, and that, I understand, is the day on which Haire started for Dublin."

"You say, you understand," said Thorndyke. "Have you not seen the account of the inquest?"

"No. But Mr Horne, my solicitor, has given me a summary of it with all the material facts, including my own untimely decease. But I needn't have said I understand, because I happen to know."

"That Mr Haire did start on that day?" Thorndyke queried.

"Yes. I actually saw him start."

"That is interesting," said Blandy. "Could you give us the particulars?"

"With pleasure," replied Moxdale. "It happened that on that day – or rather that night – I was starting for the South of France. I had left my luggage in the cloak-room at Victoria, earlier in the day, as I had some calls to make, and when I had done all my business, I strolled to Wardour Street and dropped in at Moroni's for a late dinner or supper. And there I found Haire, who had just come in on the same errand. He was taking the night train for Holyhead, and as I was travelling by the night train to Folkestone, we both had plenty of time. So we made our dinner last out and we dawdled over our coffee until it was past ten o'clock. Then Haire, who had a heavy suitcase with him, said he thought he would take a taxi across to Euston, so, when we had paid our bills, we went out together to look for a cab. We found one disengaged in Shaftesbury Avenue, and, when Haire had put his suitcase inside, he called out 'Euston' to the driver, got in, said 'good-night' to me and off he went."

"Did he say whether O'Grady had kept his appointment?" Thorndyke asked.

"He just mentioned that he had called. Nothing more; and of course I asked no questions."

"You seemed to think," said Thorndyke, "that the body that was found after the fire might be that of O'Grady. What made you think that?"

"Well, really," Moxdale replied, "I hardly know. It was just an idea, suggested, I suppose, by the fact that O'Grady went to the rooms and I didn't know of anybody else. I thought it possible that Haire might have let him use the rooms while he was away, as O'Grady lives out of town – somewhere Enfield way."

The inspector looked dissatisfied. "Seems rather vague," he remarked. "You were telling me something about a suspicion of blackmailing. Could you give us some particulars on that subject?"

"My dear Inspector," exclaimed Moxdale, "I haven't any particulars. It was just a suspicion, which I probably ought not to have mentioned, as I had nothing definite to go upon."

"Still," Blandy persisted, "you must have had some reasons. Is Haire a man who could be blackmailed?"

"That I can't say. He isn't a pattern of all the virtues, but I know of nothing that a blackmailer could fix on. And he is my cousin, you know. I think what raised the suspicion was the peculiar relations between the two men. They were a great deal together, but they were not really friends. Haire seemed to me to dislike O'Grady intensely, and I gathered from chance remarks that he let drop that O'Grady had got a good deal of money out of him from time to time. In what way I never knew. It may have been in the form of loans, but if not, it would rather look like blackmail."

There was a short silence. Then Blandy, dropping his oily manner for once, said, rather brusquely:

"Now, Mr Moxdale, you have suggested that the burned body might have been that of O'Grady. You have told us that O'Grady was in those rooms on the fourteenth of April, and you have suggested that O'Grady was blackmailing Haire. Now I put it to you that what you really suspect is that, on that day, Haire made away with O'Grady and concealed his body in the rooms."

Moxdale shook his head. "I never suspected anything of the kind. Besides, the thing wasn't practicable. Is it likely that he would have gone off to Ireland leaving the body in his rooms?"

"You are not forgetting the fire," Blandy reminded him.

"I don't see that the fire has anything to do with it. Haire couldn't foresee that someone would set his rooms on fire at that particularly opportune moment."

"But that is precisely what he did foresee," said Thorndyke. "That fire was not an accident. It was carefully prepared and started by a timing mechanism on a prearranged date. That mechanism was discovered and reconstructed by our colleague, Mr Polton."

The statement was, no doubt, a startling one, but its effect on Moxdale was beyond what I should have expected. He could not have looked more horrified if he had been accused of setting the mechanism himself.

"So you see," Thorndyke continued, "that Haire is definitely implicated; and, in fact, the police are prepared to arrest him on charges connected with both the fire and the body."

"Yes," said the inspector, "but the trouble is that we have no photograph or any sufficient description by which to identify him."

"Speaking of identification," said Thorndyke, "we learn that his teeth are rather peculiar in appearance. Can you tell us anything about them?"

Moxdale looked distinctly uncomfortable at this question, though I could not imagine why. However, he answered, somewhat hesitatingly:

"Yes, they are rather queer-looking teeth; as if they were stained by tobacco. But it isn't tobacco-staining, because I remember that they were just the same when he was a boy."

Having given this answer, he looked from Blandy to Thorndyke, and, as neither asked any further question, he remarked, cheerfully:

"Well, I think you have squeezed me pretty dry; unless there is something else that you would like me to tell you."

There was a brief silence. Then Thorndyke said in a very quiet, matter-of-fact tone:

"There is one other question, Mr Moxdale. I have my own opinion on the subject, but I should like to hear your statement. The question is, what made you go to Dublin after you had killed Mr Haire?"

A deathly silence followed the question. Moxdale was thunderstruck. But so were we all. Blandy sat with dropped jaw, staring at Thorndyke, and Polton's eyes seemed ready to start from their sockets. At length, Moxdale, pale as a corpse, exclaimed in a husky voice:

"I don't understand you, Sir. I have told you that I saw Mr Haire start in a taxi for Euston."

"Yes," Thorndyke replied. "But at the moment when you saw Mr Haire get into the cab, his dead body was lying in his rooms."

Moxdale remained silent for some moments. He seemed completely overwhelmed; and, watching him, I saw that abject terror was written in every line of his face. But he made one more effort.

"I assure you, Sir," he said, almost in a whisper, "that you have made some extraordinary mistake. The thing is monstrous. You are actually accusing me of having murdered my cousin!"

"Not at all," replied Thorndyke. "I said nothing about murder. I referred simply to the physical fact that you killed him. I did not suggest that you killed him feloniously. I am not accusing you of a crime. I merely affirm an act."

Moxdale looked puzzled and yet somewhat reassured by Thorndyke's answer. But he was still evasive.

"It seems," said he, "that it is useless for me to repeat my denial."

"It is," Thorndyke agreed. "What I suggest is that you give us a plain and truthful account of the whole affair."

Moxdale looked dubiously at the inspector and said in a half-interrogative tone:

"If I am going to be charged with having compassed the death of my cousin it seems to me that the less I say, the better."

The inspector, thus appealed to, suddenly recovered his self-possession, even to the resumption of his smile; and I could not but admire the quickness with which he had grasped the position.

"As a police officer," he said, "I am not permitted to advise you. I can only say that if you choose to make a statement you can do so; but I have to caution you that any statement that you may make will be taken down in writing and may be used in evidence against you. That doesn't sound very encouraging; but I may remind you that you are, at present, not charged with any offence, and that a statement made voluntarily in advance is more effective than the same statement made in answer to a charge."

"And I," said Thorndyke, "not being a police officer, may go farther and suggest that a statement may possibly obviate the necessity for any charge at all. Now, come, Mr Moxdale," he continued, persuasively, taking from his pocket a foolscap envelope, "I will make you a proposal. In this envelope is a signed statement by me setting forth briefly my reconstruction, from evidence in my possession, of the circumstances of Mr Haire's death. I shall hand this envelope to the inspector. Then I suggest that you give us a straightforward account of those circumstances. When he has heard your account, the inspector will open the envelope and read my statement. If our two statements agree, we may take it that they are both true. If they disagree, we shall have to examine the discrepancies. What do you say? I advise you, strongly, to give us a perfectly frank statement."

The persuasive and even friendly tone in which Thorndyke spoke evidently made a considerable impression on Moxdale, for he listened attentively with a thoughtful eye on the speaker, and when Thorndyke had finished he reflected awhile, still keeping his eyes fixed on my colleague's face. At length, having made up his mind, he said, with something like an air of relief:

"Very well, Sir, I will take your advice. I will give you a full and true account of all that happened on that dreadful day, suppressing nothing." He paused for a few moments to collect his thoughts and then continued: "I think I should begin by telling you that my cousin stood to gain four thousand pounds by my death if I should die before my uncle, Harold Moxdale."

"We knew that," said Blandy.

"Ah! Well, then, there is another matter. I don't like to speak ill of the dead, but the truth is that Haire was an unscrupulous rascal – a downright bad man."

"We knew that, too," said Blandy, "when we learned that he had set fire to the house."

"Then I need not dwell on it; but I may add that he had a deep grudge against me for being the more favoured beneficiary of my uncle's will. In fact, his jealousy had induced a really virulent hatred of me which was apt to break out at times, though we usually preserved outwardly decent relations.

"And now to come to the actual incident. I am the part proprietor of a sort of international trade directory and I do a good deal of the canvassing for advertisements, particularly in France. I live out at Surbiton and only go to the office occasionally. Now, a few days before the disaster – the eleventh of April, I think it was – I had a letter from Haire telling me that he was making a business trip to Dublin to try to arrange some agencies and suggesting that he should do some business for me at the same time. I wasn't very keen, as I knew that I was not likely to see any of the money that he might collect. However, I agreed, and eventually arranged to meet him on the fourteenth, on which day I proposed to start by a night train for the South of France. He suggested that he should call for me at my office at half-past four, that we should have some tea and then go to his rooms to talk things over.

"In due course, he turned up at the office; I finished my business, took my bag, and went with him to some tea-rooms, where we had a leisurely tea, and we then went on to his rooms, which we reached about ten minutes to six. As we passed the entrance of the business premises, I saw a man standing just inside, and he saw us, too, for he called out 'good evening' to Haire, who returned his greeting, addressing him as Mr Green; and it struck me that Mr Green looked rather hard at me, as if he thought he recognized me. Then Haire opened the street door with his latch-key and conducted me up the stairs to the first-floor landing, where he opened the door of his rooms with another latch-key, which looked like a Yale.

"Now, all the time that I had been with Haire, and especially at the tea-rooms, I had been aware of something rather queer in his manner; a suggestion of suppressed excitement, and he seemed nervous and jumpy. But when we got inside his rooms and he had shut the door, it grew much more marked; so much so that I watched him rather closely, noticing that he appeared restless and flustered, that there was a wild look in his eyes and that his hands were trembling quite violently.

"I didn't like the look of him at all, and I don't mind admitting that I began to get the wind up; for I couldn't forget that four thousand pounds, and I knew that poor old Uncle Harold was in a bad way and might die at any moment. But he was not dead yet. There was still time for me to die before him. So I kept an eye on Haire and held myself in readiness in case he really meant mischief.

"But he nearly had me, after all. He had given me a list of the Dublin firms to look at, and, while I was reading it, he got behind me to look over my shoulder. Suddenly, he made a quick move and I felt him slip a noose of soft cord over my head. I was only just in time to thrust my right hand up inside the noose when he pulled it tight. But, of course, he couldn't strangle me while my hand was there, and, seeing that, he made violent efforts to drag it away while I struggled for my life to keep hold of the noose.

"It was a horrible business. Haire was like a madman. He tugged and wrenched at the cord, he clawed at me with his free hand, he kicked me and drove his knee into my back while I hung on for dear life to the noose. By degrees I worked round until I faced him, and tried to grab his arm with my left hand while he tugged with all his might at the cord. Then we began to gyrate round the room in a kind of hideous waltz, each pounding at the other with his free hand.

"At last, in the course of our gyrations, we collided with a chair, and he fell backwards on the seat with me on top of him, his head overhanging the seat and my left hand at his throat. When we fell, the whole of my weight must have been on that left hand, for it slid under his chin and thrust it violently upwards. And as his chin went up, I felt and heard a faint click; his head fell loosely to one side, and, in a moment, his grasp on the cord relaxed. For an instant or two his arms and legs moved with a sort of twitching motion, then he lay quite still.

"Cautiously, I picked myself up and looked down at him. He was sprawling limply across the chair, and a glance at his face told me that he was dead. Evidently, the sudden drive of my left hand had broken his neck.

"Shaken as I was, I drew a deep breath of relief. It had been a near thing. An instant's hesitation with my right hand and I should now have been lying with blackening face and starting eyes and the fatal noose secured tightly around my neck. It was a horrible thought. Only by a hair's-breadth had I escaped. Still, I had escaped; and now I was free of that peril for ever.

"But my relief was short-lived. Suddenly, I realized that, if I had escaped one danger, I was faced by another. Haire was dead; but it was my hand that had brought about his death. Who was to know that I had not murdered him? Very soon, relief gave way to alarm, alarm to panic. What was I to do for my own safety? My first impulse was to rush out and seek a policeman; and that is what I ought to have done. But I dared not. As I took off the noose and held it in my hand, it seemed to whisper a terrible warning of what might yet befall me.

"Suppose I were just to steal away and say nothing to anyone of what had happened. Haire lived alone. No one ever came to his rooms. It might be months before the body should be discovered. Why not go away and know nothing about it? But, no; that wouldn't do. Mr Green had seen me enter the rooms and perhaps he knew who I was. When the body was found, he would remember that I had been with Haire the last time he was seen alive.

"I sat down with my back to the corpse and thought hard, trying to decide what I should do. But for a while I could think of no reasonable plan. The figure of Mr Green seemed to block every way of escape. Suddenly, my wandering gaze lighted on the list of Dublin firms lying where I had dropped it. I looked at it idly for a few moments; then, in a flash, I saw a way of escape.

"Haire had intended – so he had told me – to start for Ireland that very night. Well, he should start – by proxy. The people whom he was going to call on were strangers, for he had never been in Dublin before. I would make those calls for him, announcing myself by his name and presenting his card. Thus Haire would make an appearance in Dublin, and that appearance could be cited as evidence that he was alive on that day. Then, when at some later date, his body should be found, it would be beyond question that he must have died at some time after his return from Ireland. My connection with his death would have disappeared and I could snap my fingers at Mr Green.

"As soon as the scheme was clear in my mind I set to work to execute it; and as I worked, I thought out the details. First I stripped the corpse and dressed it in the pyjamas from the bed. Then, having thrown the bed-clothes into disorder, I placed the body half in the bed, half outside, with the head bent sideways and resting on the floor. The obvious suggestion would be that he had fallen out of bed and broken his neck – a mere accident implicating nobody.

"When I had folded my clothes and put them away tidily on a chair, I looked at my watch. It was barely twenty past six. The whole of this horrid drama had been played out in less than half an hour. I sat down to rest awhile – for it had been a strenuous affair while it lasted – and looked about the room to see that I was leaving no traces, but there were none, excepting my bag, and that I should take away with me. The Venetian blinds were lowered – I had noticed that when we came in – and I decided to leave them so, as that was probably how Haire was accustomed to leave them when he went away. So I sat and thought out the rest of my plan. The place was strangely quiet, for, by now Mr Green and his people had apparently shut up their premises and gone away, and there was not a sound in the room save the solemn tick of the big clock in the corner.

"Presently I rose and began, at my leisure, to complete my preparations. There was no need for hurry. It was now only half-past six by the big clock, and I knew that the Holyhead express did not leave Euston until eight forty-five. I looked over an open bureau and took from it a few of Haire's business cards and a little sheaf of his bill-heads. When I had stowed these in my bag, I had finished; and as all was still quiet, I picked up the bag, turned away with a last, shuddering glance at the grotesque figure that sprawled over the side of the bed, let myself out as silently as I could, and stole softly down the stairs.

"I need not follow the rest of my proceedings in detail. I caught my train and duly arrived in Dublin about seven o'clock the next morning. I went to a small private hotel – Connolly's – where I wrote in the visitors' book, 'G. Haire, Billington Street, London', and when I had washed and shaved and had breakfast, I went out and made the first of my calls, Brady & Co., where I stayed quite a long time gossiping with the manager. We didn't complete any definite transaction, but I left one of Haire's cards with some particulars written on the back. I made two more calls on that day, the 15th, and, during the next three days I visited several other firms, always leaving one of Haire's cards. I stayed in Dublin until the 18th, which I thought was long enough to give the proper impression of a business tour, and, in the evening of that day, just before closing time, I made a second call at Brady's, to impress myself on the manager's memory. Then, having already settled up at the hotel, I went straight to the station and caught the 7.50 train which runs in connection with the Holyhead express. I arrived at Euston in the early morning, about 5.15, and took a taxi straight across to Victoria, where, after a wash and a leisurely breakfast, I caught the nine o'clock Continental train, embarking at Folkestone about eleven.

"After that I followed my usual route and went about my ordinary business, canvassing the Bordeaux district for renewals. But I didn't complete the tour, for it happened that in an hotel at Bordeaux I came across a rather out-of-date copy of *The Times*, and, glancing through the legal notices, I was startled to see that of Horne, Cronin & Horne, announcing the death of my uncle. As this was some weeks old, I thought I had better pack up and start for home at once to get into touch with the solicitors.

"But I had to go warily, for I didn't know what might have happened while I had been abroad. Had Haire's body been discovered? And, if so, what had been done about it? These were questions that would have to be answered before I could safely present myself at Horne's office. I thought about it during the journey and decided that the first thing to do was to go and have a look at the house and see whether the Venetian blinds were still down; and if they were not, to try to pick up some information in the neighbourhood. So when I got to Victoria I put my bag in the cloakroom and took a bus to Piccadilly Circus, from whence I made my way to Billington Street. I walked cautiously down the street, keeping a sharp look-out in case Mr Green should be at his door, and avoiding the appearance of looking for the house. But my precautions were unnecessary, for, when I came to the place, behold! there was no house there! Only some blackened walls, on which the housebreakers were operating with picks.

"As I was standing gazing at the ruins, an idler approached me.

" 'Proper old blaze, that was, Mister. Flared up like a tar barrel, it did.'

" 'Ah!' said I, 'then you actually saw the fire?'

" 'Well, no,' said he, 'I didn't see it, myself, but I heard all about it. I was on the coroner's jury.'

" 'The coroner's jury!' I exclaimed. 'Then there were some lives lost?'

" 'Only one,' he replied; 'and the queer thing was that he wasn't the proper tenant, but just a stranger what had had the rooms lent to him for a few days. He was identified by a clay pipe what had his initials, CM, scratched on it.'

" 'CM!' I gasped. 'What did those letters stand for?'

" 'Cecil Moxdale was the poor chap's name; and it seemed that he had been smoking that pipe in bed and set the bed-clothes alight. Probably a bit squiffy, too.'

"Now, here was a pretty state of affairs. Mysterious, too. For the clay pipe wasn't mine. I never smoke a pipe. But, obviously, my calculations had been completely upset, and I was in a pretty tight place, for my trip to Dublin had only introduced a fresh complication. I should have to announce myself as alive, and then the fat would be in the fire. For if the body wasn't mine, whose was it? If the dead man was Haire, then who was the man in Dublin? And if the man in Dublin was Haire, then who the deuce was the dead man? It was a regular facer.

"Of course, I could have maintained that I knew nothing about the affair. But that wouldn't do; for there was that infernal Mr Green. No, I should have to make up some story that would fit the facts; and, turning it over in my mind, I decided to invent an imaginary person and let the police find him if they could. He must be virtually a stranger to me, and he must be sufficiently like me to pass as the man whom Green saw going into the rooms with Haire. So I invented Mr O'Grady and told a pretty vague story about him – but I needn't say any more. You know the rest; and now, Inspector, what about that statement that you have?"

Blandy smiled benignly, and, opening the envelope, drew from it a single sheet of paper; and when he had quickly glanced at its contents, he positively beamed.

"Dr Thorndyke's statement," said he, "is, in effect, a very brief summary of your own."

"Well, let's have it," said Moxdale.

"You shall," said Blandy, and he proceeded, with unctuous relish, to read the document.

" 'Summary of the circumstances attending the death of Gustavus Haire as suggested by evidence in my possession.

" 'Haire had planned to murder Cecil Moxdale, presumably, to secure the reversion of a bequest of four thousand pounds, and then, by means of a certain mechanism, to start a fire in the rooms while he was absent in Dublin. He prepared the rooms by filling them with inflammable material and planted certain marked, uninflammable objects to enable Moxdale's body to be identified. On the 14th of April, he set the mechanism to discharge in the early morning of the 19th. At about six p.m. on the 14th he brought Moxdale to the rooms and attempted to murder him. But the attempt failed; and in the struggle which ensued, Haire's neck became dislocated. Then Moxdale, knowing that he had been seen to enter the premises with Haire, and fearing that he would be accused of murder, decided to go to Dublin and personate Haire to make it appear that Haire was then alive. He started for Dublin in the evening of the 14th, and remained there until the evening of the 18th, when he apparently returned to England.'

"That is all that is material," Blandy concluded, "and, as your statement is in complete agreement with Dr Thorndyke's – which I have no doubt is supported by conclusive evidence – I, personally, accept it as true."

Moxdale drew a deep breath. "That is a blessed relief," he exclaimed. "And now what is to be done? Are you going to arrest me?"

"No," replied Blandy, "certainly not. But I think you had better walk back with me to Head Quarters and let us hear what the senior officers propose. May I take your summary with me, Doctor?"

"By all means," Thorndyke replied; "and make it clear that I am ready to produce the necessary evidence."

"I had taken that for granted, Doctor," said Blandy as he put the envelope in his pocket. Then he rose to depart, and Moxdale stood up.

"I am thankful, Sir," said he, "that I took your advice, and eternally grateful to you for having dissipated this nightmare. Now, I can look to the future with some sort of confidence."

"Yes," Thorndyke agreed, "I don't think that you need feel any great alarm; and I wish you an easy passage through any little difficulties that may arise."

With this, Moxdale shook our hands all round, and, when the inspector had done likewise, the two men moved towards the door, escorted by Polton.

CHAPTER NINETEEN

The Evidence Reviewed

"A brilliant finish to a most remarkable case," I commented as our visitors' footsteps died away upon the stairs, "and a most magnificent piece of bluff on the part of my revered senior."

Thorndyke smiled and Polton looked shocked.

"I shall not contest your description, Jervis," said the former, "but, in fact, the conclusion was practically a certainty."

"Probability," I corrected.

"In practice," said he, "we have to treat the highest degrees of probability as certainties; and if you consider the evidence in this case as a whole, I think you will agree that only one possible conclusion emerged. The element of bluff was almost negligible."

"Probably you are right," I admitted. "You usually are, and you certainly were in this case. But the evidence was so complex and conflicting that I find it difficult to reconstitute it as a whole. It would interest me very much to hear you sort it out into a tidily arranged argument."

"It would interest me, too," said he, "to retrace our investigation and observe the curious way in which the different items of evidence came to light. Let us do so, taking the events in the order of their occurrence and noting the tendency of the evidence to close in on the final conclusion.

"This was a very singular case. The evidence did not transpire gradually but emerged in a number of successive and perfectly distinct stages, each stage being marked by the appearance of a new fact which reacted immediately on our previous conclusions. There were seven stages, each of which we will examine separately, noting how the argument stood at the end of it.

"The first is the inquest, including the post mortem. Perhaps we had better deal with the body first. There were only two points of interest, the neck and the teeth. The dislocation of the neck appeared to me to have occurred before death and I took it to be, most probably, the immediate cause of death. As to the teeth, there was nothing very striking in their appearance; just a little pitting of the enamel. But from the arrangement of the little pits in irregular transverse lines, corresponding roughly to the lines of growth, I did not believe them to have been due to the heat but to have existed during life. I thought it possible that deceased might have had mottled teeth which had been bleached out in the fire; but, as I had never seen a case of mottled teeth, I could not form a definite opinion. I just noted the facts and satisfied myself that the pitting showed clearly in Polton's photograph of the dead man's face.

"And now let us consider the body of evidence which was before us when the inquest was finished and the inferences that it suggested. To me – and also to Blandy – the appearances as a whole conveyed the idea of deliberate arson; of a fire which had been arranged and started for a definite purpose. And since the death of Cecil Moxdale seemed to be part of the plan – if there was a plan – it was reasonable to suspect that this was the purpose for which the fire was raised.

"What especially led me to suspect arson was the appearance of preparation. The room, itself, crammed with highly inflammable material, seemed to have been expressly prepared for a fire. But most suspicious to me was the information given by Haire to Green. It seemed designed to create in Green's mind (as it actually did) the fear that a fire might occur. But more than this; it prepared him, if a fire should occur, to decide at once upon the way in which it had been caused. Nor was that all. Haire's statement even suggested to Green the possibility of a fatal accident; and in the event of such a fatality occurring, it provided Green in advance with the data for identifying any body that should be found.

"Then there were the objects found in the ruins which confirmed Green's identification. They were marked objects composed of highly refractory material."

"They would have to be," I objected, "if they were found. All the combustible objects would have been destroyed."

"True," he admitted. "But still it was a striking coincidence that these imperishable objects should happen to bear the initials of a man whose corpse was unrecognizable. The clay pipe was especially significant, seeing that people do not usually incise their initials on their pipe-bowls. But a clay pipe is, as nearly as possible, indestructible by heat. No more perfect means of identification, in the case of a fire, could be devised than a marked clay pipe. To me, these most opportune relics offered a distinct suggestion of having been planted for the very purpose which they served.

"But there is one observation to make before finishing with the positive aspects of the case. It was assumed that the man who was in the house when the fire broke out was a live man; and it was agreed that that live man was Cecil Moxdale. Now, I did not accept, unreservedly, either of these assumptions. To me, the appearances suggested that the man was already dead when the fire started. As to the identity, the probability seemed to be that the man was Moxdale; but I did not regard the fact as having been established conclusively. I kept in my mind the possibility of either a mistake or deliberate deception.

"And now, what conclusions emerged from these considerations? To me – and to Blandy – they suggested a crime. My provisional hypothesis was that Haire had made away with Moxdale and raised the fire to cover the murder; that the crime had been carefully planned and prepared; and that, for some reason, Haire was especially anxious that the body should be identified as that of Cecil Moxdale. That, as I said, was the positive aspect of the case. Now let us look at the negative.

"There were two facts that conflicted with my hypothesis. The first was that when the fire broke out, Haire was in Dublin and had been there for five days. That seemed to be an unanswerable alibi. There was no trace of any sort of fire-raising apparatus known to the experts or the police; indeed, no apparatus was known which would have been capable of raising a fire after an interval of five days. The large and complicated appliances used for the automatic lighting of street lamps do not come into the problem; they would not have been available to Haire, and, in fact, no trace of anything of the kind was found. Apparently, it was a physical impossibility that the fire could have been started by Haire.

"The second objection to my hypothesis was in the nature of the injury. A dislocation of the neck is, in my experience, invariably an accidental injury. I have never heard of a homicidal case. Have you?"

"No," I answered; "and, in fact, if you wanted to dislocate a man's neck, I don't quite know how you would go about it."

"Exactly," he agreed. "It is too difficult and uncertain a method for a murderer to use. So that, in this case, if the broken neck was the cause of death, the man would appear to have died from the effects of an accident.

"Thus, the position at the end of the first stage was that, although the case as a whole looked profoundly suspicious, there was not a particle of positive evidence of either arson or murder.

"The second stage was introduced by the disappearance of Haire. This was most mysterious. Why did Haire not return at the expected time? There was no reason why he should not, even if my hypothesis were true. For if he had raised a fire to cover a murder, his plan had succeeded to perfection. The fire had been accepted as an accident, the body had been identified, and the man's death had been attributed to misadventure. And not only was there no reason why Haire should not have come home; there was a very good reason why he should. For his absence tended to start inquiries, and inquiries were precisely what he would have wished to avoid. I could think of no explanation of his disappearance. There was a suggestion that something had gone wrong; but there was no suggestion whatever as to what it was. Nevertheless, the fact of the disappearance tended to make the already suspicious group of events look even more suspicious.

"The third stage was reached when we learned that Moxdale senior was dead and heard of the provisions of his will. Then it appeared that Haire stood to benefit to the extent of four thousand pounds by the death of Cecil Moxdale. This, of course, did not, by itself, establish a probability that Haire had murdered Moxdale; but if that probability had already been suggested by other facts, this new fact increased it by supplying a reasonable and adequate motive. At this stage, then, I definitely suspected Haire of having murdered Moxdale, though still not without some misgivings. For the apparently insuperable difficulty remained. It seemed to be a physical impossibility that Haire could have started the fire.

"Then came Polton's astonishing discovery; and immediately the position was radically altered. Now, it was shown, not only that it was possible for Haire to have started the fire, but that it was nearly certain that he had done so. But this new fact reacted on all the others, giving them an immensely increased evidential value. I had now very little doubt that Haire had murdered Moxdale.

"But the mystery of Haire's disappearance remained. For he was all unaware of Polton's discovery. To him, it should have seemed that all had gone according to plan and that it was perfectly safe for him to come back. Then why was he keeping out of sight? Why did he not return, now that his uncle was dead and the stake for which he had played was within his grasp? I turned this problem over and over in my mind. What was keeping him away? Something had gone wrong. Something of which we had no knowledge. What could it be?

"Once more, that dislocated neck presented itself for consideration. It had always seemed to me an anomaly, out of character with the known circumstances. How came Moxdale to have a broken neck? All the evidence pointed to a murder, long premeditated, carefully planned, and elaborately prepared. And yet the murdered man seemed to have died from an accidental injury.

"Here another point recurred to me. The body had been identified as that of Cecil Moxdale. But on what evidence? Simply on the hearsay evidence of Green and the marked objects found in the ruins. Of actual identification there had been none. The body probably was Moxdale's. The known facts suggested that it was, but there was no direct proof. Suppose, after all, that it were not. Then whose body could it be? Evidently, it must be Haire's, for our picture contained only these two figures. But this assumption involved an apparent impossibility; for, at the time of the fire, Haire was in Dublin. But the impossibility disappeared when we realized that again there had been no real identification. The men whom Haire called upon in Dublin were strangers. They knew him as Haire simply because he said that he was Haire and presented Haire's card. He might, quite easily, have been some other man, personating Haire. And if he were, that other person must have been Moxdale.

"It seemed a far-fetched suggestion, but yet it fitted the facts surprisingly well. It agreed, for instance, with the dislocated neck; for if Haire had been killed, he had almost certainly been killed accidentally. And it explained the disappearance of the Dublin 'Haire'; for Moxdale's object in personating Haire would have been to prove that Haire had been alive after the 14th of April, when the two men had been seen to enter Haire's premises together; and for this purpose it would be necessary only for him to 'enter an appearance' at Dublin. When he had done that, he would naturally return from Ireland to his ordinary places of resort.

"Thus the fourth stage of the investigation left us with the virtual certainty that Haire had raised the fire, the probability that he had murdered Moxdale, but the possibility that the murder had failed and that Haire had been killed accidentally in the struggle. There were two alternatives, and we had no means of deciding which of them was the true one.

"Then, once more, Polton came to our help with a decisive fact. Haire had mottled teeth and was a native of Maldon. Instantly, as he spoke, I recalled the teeth of the burned corpse and my surmise that they might have been mottled teeth. At once, I got into communication with a dental practitioner at Maldon, who, though I was a stranger to him, gave me every possible assistance, including a wax denture of mottled teeth and some spare teeth for experimental purposes. Those teeth I examined minutely, comparing them with those of the body as shown in Polton's enlarged photograph of the face; and, disregarding the brown stains, which the fire had bleached out, the resemblance was perfect. I did, as a matter of extra precaution, incinerate two of the spare teeth in a crucible. But it was not necessary. The first comparison was quite convincing. There was no doubt that the burnt body was that of a man who had mottled teeth and very little doubt that it was Haire's body."

"But," I objected, "Moxdale might have had mottled teeth. He was Haire's cousin."

"Yes," Thorndyke agreed, "there was that element of uncertainty. But there was not much in it. The mere relationship was not significant, as mottled teeth are not transmitted by heredity but are purely environmental phenomena. But, of course, Moxdale might also have been born and grown up at Maldon. Still, we had the definite fact that Haire was known to have had mottled teeth and that the dead man had had teeth of the same, very rare, kind. So this stage left us with the strong probability that the body was Haire's, but the possibility that it might be that of Moxdale.

"But at the next stage a question was settled by the reappearance of Moxdale in the flesh. That established the identity of the body as a definite fact. But it also established the identity of the personator. For if the dead man was Haire, the live man at Dublin must have been Moxdale. There appeared to be no alternative possibility.

"Nevertheless, Moxdale essayed to present us with one in the form of a moderately plausible story. I don't know whether Blandy believed this story. He professed to; but then Blandy is – Blandy. He was certainly puzzled by it, as we can judge by his anxiety to bring Moxdale here that we might question him, and we have to remember that he did not know what we knew as to the identity of the body. For my part, I never entertained that story for a moment. It sounded like fiction pure and simple; and a striking feature of it was that no part of it admitted of verification. The mysterious O'Grady was a mere shadow, of whom nothing was known and nothing could be discovered, and the alleged blackmailing was not supported by a single tangible fact. Moreover, O'Grady, the blackmailer, did not fit the facts. The murder which had been so elaborately prepared was, specifically, the murder of Cecil Moxdale. Not only was it Moxdale whose identification was prepared for; the motive for the murder was connected with Moxdale.

"However, it doesn't do to be too dogmatic. One had to accept the infinitely remote possibility that the story might be true, at least in parts. Accordingly I grasped at Blandy's suggestion that he should bring Moxdale here and give us the opportunity to put the story to the test of comparison with the known facts.

"We need not consider that interview in detail. It was an ingenious story that Moxdale told, and he told it extremely well. But still, as he went on, its fictional character became more and more pronounced and its details more and more elusive. You probably noticed that when I asked for a description of O'Grady, he gave an excellent one – which was an exact description of himself. It had to be; for O'Grady must needs correspond to Green's description of the man whom he saw with Haire, and that description applied perfectly to Moxdale.

"I followed the narrative with the closest attention, waiting for some definite discrepancy on which one could fasten. And at last it came. Moxdale, unaware of what we knew, made the inevitable false step. In his anxiety to prove that Haire was alive and had gone to Dublin, he gave a circumstantial account of his having seen Haire into the taxi *en route* for Euston at past ten o'clock at night.

Now, we knew that Haire had never gone to Dublin. Moreover we knew that, by ten o'clock, Haire had been dead some hours; and we knew, also, that, by that time, the personator must have been well on his way to Holyhead, since he appeared in Dublin early the next morning.

"Here, then, was a definitely false statement. It disposed at once of any possibility that the story might be true; and its effect was to make it certain that the Dublin personator was Moxdale, himself. I was now in a position to tax Moxdale with having killed Haire and carried out the personation, and I did so with studied abruptness in order to force him to make a statement. You see there was not very much bluff about it, after all."

"No," I admitted. "It was not really bluff. I withdraw the expression. I had not realized how complete the evidence was. But your question had a grand dramatic effect."

"That, however, was not its object," said Thorndyke. "I was anxious, for Moxdale's own sake, that he should make a true and straightforward statement. For if he had stuck to his fictitious story, he would certainly have been charged with having murdered Haire; and, as Blandy very justly observed, a story told by an accused man from the witness-box is much less convincing than the same story told voluntarily before any charge has been made. Fortunately, Moxdale, being a sensible fellow, realized this and took my advice."

"What do you suppose the police will do about it?" I asked.

"I don't see why they should do anything," he replied. "No crime has been committed. A charge of manslaughter could not be sustained, since Moxdale's action was purely defensive and the death was the result of an accident."

"And what about the question of concealment of death?"

"There doesn't seem to be much in that. Moxdale did not conceal the body; he merely tried to dissociate himself from it. He did not, it is true, report the death as he ought to have done. That was rather irregular and so was the personation. But I think that the police will take the view that, in the absence of any criminal intention, there is no need, on grounds of public policy, for them to take any action."

Thorndyke's forecast proved to be correct. The Assistant Commissioner asked us for a complete statement of the evidence, and when this had been supplied (including a demonstration by Polton) he decided that no proceedings were called for. It was, however, necessary to amend the finding of the coroner's jury, not only for the purposes of registration, but for that of obtaining probate of Harold Moxdale's will. Accordingly, Thorndyke issued a certificate of the death of Gustavus Haire, and thereby put the finishing touch to one of the most curious cases that had passed through our hands.

R Austin Freeman

The D'Arblay Mystery
A Dr Thorndyke Mystery

When a man is found floating beneath the skin of a green-skimmed pond one morning, Dr Thorndyke becomes embroiled in an astonishing case. This wickedly entertaining detective fiction reveals that the victim was murdered through a lethal injection and someone out there is trying a cover-up.

Dr Thorndyke Intervenes
A Dr Thorndyke Mystery

What would you do if you opened a package to find a man's head? What would you do if the headless corpse had been swapped for a case of bullion? What would you do if you knew a brutal murderer was out there, somewhere, and waiting for you? Some people would run. Dr Thorndyke intervenes.

R Austin Freeman

Felo De Se
A Dr Thorndyke Mystery

John Gillam was a gambler. John Gillam faced financial ruin and was the victim of a sinister blackmail attempt. John Gillam is now dead. In this exceptional mystery, Dr Thorndyke is brought in to untangle the secrecy surrounding the death of John Gillam, a man not known for insanity and thoughts of suicide.

Flighty Phyllis

Chronicling the adventures and misadventures of Phyllis Dudley, Richard Austin Freeman brings to life a charming character always getting into scrapes. From impersonating a man to discovering mysterious trapdoors, *Flighty Phyllis* is an entertaining glimpse at the times and trials of a wayward woman.

R Austin Freeman

Helen Vardon's Confession
A Dr Thorndyke Mystery

Through the open door of a library, Helen Vardon hears an argument that changes her life forever. Helen's father and a man called Otway argue over missing funds in a trust one night. Otway proposes a marriage between him and Helen in exchange for his co-operation and silence. What transpires is a captivating tale of blackmail, fraud and death. Dr Thorndyke is left to piece together the clues in this enticing mystery.

Mr Pottermack's Oversight

Mr Pottermack is a law-abiding, settled homebody who has nothing to hide until the appearance of the shadowy Lewison, a gambler and blackmailer with an incredible story. It appears that Pottermack is in fact a runaway prisoner, convicted of fraud, and Lewison is about to spill the beans unless he receives a large bribe in return for his silence. But Pottermack protests his innocence, and resolves to shut Lewison up once and for all. Will he do it? And if he does, will he get away with it?